ADRIAN'S UNDEAD DIARY

Chris Philbrook

Book One

DARK RECOLLECTIONS

Adrian's Undead Diary: Dark Recollections
Copyright © 2010 Christopher Philbrook

Published in the United States of America

First Publishing Date October, 2010

Cover design and interior layout by Alan MacRaffen

For my Dad.
I am the man I am today, because of the man you were for me
yesterday.
I miss you, I love you.

-Chris

Also by Chris Philbrook:

Elmoryn - The Kinless Trilogy
Book One: Wrath of the Orphans

Coming Soon:
Book Two: A Motive for Massacre
Book Three

Adrian's Undead Diary
Book One: Dark Recollections

Coming Soon:
Book Two: Alone No More
Book Three: Midnight
Book Four
Book Five
Book Six
Book Seven
Book Eight

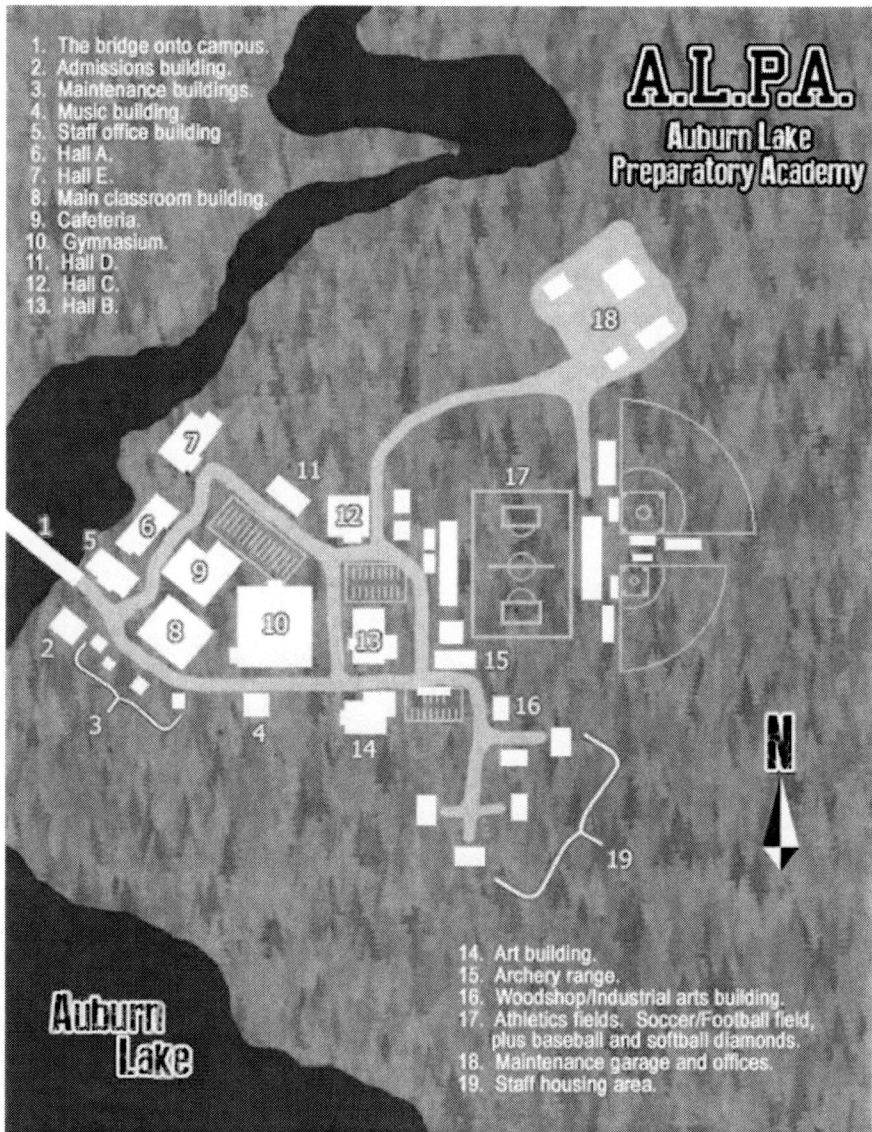

A.L.P.A.
Auburn Lake
Preparatory Academy

1. The bridge onto campus.
2. Admissions building.
3. Maintenance buildings.
4. Music building.
5. Staff office building
6. Hall A.
7. Hall E.
8. Main classroom building.
9. Cafeteria.
10. Gymnasium.
11. Hall D.
12. Hall C.
13. Hall B.

14. Art building.
15. Archery range.
16. Woodshop/Industrial arts building.
17. Athletics fields. Soccer/Football field,
    plus baseball and softball diamonds.
18. Maintenance garage and offices.
19. Staff housing area.

N

Auburn
Lake

TABLE OF CONTENTS:

September 2010

September 21st

It's pretty fucking cold out tonight. The big ass plastic thermometer on the tree outside says its 35F out tonight. I'm glad I figured out where the emergency generator is here, otherwise I would be freezing my balls off now. Despite the fact that this place was kind of a bitch to clear out, I'm glad I did it. It's got everything I need to survive for a long time.

I don't even really know where to start. It's a Tuesday today. At least I know what day it is. Someone in the main office building was wise enough to buy their calendar early this year so it'll be easy for me to keep track of the days until the end of next year. After that I guess I'll have to use some of the graph paper and make my own calendar. That's being pretty optimistic though. The way the last few months have been I'll be goddamn lucky to make Christmas, let alone next Christmas.

I decided to start writing this mainly to keep track of my daily activities and to have a way to purge my nugget. Frankly I talk to myself way too goddamn much to be mentally healthy and I was always told that writing a journal helped. Sooo.. let's call this my journal. Thank God for spell check. I also realize that now is not the best time to be writing. I'm using up some of my gasoline to run the generator, which is basically a waste, and honestly having any lights on at night draws them in. Moths to a flame as the old saying goes. But I can't sleep and I've been meaning to do this for a long time now. Having the electricity back has set a fire under my ass to do this.

My name is Adrian Ring. I lived what I would now call as only a moderately successful life. I was happy, but I had pretty low standards. I had a girlfriend, I had a small condo downtown, I still have my cat (score!), and I have thus far avoided being eaten by the undead. Surprise! There's the twist in the story. I fucking love horror movies. Like seriously. I watched well over a thousand of them and always used to plot and plan should zombies ever rise from the dead and take over the world. Irony in all that is that when the shit hit the fan it happened so fast that any kind of plan would've been almost impossible to execute.

I was at work the night it started. I used to work third shift at a private school as a dorm supervisor. It was out of the way up in the hills outside of downtown, and only had about 100 students. Over 100k a year to attend. Very elite, very snooty, and basically the best job you could ask for. I had 9 hour shifts where I basically just made sure the kids didn't run away, and had their needs taken care of. Most nights I would do maybe an hour of work. I spent the rest of the time fucking around online looking at stupid videos and screwing around on the big ole f-book. God I wish I could update my status right now. Something really witty like "hasn't been eaten yet, so is pretty stoked." Or maybe something like, "wishes he grabbed more bullets when he raided the gun store in town." I dunno. Something cool.

Anyway, I was at work when it all hit. Working nights meant I was totally alone aside from the three other overnights and the sleeping kids, so when I checked the news websites and saw the few updates about "zombie hoaxes" I laughed. After a few hours more and more popped up on other websites, but I didn't take it too seriously. After all Halloween was coming up soon I figured it was some kind of stunt to promote a new movie or tv show. It wasn't until the morning when half the day shift people didn't show that I really realized something was up.

I went home as I normally do, and nothing seemed amiss. I called my girlfriend on the short drive home and we chatted. I asked her about it and she basically said she thought it was a hoax or some stunt. She was still half asleep though, so who knows what she really saw or heard on tv. Plus she was getting ready for work herself. She was gone by the time I got home, and I never saw her again. I think she was killed at work, or maybe on the drive home from work. I'll never know. The cities are far too dangerous for me to attempt to go to, and to be honest, as much as I loved her, it scares the shit out of me when I think of getting eaten alive. If you can read this babe, I love you.

I went to bed after watching a few minutes of the news and eating a banana. I can still remember the weird vibe on the good morning shows. Kinda tense, but sort of laughing it off. I can still remember the look on the dude's face as he reported it, kinda like he was waiting for an "april fools!" to pop up on his teleprompter. Never came I guess. So I went to bed.

I slept pretty good until about 3pm. I remember distinctly waking with a start, jarred awake. It took me a few minutes to piece together what actually woke me up, but the second gunshot kinda solved that riddle. It came from outside my window in the condo complex and I knew instantly something was very wrong.

My curtains are taped right to the window frames to block out the light, so I pulled on my gym shorts and hustled downstairs to look out the glass slider on the back side of the house. The action had ended by the time I got down there, but about thirty feet from where my place is I could clearly see a dead body laying in the parking lot. Have you ever seen someone take a shotgun blast to the head? Its horrible. There's no head left to speak of, first off, and secondly the body just empties the blood out of what's left of the head. More of a neck by that point really.

The body, a woman incidentally, was kind of laying towards my place, kinda downhill, and the blood was running into the mulch at the foot of the pine tree right behind my place. I've seen dead bodies before, I've been around violence plenty of times, but this was weird. It was in my neighborhood. You know, your sanctuary? I imagine the way I felt looking at her head-stump empty was a lot like watching your house burn down, or coming home to realize your house had been broken into. I felt violated. Anyway, I grabbed my sweatshirt, my cell phone, slipped my sandals on and sprinted out the back, dialing 911 as I went. I tripped over a root from the fucking pine tree and ate shit on the way, but I got there.

She was dead, of that there was no doubt. Her head was absolute demolished. She was wearing a garish flowery pattern shirt that looked a lot like the kind of shirts that a pediatric nurse would wear. She definitely had pants that looked a lot like those greenish scrub pants you see nurses wearing. I made my decision. Headless shotgun woman had been a nurse only a short time ago. At that point I realized my 911 call wasn't going through. Getting the all circuits' busy bullshit, which instantly set off my oh-shit radar. My groggy ass brain finally started to put two and two together. The zombie shenanigans from last night may not have been a hoax.

I don't own a gun. My girlfriend was kinda twitchy, and she had a little bit of a temper, and I really didn't want a firearm around that cocktail. It was far too foreseeable to see me getting shot because she thought I was a robber or something. So no guns. I did however own a few very high quality swords. Competently made and purchased at a few nerd festivals over the years. I really didn't want to grab a sword and just go driving around on the outside chance that this was just a random shooting, but I knew I had to get the fuck back inside one way or the other. If this was a random shooting, the random shooter was still pretty fucking nearby and I was not in the mood to get head-stumped myself.

So I ran inside. This time I did not eat shit on the root from the pine tree, and made it inside like an Olympic sprinter. I do remember being really pissed at myself because I left the slider open and my frigging cat Otis was sitting right on the fringe watching me the time. I didn't want him to get out, as he's an inside cat. He's a Maine Coon, so he's a beefy guy, but I woulda been pissed if he got hit by a car, or shot by a psycho with a twelve gauge. Seems like a reasonable concern considering the prior events, right? Whatever dude. I love my cat. He's my homeboy.

So by then I'd tried dialing 911 like 4 times. I had the

number for the police station already in my contacts so I called that line, and I got their automated response. The emergency choice just routed me to 911, and I was right back where I started. At that point I knew shit was bad. Can't be a coincidence. I hit the tv on and there it was, the EAS message. You know that irritating noise you hear when they're testing the emergency system? And very fucking rarely is there ever an emergency. I mean I guess in the midwest when they get tornadoes, or in the south when a hurricane is coming it's more relevant than here. All we ever get is shit like "emergency snowstorm warnings," or shit like road closures or accidents.

I'll never forget the message from that day:

State and local agencies are reporting widespread attacks on citizens across the region. Authorities are advising people to stay inside, lock their doors, bar their windows and only open doors for known friends and family who respond intelligently.

That was it. No mention of a virus, aliens attacking, zombies, vampires, or any such nonsense. I mean, I know now after having seen it a few hundred times we're dealing with zombies, but that message had no info at all. For the astute horror fan though, that's when I knew it was "on." You know, as in "it's on like Donkey Kong." I tried calling my girlfriend, both on her cell phone, and at her work extension, but no dice. I'm pretty fortunate in that I don't panic, like, ever. I've got years of experience dealing with violence, and I just don't lose my cool when the shit hits the fan. I'm the kind of dude you want making decisions in dangerous situations. Enough about me, I'm writing history now. More about me later when I have less to write about.

I knew she was dead. Or at least, damn close to it. None of the channels would work so I grabbed my laptop and fired it up. After connecting to my network I went to all the news websites and immediately found out I was right.

14

Picture after picture after cell phone video after news broadcast. All showing the zombies. Of course, no one had the fucking balls to call it like that. People were calling it everything but. Theories abounded everywhere I pointed the mouse. But I knew. You could see it. They were dead already, and didn't attack others until they'd passed on. I knew I needed to know a few things immediately about whatever it was that was doing this, so I got all scientific, and went to the CDC website.

They were on the ball, thankfully, and had the info as best as they could, already up. I needed to know a few things specifically:

• Transmission. How did it get transmitted? According to the CDC transmission occurred only via bite. Scratches did not seem to pass along the sickness/curse/virus/evil. Further, they had confirmed that the illness did not spread to non-human victims. Apparently a farm in Pennsylvania had all their cows eaten by the zombies and they stayed dead. (Of course later on I realized that this was somewhat wrong. You see by that point I don't think they had realized that anyone who died and didn't get their nugget wrecked immediately would get back up, seeking out flesh, being a general motherfucking nuisance to the living. But, I worked with what I knew at that point)

• Did they eat flesh? The CDC confirmed that yes, they did indeed eat the flesh of the living.

• Were the undead/sick/ill/terrorists that ate flesh more or less dangerous than a normal human being? Once again the CDC reported that the ill were slow, had diminished capacity for thought and reason, and were hostile to other human beings as well as animals. They were uncoordinated, couldn't move much faster than a clumsy trot at best, and showed no ability to communicate, or to make plans of any sort.

•Where did it all start? How close was I to "ground zero?" The CDC had no fucking clue. They said that there were about ten dozen simultaneous reports from all over the world. Plus or minus a few hours, which globally speaking is pretty fucking simultaneous. As best as I could figure, I was about a two hour drive from the closest outbreaks on the eastern seaboard.

•Could they be killed, and if so, how were they killed? According to the CDC (by now my most trusted source for news regarding the current and ongoing Zombie apocalypse) any significant damage done to the brain would drop them again. So Romero, dude you were totally spot-on. Fucking A brother.

So there it was. Despite the fact that even the CDC avoided calling it a "zombie outbreak" or the "apocalypse" I fucking knew. Well, at the very least, I wasn't about to risk it. I grabbed up my phone and tried to make a few more phone calls, but no joy. All circuits still busy. So, I formulated my plan.

Mom lived about a mile away, right near downtown, right near the schools, and I knew I would swing by her place to see if she was okay. I had a few friends who lived right around town too, and I wanted to check on them. More importantly though, was a long term survival plan. My condo was shitty in terms of a place to hole up, so I needed a place to go. I knew almost immediately I would come here, back to the school. It had everything.

I would get guns, some supplies, food, and then head to the school. Ride it out from there and see what happens. As you can tell, I made it here in one piece. But that doesn't tell the whole story. Unfortunately my guilt over wasting this gas has finally reached its boiling point. Plus I'm getting really fucking tired and I need to lock the upstairs down so I can sleep soundly.

I think for my next entry I'll talk about the trip to get here. And what I found when I did.

Until next time Mr. Journal.

-Adrian

September 27th

Hi Mr. Journal. I think it's all starting to get to me. I did not have a very good week here at all. Nothing bad happened, which is awesome really, but I think spilling my guts last Tuesday opened up some fucking epic wounds I had really forgotten about.

I'm sitting here with tears welling up in my eyes as I think about the fact that I did not go and at least try and find Cass. Cassie. Just typing her name is hard for me to do right now. I sat here looking at this blank white sheet of pixilated paper for almost an hour just trying to think of something to write about but I couldn't. All I could think about was the fact that my awesome goddamn plan that day didn't include at least trying to rescue the woman I should've married.

I mean, I'm alive, and that's good, but it all seems pretty fucking pointless without her here. Like, why do I even bother to make myself dinner when she's not here to tell me how bad my cooking is? We were together for so long and I just don't know why I didn't ask her to marry me sooner. Fear of commitment? Wedding was too expensive? Was I afraid her parents would say no? Shit I don't know. And it kills me I never will know. My mouth is bone dry right now. I can't even swallow.

I've sat in bed, snuggled up with Otis and just laid there thinking about this. I've been so busy getting this place safe from the zombies that I haven't had time to really think about it until now. She has to be dead, right? She was never

17

the "survivor" type. She lost her goddamn mind when there was a spider in the house, I can't envision her keeping her shit together when people are dying all around her, then sitting up and attacking her too. My most frequent delusion about her death is that she died in a car accident trying to get out of the city. You know, she would've taken the stairs to get out of the building, ran to her car, dodging the undead's awkward lunges. I can see her starting her little car, backing out into the street, and then getting creamed at an intersection by some fucking asshole in a giant SUV trying to do the same thing as her. In my guilt filled vision she not only is killed instantly, but is either decapitated, or is so mangled that she can't get back up as the undead.

I think thinking of it that way makes me feel like it's better that way. At least if she died that way she isn't hurting anyone else, and at least that way I will never have to worry about seeing her disintegrating body shambling towards me someday. Man I hope that never happens. I don't think I could take seeing that. Seeing her beautiful face all ashen and bloody, teeth bared, slowly clawing at the air as she comes toward me.

Just typing that makes my fucking skin crawl.

There's this enormous part of me that says I should go get a truck from the maintenance barn and make my way to her work. For closure. I know I won't find her, at least, I know I won't find her alive. I think if I did find her car smashed to shit in an intersection I might feel better about myself. About my decision that day. You know at least I could say that I was right about not going to try and find her. She was probably already dead by the time I even knew what was going on that day. There was no chance that I could've saved her.

Then the little prick inside me says; "Adrian, but what if you find her dead, walking along the road, slowly making her way home, slowly making her way back to you?" And my ambition to go get closure just dries right the fuck up. I think that little prick, that little voice inside me is my

18

cowardice. I never thought of myself as a coward. Really. I've waded into some pretty dangerous shit in my 34 years on this planet, and not once did I give it a second thought.

Why the fuck did I give up on her so easily that day?

Fuck you Mr. Journal.

-Adrian

September 28th

Mr. Journal I'm profoundly sorry for my outburst at the end of the last journal. Good sentence right there. I think a few of my English teachers just rolled over in their graves. Well actually a few of my English teachers probably just burped up the entrails of a few of my math teachers, but you get the idea. Sorry surviving English teachers, that was pretty tasteless.

Pun not intended.

I feel better about myself today. I think yesterday's journal entry was cathartic for me. Finally admitting out loud that I failed myself and Cass that day has relieved me of some guilt. I actually slept pretty good last night for the first time since my first journal entry. I've been restless for a long time, and it was really rejuvenating to get a full 8 hours of sleep. Otis can sense my troubles too, and it has had him on edge. He's been largely avoiding me for a few days now, and finally this morning he actually came up to me as I woke up and looked for some attention. Apparently he can figure out when I'm emotionally capable of giving him some affection. I am so thankful he's still around.

After I gave him his love this morning I had a bit of a startle. The campus here is pretty fucking out of the way. We're at the end of a country dead end road in a small town, miles from anything even remotely looking like civilization.

There are maybe fifteen houses along the five miles heading up the hills to get here. Our campus is surrounded by water. There is a lake all along one side of the property, and the lake has a river draining down the hill we're on that skirts the other side of the property. Shit, you need to cross a bridge to get here. It's as close as you can get to an island without needing a boat. Hence part of its allure as a last ditch place to hold up. I parked two of the transport vans we used to use to get the kids around use on the far side of the bridge and there's no way anything can get across. Someone could climb across the top, but the zombies are far too stupid to put that plan together. Living people would need to get out and cross on foot if they were coming to visit.

I hate using my guns now. A: It's a waste of ammunition, B: we have an archery range here, and arrows are reusable if I do it right, and C: guns are loud, and could theoretically draw unwanted attention. Anyway, when I went out to check the campus for dead folk, lo and behold there were two zombies shuffling and milling about on the far side of the vans. I don't think they knew I was here, but honestly, I didn't ask them. It took me three arrows to hit both of them in the head and re-kill them, so to speak. My first shot just thunked right into the dry, empty eye socket of the first zombie. He dropped like a bag of wet laundry. My second shot sailed pretty wide right, not sure why, it felt good when I let it go. But, third time's the charm, and I hit the other zombie squarely in his brainpan. I sat still for a bit, waiting to see if there were any other undead dudes on the other side of the bridge, and after a bit, I crossed carefully and retrieved all three arrows. All three were fine for use again.

I really didn't want to leave those bodies there, so I got my rubber gloves, my shitty overalls, and got the four wheeler with the little trailer on it, moved the vans, and drove the two corpses to the far back side of the campus, out where the faculty residences are. Or used to be. Not sure what the proper tense is on that. I mean technically, the residences are still there, but the faculty that used to live in them is long since gone. I guess it doesn't matter. Both of the bodies were heavy as hell, and smelled fucking awful. Not the sick, rotting putrid flesh smell, more of a rotting fecal matter and kelp odor. I know, charming.

Anyhoo... moved the vans back, chilled out for a bit to make sure everything was quiet, and I hit the campus cafeteria and snagged some canned stuff to eat for the day. I'm finally getting accustomed to moving about without the constant fear of being attacked around every corner. At first, right after all the shit started, I moved through life in a slow and smooth combat walk, gun at the ready. Every single door was breached like I was either a super secret sneaky spy, or like I was kicking in a door in a slum in Baghdad, looking for wahabi.

It's only been the last few days that I've felt safe enough to basically just live life like "normal." Lol. Normal. What the fuck is that now? Normal is not being pretty okay with watching a dead human being gnawing away at the flesh of a slowly dying person. Normal is not reasoning with yourself that everything in that situation is okay, because the zombie is busy eating that person, and will thus not attack you for some time, ergo, you are "safe." How fucked up is that?

So I'm feeling pretty good right now. I have some warmed up canned corned beef hash, a couple slices of canned brown bread, and some hot instant coffee. I'm feeling a little better about my utter scumbaggery re: leaving the love of my life to die a bitter, lonely death, and I actually feel like dropping more into this journal. Sound okay to you Mr. Journal?

I thought you'd like the attention. Soon as I get Otis off the screen of the laptop, I'll tell you a story.

There we go. I'm sure he'll be back up in my lap shortly anyway. I'll get done what I can in the meantime.

Where was I? So I had formulated a plan to get to what I felt was relative safety. Food, supplies, guns, check on friends and family, and get here to the school. Not necessarily in that order. I live about 2 miles from the local gun store. I could see and hear cars still driving by on main street outside the complex so I knew it wasn't total devastation. Probably panicked, probably fucked up a lot, but probably still, you know, held together.

After I got dressed, I grabbed a mess of shit and loaded my car. A suitcase and a duffel bag of clothes were first. I grabbed my two best swords, and strapped my dad's old hunting knife to my belt. It's a badass knife my uncle made a long time ago out of a piece of heavy duty file. It looks like something straight out of horror movie. I use an old K-Bar sheathe for it for when I go hiking, so it looks even more badass. Like how badass I look is going to help when I am getting mauled by the undead, right? Very feminine of me to think about how I look at a time like that. Cass always said I was sensitive.

I snagged an old plastic milk crate and loaded all the food in the kitchen that would last into it. Everything canned, everything frozen, anything bottled. I filled every water bottle we had, and dumped out the milk jugs, and filled those with water too. No idea how long running water would be available, and I wanted as much as possible. I grabbed Cass' sewing kit, my dad's old fishing rod and tackle box, our first aid kit, and my toolbox. I grabbed a few other odds and ends like boots and shoes, miscellaneous items that might come handy, books, some hobby oriented shit, and then I got Otis into his travel cage thingy. He fucking despises that thing with a passion. Some of worst scars have come from him fighting me when I try and get him in there. That day though, he was pretty good.

I remember vividly one of my last memories of my condo that day was seeing that nurse's body in the parking lot again. Her blood wasn't anywhere near as red on the pavement anymore. It had already started to turn a muddy, rusty brown color, which is normal. Blood is bright red, especially when it's arterial blood, which is what she had been squirting all over the place when I first saw her. I can remember still that seeing her body the second time around didn't weird me out at all. I think I can attribute that to two things; first, my natural sense of calm when the shit hits the fan, and second, I knew that the nurse was probably undead when she was shot. It kind of made me feel good to know that someone had the presence of mind to drop her quickly. Of course I also wonder today that maybe someone just blew her head off and was going to use the whole zombie thing as an excuse. The more I think about it, the more plausible some variation of that idea seems right. After all, when you kill a zombie, they don't really bleed, they just kinda... ooze. She was totally squirting. Sounds totally dirty. Maybe she had just been bitten, was still alive, and then she got shot? Who knows.

My last memory from my place was seeing her body in the parking lot. I loaded Otis in the car, double checked that I had everything I would need, and we were off to Moore's Sporting Goods. Moore's was a scene straight out of an end of the world movie. There was a cop in the parking lot providing barely adequate security as like 30 cars filled with people stormed in and out of the shop, buying everything in sight. I remember being suddenly doubtful of me being able to get anything at all there, but I was there, and I had to go in.

I know all the cops in town on a first name basis, or at least by face, and the cop in the parking lot was one I've known for years. Officer McGreevy. Big dude, bigger than me, and that's saying something. Bald as shit though, which is something I'm not. He was struggling trying to talk to a few panicked older people and we exchanged glances. I knew just from the look on his face shit was bad all over. He had that no nonsense, shit was bad look on his face. You know the one.

There was almost a line to get into the shop. Luckily Moore's had extra people behind their counter, so they were ringing people up pretty quickly. I noticed a few big hastily scribbled signs taped up in conspicuous places around the shop, each said the same thing;

There is a one rifle, one handgun, and one shotgun limit per customer. Thank you, Moore's.

Good enough. If you couldn't figure out how to get through this with all that, you were fucked anyway I think. I waited patiently in the three deep crowd at the counter until one of the clerks finally motioned for me to come up. I can remember his nametag was crooked, like the little safety pin had come undone in the back. His name was Phil. Phil was overweight like I was, had salt and pepper hair, and the look of a person who had had fucking enough. I made my decision to keep it professional.

I calmly requested to Phil that I was interested in a Glock handgun, preferably a 9mm or .40 caliber, a pump or semi auto shotgun, preferably 12 or 16 gauge, and a semi-automatic .22 caliber rifle, one preferably with a magazine. He told me they were flat out of Glocks entirely, but they did have a few Sig 9mm's left. I told him that was fine, and he got the rest of my order.

Now I'm not saying the fine folks of Moore's made a poor decision that day, or that our legal system failed our nation, but there was NO background check performed on anyone while I was there. Now I have a clean record, but some of the folks there were Shady as hell. Capital S added for extra emphasis on Shady.

Phil was nice enough to sell me 2,000 rounds of the .22 cal ammo, 200 rounds of 9mm, and 48 12 gauge double ought shells. He told me he was giving me the "hook up" and even sold me two spare magazines (that's a clip, for the uninformed) for both the rifle and the pistol. Those would be a big deal as you'll see in later entries. I also got a few extra things of gun oil, a fresh gun cleaning kit, as well as a holster and a hunting vest to wear for the shotgun shells and supplies.

The line had died down pretty dramatically while Phil

waited on me, and he and I chatted a bit. The folks here were in tight with the cops and they had a better local feel for what was up. Apparently there were no zombies from here, yet. The few zombies seen nearby were people who had come in from out of state already bitten, or already sick somehow. Of course, those few folks had bitten some other folks, and it was slowly spreading. The cops were doing a great job of containing shit from the sound of it, but even after hearing that, I wasn't fucking around. I had Phil charge it all on my credit card, and walked out more or less armed to the teeth.

Officer McGreevy was currently unimpeded by panicked customers when I walked out, so I waved hello, and he tiredly waved back. I loaded up my weapons, illegally, right in front of him in the parking lot, and we exchanged one last wave.

As I drove away down the road, I heard a few gunshots from behind me, back down where the shop was. I stomped the brakes, threw it in reverse, and backed down the road into the parking lot. A new car with out of state plates was in the lot, and McGreevy had his weapon drawn on the vehicle. One of the Moore's employees (not our intrepid hero clerk Phil) was in the doorway, handgun drawn as well. From inside my car I could see that the driver of the out of state sedan was face down on the ground, bleeding a circle out underneath him. The passenger of the car was a little boy, maybe 14 years old, brown hair, screaming bloody murder. McGreevy's pistol shot once more, caving in the back of the dude's head, splattering shit everywhere on the fender of the car. I noticed then that the guy had a huge red mark on the sleeve of his dress shirt. Looked an awful lot like a big fucking bite mark.

My guess was he looked sick, McGreevy saw the bite mark, and made a quick decision. I could see clearly from his face the cop was not cool with what had just happened. I could also see the Moore's guys coming out, practically celebrating that they had "gotten one." McGreevy looked up at me in my car, sighed once, and nodded really slightly. The kid was still screaming.

I never saw any of them again.

-Adrian

October 2010

October 4th

Hello again Mr. Journal. You know all this week I was wondering to myself why I sort of randomly decided that you were Mr. Journal, as opposed to Ms. Journal, or Mrs. Journal, or even Miss journal. Maybe I am subconsciously only comfortable spilling my guts to an artificial male? Dunno. Maybe at a later date I'll decide to spill my guts to a new target audience and change it (you)to Miss Journal. Maybe Miss Journal will want my shit, and I'll get laid again. Guess I should make my stories good then eh? Another thought occurs to me though; if I change Mr. Journal to Miss Journal, and I'm hoping Miss Journal wants my shit does that mean I'm into trannies? Now there's a Zen train of thought for you.

It's been a pretty good week since my last entry. Not much of anything has happened here on campus. I spent the majority of my time working in the vocational building in the woodshop. We had a shit-ton of lumber stored there and I was working on making myself some barricades. The dorms here aren't like you'd imagine for a normal boarding school. They aren't like Hogwart's, and they aren't like apartment buildings. We have five dorm buildings all broken up by age groups and grades. Each building is more or less like a giant house. Three of the dormitories are two floors, one is three floors, and one is just one floor. Stylistically they are all pretty similar to houses, but they're beefed up and industrialized.

Each dorm's exterior doors are all fire doors with heavy duty locks. That means they are steel, lock when they close, and are set in heavy duty frames. Perfect for fending off zombie attacks basically. Now each dorm has certain perks going for it. Hall A is good because it's dead center in campus. Windows in the dorm face in all directions, and it's got a great view of the bridge that people (or the undead) would cross to get here. Hall A is shitty because the first

28

floor is very low to the ground. Its windows would be easy to break, and there are a lot of windows for the breaking. The second floor is good because the two stairwells are separate from the first floor, both are behind fire doors, and they're on separate ends of the building. Plus the second floor has a little balcony off the staff apartment that used to belong to Mr. Trendwell, the physics teacher.

Hall E is about 200 feet down the sidewalk from A. Both Hall E and Hall A are near the river that skirts campus, which is nice when you open a window. You can hear the babbling of the water, and it's relaxing. Hall E has a lot of things going for it. It's kind of on the edge of a hill, and there are no windows on ground level. The bottom of the windows start at about five feet above ground level, so breaking a window would be difficult for a zombie. I've already got those windows barricaded with 2x4's and plywood, so that's covered. I was clever and only blocked off the bottom two thirds of the windows so I could still see out the window, or shoot out them if necessary. Other benefits of Hall E are as follows: Full kitchen, three floors, two living rooms, standard issue double fire doors at both entrances, and 18 bedrooms. Hall E seemingly had the least drawbacks, so that's where I'm set up now.

I'll tell more about the campus and the other buildings here later. Just about every building here has some kind of fucked up story to tell about it, and I don't want to miss any of the juicy details. Gotta impress Miss Journal for when she shows up, right?

The barricades I worked on this week were for some of the buildings that are low to the ground here. Specifically I really want to get the deck on the end of Hall E more secure. It's on the edge of the building that's overhanging the hill, so it's about 8 feet off the ground, but I really want to shore up the railings in the event I'm swamped and trapped here. So that was my project this week. I had enough lumber, skill and ambition to get that project done. Huzzah me. The whole time I was working in the shop I kept my shotgun handy, and didn't use any of the power tools. Noise is bad, and plus there's no sense in wasting my gas. My supply is obviously limited, and it's not like I've got more important shit to do. Handsaws for the win.

I think I should probably fill in more details about my trip here though. There's still so much story left just from the day the world fell apart. I'll be talking about it in journal entries until Thanksgiving more than likely.

So I think I said earlier that things happened so fast a plan was kind of impossible. Everything according to my plan had gone pretty much perfectly up until the shooting at Moore's. And really, that incident didn't change my plan at all. That was the first really fucked up thing I was sort of involved in that day, so I kind of look at that as the tipping point where things started to seriously come undone for me.

So I left the gun shop and started to update my plan. I now had guns and ammo. The most important and useful things from my house were in my trunk and backseat, so all I needed to do was to check on my friends, and stock up on food. Non-perishable stuff of course. As I got off the side street Moore's is on I saw the local agriculture store and it suddenly dawned on me I might need to grow food. I also noticed that the parking lot was almost empty so I made my first detour. Everyone in the store was huddled at the counter listening to the radio, and the news streaming out of it from NPR. I didn't want to waste any time, as it was already starting to get late, so I just went straight to the seed display. I literally grabbed one little pouch of everything they had, and snagged one of those garden weasel dealies. I knew the grounds keeping equipment at the school would probably have whatever else I needed. I remember it took me asking about ten times before the chick running the register even realized I was waiting to pay. She rang me up totally wrong, and only charged me like 15 bucks for everything. I had enough cash, so I paid, took my bag and garden aero-ater thingamabob, and walked out totally unnoticed.

All that shit went into the backseat and I was off again. When I was about to pull out of the parking lot one of the town ambulances flew by, headed down the road Moore's was on. I assumed they were headed to deal with the shooting. Another one of our town's finest was right on the ambulance's ass as well. That was actually the last time I saw a cop. Weird now to think that it's been months since I've seen a cop. Weird now to think that the dead come alive and feast on the flesh of the living too. Lols and whatnot.

Sooo.... Our local chain grocery store is on the other side of downtown, about 3 miles or so from where I was. I knew it'd be a madhouse, but I really needed food. I drove just under the speed limit mostly because I wanted to scan the surroundings for weirdness. Oddly enough, I saw little. There were a lot of people packing their cars, and I saw a lot of dads and son out in the yard hammering nails into sheets of plywood covering windows. I saw one desperate dude hammering up a door over a window and had to laugh. I wonder still how many of those folks are still holed up in their houses. I haven't done any tests, but I imagine a sheet of plywood wouldn't last long against a bunch of the undead hitting it over and over. Granted, they are weaker than a person, but they don't fucking get tired. The only "break" they take is to gnaw your flesh off your bones. Otherwise, they just keep at it, whatever it is they're doing.

Anyway, downtown was pretty tame. The power was still on, and I ran the red light cautiously in the center of town. There was no traffic, and I wanted to get to the store to get food before it was literally gobbled up. The final two miles to the store was more or less uneventful. I got passed on the road twice by jackasses driving giant pickup trucks. One of them flipped me off as he passed me on a solid yellow and I just had to laugh. World is ending and this guy is such a dink that he has give me the finger for not doing 60 in a 30. Some people are just assholes. I hope he got eaten by another asshole. The second guy who passed me was much nicer though. No middle finger.

The grocery store was mobbed, as I thought it would be. I parked on the edge of the parking lot and locked up the car. I slipped on my hunting vest, loaded it up with the shells Phil hooked me up with, and slung the shotgun over my shoulder. It was that moment that realized I needed to shorten the barrel and stock on the shotgun somehow. It was a little long and would be difficult to use in a building. I made a mental note to myself on that for later. I could clearly see other folks leaving the store carrying hunting rifles, so I wasn't too worried about the "social norm" of carrying a 12 gauge. I did get the opportunity to watch some woman in a minivan fucking cream a dude walking in the parking lot though. She must've not seen him, cuz she just plowed through his ass and just drove on. The ass end of the minivan hopped up like it was on springs when she drove over him. A bunch of folks rushed over to help him right after, so I didn't feel obligated to. I snagged a cart out of the corral and just like Johnny Shopper, I went in the automated door, and straight into retail hell.

You ever been grocery shopping the week of Thanksgiving? Or right before Christmas, when all the soccer moms lose their fucking mind and fight over boxes of shitty stuffing mix and cranberry relish? Well imagine that, and then add an "end of the world" flavor to it. That'll get you in the ballpark for the mood everyone had in the store that afternoon. I think it was about 5 or 5:30 at that point. Just starting to get dark-ish, and I can remember the temp getting low as the sun was setting.

Anyway, the lines were packed, and people were literally running their carts around the store, up and down the aisles like with reckless abandon. There were kids hollering at the top of their lungs as their moms and dads shopped literally like there was no tomorrow. I can't even imagine what a six year old would make of the situation. PTSD without a doubt for our children now. If there are any children left. Like all grocery stores, the majority of the canned goods are in the center of the store. Most of the folks were in those two aisles, so I decided to start on the fringe, and get other shit first. By the time I was done I had grabbed an entire shopping cart of food and supplies. Felt like I was pushing a pallet of bricks. I hit the pharmacy area hardcore and loaded up on bandages, ibuprofen, cold remedies, vitamins, melatonin, bacitracin, etc. You name it, I grabbed it. I wasn't about to worry about running out of that stuff.

For those of you who are curious, yes, I did grab several boxes of yellow, crème filled snack cakes. I didn't want to risk wanting one and having to come back to get them. So I snagged a mess of frozen veggies and shit like that, and I eventually intimidated my way into the canned goods aisles. Six foot one with scary tattoos is > a soccer mom. I knew the school kept a lot of canned shit on hand, so I made sure to grab the stuff I knew they would likely have little or none of. Boyardee stuff obviously, and I grabbed a lot of tuna pouches, canned veggies and that righteously yummy canned brown bread you eat with beans. I also got the beans to go with it. Sneaky motherfucker that I am I slipped behind the deli counter when the clerks weren't looking and grabbed a few whole, still sealed slabs of meat. One each of turkey, ham and bologna.

Sooooo… my shamefulness comes back. The deli is kinda near the exit and it took about two seconds of deliberation before I decided I was going to walk the fuck out without paying. What were they going to do anyway? Every employee had either left already, or was gooch-deep in customers. The only shitty problem was that my groceries would not be bagged. Not a real problem. I'll deal with that.

Out the door I went, snagging two bunches of bananas on the way. Outside things had gotten much fucking worse. Our grocery store patron who had been creamed by the soccer mom in her minivan was not doing well at all. Actually he had died, and someone had thrown a heavy duty blanket over him. One of those gray, industrial blankets people steal out of the back of moving trucks. I gave the crowd around his body a wide berth and made it about fifty more feet before I heard them start screaming. I stopped dead in my tracks, turned around, and watched the crowd scatter like dandelion fluff in the wind. I have never seen such fat people move with such vigor before. One lady with a mega-fupa was literally tearing up pavement as she ran. I still laugh today thinking of her jiggling rolls as she nearly ate shit getting into her far too small compact car. It might've been the springs, but I swear to this day I heard her car cry out in pain when she got in it.

Anyway, our poor accident victim had sat back up. From my angle at the time he was kind of facing away from me, and he still had the blanket covering his front side. He was blind basically with the blanket over his face. Morbid curiosity found me unslinging the shotgun, and approaching the dude. I racked up a round in the chamber and slowly circled him at about ten feet. You could just tell from his body language that he was fucked up. Plus he was making this rattling noise with his quasi-breathing that was just not normal. Well that's not entirely true. Ever give someone CPR? Frequently when you're giving real CPR air gets down into the stomach. When the air escapes it sometimes does this burpish-gurgle deal that's kind of unsettling. It's the death-rattle you read about. This dude was doing it, and he was moving around at the same time. Didn't make sense. I knew what it really meant though.

Just about when I got to his 10 o'clock the blanket slipped off his face, and I saw my first zombie. He was lit the fuck up. That accident had made him royally fucking nasty, and add to that all his color had drained away. His skin was this ashen white with a blue tinge. Dried blood crusted the edge of his mouth. He tried to stand up to come at me but both his legs were shattered. He kinda half fell over in my direction and face planted on the pavement. I remember laughing nervously when he started crawling at me because I saw his face had left a bloody wet mark where it had hit down.

His eyes had totally glazed over and were almost whitish-grey. He wasn't moaning like they do in the movies either. It makes a lot of sense now that I've seen so many real zombies. Moaning requires breathing, and these things do not breathe. Once he had finished his charming death-rattle, he was silent. That's actually one of the things that keeps me up at night. If you don't hear the shuffling of their feet, see them coming, or smell them coming, they are almost entirely silent.

After I made the mental decision that this man was indeed a newly minted zombie I took a deep breath, drew a bead on his face, closed my eyes, and pulled the trigger. The Mossberg bucked hard, and I felt something hit the front of my pants. I opened my eyes and saw that his face was totally annihilated, and some of the splash had hit me in the legs. I panicked for a second, wondering if this shit was contagious. I took another deep breath and chilled myself out. Couldn't worry too much about it right then. I racked up another shell in the shotgun, noticed the startling amount of people looking at me with shocked expressions, and walked back to my cart. You know there were at least ten guys in the parking lot at that moment with a gun just like me. Why didn't they do anything? Was I the only one with balls? I suspect I have just watched too many horror movies.

The crowds parted like I was mother-fucking Moses and they were the Red Sea. I'm a big dude, and frequently people see me and my tattoos and I get a wide berth anyway, but this was an adult-strength wide berth. 20 feet solid. That kinda felt good. I was getting a hardcore adrenaline rush the whole time and I'm not gonna lie, it felt kind of good.

I scooped my groceries into the trunk of my car, topping it off. I grabbed the box of shotgun shells from the passenger seat of my car, loaded a replacement shell in for the one I just shot, and got in the car.

Next stop: Friends and family.

See you soon Mr. Journal.

-Adrian

October 7th

I am kinda bored Mr. Journal. Instead of my planned once weekly entries I'm doubling up this week. I know I've got enough gas to power the generator to keep me in heat and electricity for winter so I can waste a little juice on keeping the laptop running.

It's Thursday, I just ate some lunch, and things are pretty good here. Got my deck fully reinforced and I pulled up all the stairs leading off of it. Now there's no way they can get in via that entrance. Hall E has all the windows on the first floor barred up adequately and the fire doors are strong enough to hold back a siege. I've also got clear lines of sight to all entrance to pick off a ton of Zombies should things get desperate. I have a lot of lumber left over as well so I'm starting to think of what else I should really be reinforcing. I don't know yet, this place is pretty huge and I don't want to waste the wood.

Otis is well, nice of you to ask. I'm definitely wishing I had grabbed more cat food for him though. I only thought to grab two large bags of food, and that's getting low. I know I can share my food with him, but that's not ideal cat food, ya know? I guess eventually I'll have to seriously consider a run back into town to restock. There has to be food still in town somewhere, and I can't imagine that our residents thought to grab up all the cat food. In all honesty, I really ought to start formulating a plan to get down there as soon as possible. I'm starting to notice food choices are getting slim at dinner, and if there are other survivors in town, I want to make sure I get the food before them. Selfish, but it's the reality now. I'm as likely to get shot and killed by another living person as I am to get eaten alive by the undead.

I'll start to look at my options this week. I can tell it's gonna be a pisser of a winter, and I don't want to have to leave here in a snowstorm. I should also stop by my house and get more of my own stuff. I'll be cooped up inside for most of the coming winter and I don't want to get stir crazy. It's entirely possible boredom might drive me to desperate measures, and I'd rather cut that off at the pass.

What to talk about? Me? The past? More of the story from the day it all started? I don't really want to say much about myself. I think we are all delusional about our self image anyway. What I type in this little journal will be just a vision of myself, not a real accounting of reality. I guess eventually I'll have to say something, but for now, go fly a kite. You already know my name, my height, and that I've got a lot of tattoos. I also mentioned briefly that I had experience with violence. I worked concert security and did bouncing for 13 years on the weekends. I also did some bodyguard work here and there, and did my stint in the Army. Plus Dad and three brothers were all military so that was my culture at home. Anyway, I'm feeling like dropping more history now about the day the world ended, so let's get that ball rolling.

Ha, had to open my last journal entry to see where I left off. So by the time I got all my groceries into my truck it was 6pm. I figured I had another solid hour of twilight before dark, and I really wanted to be done here in town before it was dark. The thought of wandering around in the dark with the undead wandering still sends ice water through my veins. I checked Otis to make sure he was okay, which he was, and I formed a mental map of town and where my friends were, and in what order I needed to check on them in.

Mom was first. She was probably the closest, likely the least capable of dealing with the crisis, and had some skills that I knew would be useful if this thing got dragged out. In retrospect, I fucking despise being around my mother, and I really should've thought of that. Second was my good friend and co-worker Steve. Steve lived on main street, but he was good to go by himself. He was smart, resourceful, had a decent car, and probably wasn't home anyway. He frequently went into the city after he woke up so there was a good chance he was already gone. Third was Cass and I's friends John and Dorothy. They lived outside town with their four year old daughter and I really wanted to try and get them to come with me to the school. They would be last though, as they were the furthest out. The rest of my family all lives in the city or just outside of it, so they were too risky, at least for tonight.

Mom lives on School street downtown, weirdly enough, next to the school. She was getting up there, about 70, and she had just moved into senior housing a few months earlier. She hated it, but she couldn't afford much else. Cass and I both felt her moving in with us was not an option. I left the parking lot of the grocery store driving slowly. This time though I had the Sig in my lap as I drove. Things were much more serious in my mind now. I'd just seen a zombie, just shot a zombie, and I now knew for sure it was happening right here, right now.

School street was maybe a mile away. The short drive to mom's place put things in perspective for me. I didn't see a single zombie on the way there, but that makes total sense. Unless you were bitten, or died of some other cause, there would be no reason to see one. Mind you, I was still operating partially thinking the CDC was right about how transmission was only by bite. I hadn't quite fully made the connection that parking lot zombie had never been bit yet. Anyway, I realized there was probably a bit of a buffer of time still until people started to die. As long as I could avoid human on human violence, I should be pretty good.

Keeping suit with my new criminal side I ran the light again, but this time turned onto School street heading toward mom's. There were way more people out and about now. Lots of folks still boarding up their places, and even more loading up their cars and vans with shit to get out of town. I imagine a lot of people were going to head north to get to even more rural areas. No idea how that panned out. Judging by my success, as long as they weren't total idiots, a lot of them should be just fine.

I saw a few more fender benders before I got to mom's place, but nothing that would generate a dead body, so no worries there. The senior housing place mom lives in is a huge two floor building. Imagine a hospital style setting only less sterile, and mildly more homey-feeling. I pulled my sedan into the parking lot, right near the entrance closest to my mom's apartment, and got out. The scene there was also pretty hectic. From the looks of things people were picking up their elderly family members and getting the fuck out of Dodge. Lots of old folks getting wheeled out in wheelchairs at top speed to waiting cars. I hopped out, locked the car, and headed towards the door. I left the Mossberg behind in favor of the Sig. The barrel of the shotgun was probably going to be longer than needed, and would likely be a hindrance if shit hit the fan.

Speaking of that, just as I got to the big glass doors, someone burst out, nearly smashing me in the face. I remember stumbling backwards a few steps when I saw blood on them. It was a middle aged man, somewhere around 45 maybe. I recall his hair was receding pretty badly, and he had an epic comb over, and really thick eyeglasses. His palms were slick with blood, and his sleeves were streaked with red all the way up the elbows. His neck was also covered in what looked like a spray of bright red blood too. He just blew right by me in a total panic. I couldn't see any wounds or bites, so I didn't think to stop and ask him what was up. After watching him sprint across the parking lot to his waiting car, I pulled open the doors and headed in, drawing the Sig.

There were bloody footprints all along the carpet in the lobby. The bloody tracks headed through the nurse-station area, originating down the hallway my mom's apartment was. I instantly got a really bad feeling. I started to move really slow, handgun up, taking wide berth of doors. The intersection where the bloody footprints turned was a four-way, and you could see huge smears of blood on the walls and on the handrail that ran everywhere in the place. I swept around the corner and saw a cluster of people huddled in the middle of the corridor about 20 feet away.

I don't remember exactly what I said, but it was something along the lines of "hey there." But loud, like, attention grabbing. The people stood up slowly, and turned. At first I just thought they were old, and moving in an arthritic fashion, but once I got a clear look at them turned around I knew they were dead. Two old ladies and an old man, sallow and sunken faced, covered in blood and gore. The lady closest to me had a massive wound in her neck that was ragged and semi-circular, like a bite. The three of them had been eating someone on the floor in the hallway and my shout had interrupted them.

The trio of old zombies started to shuffle towards me. If it wasn't so fucking gross it might've been kinda funny. Older people zombies or injured people zombies seem to reanimate in as good a condition as they were in life, this is something I've learned. They stumbled, bumped into the walls and moved at a crawl towards me, dripping blood all the way. I took a quick check behind myself to make sure there wasn't any behind me, and once I noticed it was all clear, I dealt with the three Methuselah. I am a pretty good shot, thankfully, and put one in the face or forehead of all three of them. Start to finish the entire encounter maybe lasted six seconds. At the time it felt like forever, but adrenaline has this neat effect of slowing time down for you. Thank you for that big person upstairs.

I checked behind me again, and it was all clear. From the other side of the building I could hear the screams of people fleeing from the gunshots (or perhaps other elderly zombies) so I knew I had a little time. Of course this changed my estimates on my time buffer. These older folks had obviously died of natural causes and reanimated, so I knew at that point there was a much higher chance of there being more walking dead. I slowly approached the three bodies, and gave them a good kick. I can remember wishing I had bought sturdy work boots. Those are harder to bite through.

The body in the hallway was my mom. I could've built it up all dramatic like, but honestly I don't have the writing skill. I think I knew, because when I got close enough to the body I wasn't surprised at all that it was her. Her gray bushy hair, the silly track pants she always wears, and the ugly housecoat/nightgown thing she thinks is still stylish. I might've seen it in the fray maybe, I don't know. I just remember not being surprised or moved really. She was in pretty bad shape though. Her clothes were ripped apart pretty good and her chest had been chewed at. The burgundy rug in the corridor was stained a terrible black brown around her from all the blood she'd lost. Her breast had been ripped or bitten off, leaving a gaping wound. She did have a peaceful look on her face, but I was pretty creeped out by her open eyes. I kneeled down, and slowly closed her eyelids.

Stupid move, majorly big-time dumb. She snapped at me as I pulled my hand away, and was about a pubic hair's width from taking a finger right the fuck off. I can distinctly remember the clicking noise her teeth made when they clamped at the open air. I kicked away, launching my back right into the hall wall. That fucking hurt badly. She rolled over and started crawling towards me, pulling at my jeans to get closer. I fired a half dozen times from the hip as fast as I could pull the trigger, and at least two or three shots hit her in the face. God I hate what that does to the face. Just fucking nasty. I got hit in the side of the neck by a few of the ejected shell casings, which gave me a nice little burn or two.

She then slumped into my lap, and proceeded to ruin my pants that I had kinda hoped to salvage at a later date. At this point in the end of the world I still didn't know if I would be able to wash gore out with normal laundry detergent. I got her off me, calmed myself down thought about what, if anything she could have in her house that might be useful to me, and made my next plan. One amusing thing that occurred to me at that moment was the fact dear old mom had false teeth. Would she have been able to infect me with falsies? It was the clicking noise that made me think about it. Food for thought I guess.

And that's the story of how I shot my mom. Think less of me yet?

-Adrian

October 11th

The weather seems to have taken a turn for the mild. It's gone up about 20 degrees on average over the last week, which is pretty awesome. Those 35 degree nights are going to be bad enough in January, let alone all frigging October and November. Of course there's nothing I can do about it, one way or the other. Can't change the weather. I can however change how I stay warm. This weekend I actually did some work on what exactly I needed to do to stay warm.

I think I mentioned earlier on that I had electricity. Which I do. There was a good sized generator in the basement of Hall E (where I am) that I got running. That makes it sound like I'm a mechanical miracle worker though, which I'm not. It just needed a refill of gasoline, and some basic cleaning. With the fuel I have in the tanks of all the vehicles parked around campus I figure I have enough gasoline for electricity for maybe 6 hours a day. What I really need to think about is the fact that the heat here is supplied via oil furnace. The furnace has electric ignition though, which means it will only fire when there's electricity supplied to it.

So there's a few problems I need to deal with. I checked the various oil tanks on campus, and there's a metric fuck-ton of oil for me to burn. Each building has oil heat, and almost every building has a pretty full 500 or 1,000 gallon tank. I should have oil for years. However, I do not have enough gasoline to run the generator for years. There's about

20 vehicles on campus, and most of those have less than half a tank of gas. I figure that's about 200 gallons of gas, at most. I will need heat overnight at the very least during winter, which is at least 6 hours, which means all my gasoline will be used up generating electricity, strictly to keep my furnace running. Not really a great situation. I definitely need to address two problems:

1)I need way more gasoline. I need gas for the cars, should I need to leave here, and I need gas to power the electric generator.

2)I need a more renewable heating system. Something like a wood stove. There's trees all over the place here, and I will never run out of firewood. Shit, there's enough downed trees to keep me in firewood for this year just on campus.

So now what? What's my first step to solving the heat and gasoline riddle? I have no additional reserves here on campus to tap into that I am aware of, so that means going into town. Well, at least that means going to a convenience store or something where I can get more gas. Worst case scenario there's a small gas station about 4 miles from here down the road I can hit. I know there are manual cranks to get the pumps working, and If I can scrounge up some gas cans, I think I can get myself set up pretty good. I know very frigging little about installing wood stoves though. I don't even know where to find one.

So I guess I should start thinking about how to hit the gas station. If I'm even a little lucky the electricity will still be on down there, though if my power is out here, it's probably out down there. I was surprised how long the power stayed running though, almost 6 weeks before it shit the bed.

There's about 12 houses in the little neighborhood where the store is. There's also a country store with gas pumps about half a mile from there too, which is an option. I'm betting there might be food at both places still. It stands to reason that if people downtown went out after the shit got bad to get food, they probably went to the grocery stores and the shops downtown. These fringes of town places might not have been picked over yet. I guess yet is the operative word here. I guess the sense of urgency in getting to any leftover supplies should motivate me to get my ass in gear.

Alright, here's my plan: Find as many gas cans as possible first off. Maintenance has two F-150 dump body trucks. Those are pretty sturdy vehicles, and the dump body is big, and could be used to climb into if I get surrounded. It's pretty high off the ground and the solid steel is obviously tough as hell. Plus I checked, and truck #1 still has a full tank, so that's a plus. Take truck #1, load up the guns, sword, and ammo, and head to the closest convenience store.

At the store, my main plan is to get gas into all gas cans. That's my primary need. I have enough food to last me for winter and then some, so that's a secondary thing. However, if the coast is mostly clear, and I'm feeling good, I'll check the store(s) for anything food or supply related that I could use. It'll be a thrill for sure to head back out into the scary world again. What are the downsides of doing this though? I haven't really considered that yet.

Getting killed is obviously one. I really don't want to be eaten alive, and I sure as shit don't want to get killed by another survivor. I could definitely lead zombies or survivors back here too. The school is at the end of a dead end road, so if anyone sees me make the turn up here, all they gotta do is go straight to find me. I know the zombies are stupid, but one thing they can do is go straight for a long time. If one sees me turn, I could lead them back here. That'd lead to me defending the campus with guns I'm sure, which might make enough noise to get more up here, spiraling everything into an enormous shit storm. Let's face it, no one likes a fecal tornado.

Good, positive thoughts are important at a time like this. Sigh.

I'm sure there's more that could go wrong. But, the simple fact is this: at the rate I'm burning through gasoline I will not make it through winter. I will freeze. Scary thought really. I also really need to think about alternative heating sources like the wood stove or something. Maybe I can look into solar panels or something? You know a woodstove would be great for cooking too, it'd save on the gas consumption big time. The electric stove is killing me I'm sure. That and running the fridge. Well not so much anymore really, as I don't have anything perishable in there anymore to speak of. Leftovers. In the Winter I can easily just set my leftovers outside somewhere the bears can't get at. Oh yeah, we have bears up here. Forgot to mention that.

I'm gonna go check around campus tomorrow to see if there are spare gas cans. I'll also double check around truck #1 to make sure that it's in good shape for a run outside. I probably ought to be starting these cars more often and letting them run for a bit. Families of squirrels and field mice are probably inside all of them by now too.

I'll keep you updated on how things go.

-Adrian

October 12th

Okay, my recon mission around campus is complete. I think.

Down in the maintenance garage way in the back of campus I found three gas cans. They are whopping 2 gallons cans. I searched all over the rest of campus, each and every building that was likely to have a gas can, and no luck. I did however find another 2 gallon canister in the trunk of someone's car though, parked in the employee lot. So that's 8 gallons total. Not even worth a trip really.

So, plan B. Instead of taking truck #1, I'm going to take truck #2. Truck #2 has about a quarter of a tank of gas, which is more than enough to get me down there. According to the manual in the glove box, the truck has a 36 gallon tank. I figure I'll get about 30 gallons in the tank, which I can siphon off later, and then I can get 8 more gallons in the small gas cans. If I'm lucky, they'll have more gas cans at the store. At the very least, roughly 38 gallons of extra gas will stretch out my fuel reserves. Plus if it goes well I can start making more frequent trips and just fill up the gas tanks of the vehicles around the school. Is it an ideal solution? Shit of course not. Will it work for now until I figure this shit out? I surely hope so.

I think this will work out. I can't imagine the area the store is at will be flooded with zombies. There's what? 12 houses there? At absolute worst there should be no more than like 40 zombies. That's assuming most houses are producing 3-4 zombies per house. That's unlikely. Some of those people have to have left town, or holed up somewhere else.

I'll guess I'll find out tomorrow. Until then Mr. Journal, I bid you adieu!

-Adrian

October 12th (2nd entry)

Well I sure as shit can't sleep. I am all kinds of nerved up over going out tomorrow morning. I definitely decided morning was best. If something does happen and I need to come back on foot, I want as much daylight as possible to make it back. Moving around in the dark now absolutely petrifies me. There's some sense in thinking that the zombies are less dangerous at night, as their vision probably sucks ass compared to living people vision, so dark would be easier to move around. I'm still of the school of thought that my vision is compromised at night, and with these fuckers being so quiet I'd rather use daylight to have a better chance of seeing them.

So morning it is. After I finished typing today's earlier entry I broke down all my guns and cleaned them. I'm only taking the 12 gauge and the Sig tomorrow, but I cleaned the . 22 and the .30-06 as well. I'm sure I'll fill in the story how I got that at some point. Don't feel like talking about it right at the moment though, I'm busy, and it's kind of a sore subject still. I should have plenty of gun cleaning supplies to last me indefinitely. Pat myself on the back for grabbing the gun cleaning kit and the extra gun oil at Moore's that day.

I guess I can try and exhaust myself by talking more about 'that day.' There's still a lot to tell. So where was I? Just checked my last entry to remember and as it turns out, I left off with me being an awesome son, and shooting my mother in the face.

So I shot her in the face with the Sig, and she slumped down on top of my lap with her head leaking all over me. I'm pretty sure I was in some kind of shock for a few seconds after I got up. Didn't last long though. As gross and weird as this sounds, shooting my mom in the face actually made it go away quicker I think. With her face gone I couldn't like, look at her and see what I'd done. With her face so mashed up it could've been any old lady's body laying in front of me. It was like she was anonymous.

So like I said earlier I thought about what my mom might have had that would be useful. Plus I knew at this point I needed to stay busy or I might start getting emotional about shooting my mother. My mom was kind of a douche to me in life, but shit, she was Mom, right? I was having trouble thinking clearly, and I knew I needed to get out of the hallway anyway, so I decided to go inside the apartment where she lived. At least I could shut the door behind me for some semblance of safety, and look first hand at her place.

I stepped over her body and got out my keys and let myself in. Her place was pretty normal, no mess, or signs of the struggle that evidently did her in. Probably got jumped heading here, or got pulled out into the hall if she opened the door. No idea. Her place stank of stale cigarettes. If it wasn't for the end of the world zombie plague and getting her body torn apart I swear lung cancer would've gotten her shortly. At the rate she chimneyed those fuckers she HAD to have been at least a little cancerous. (physically at least, her personality had always been cancerous)

Once I got inside and calmed myself a bit I instantly remembered that my mom was a food hoarder. She was Italian, and Italians love to cook overly large meals. I knew she had canned goods out the wazoo. I headed into her kitchen and started flinging cabinets open and revealed a cornucopia of food. I actually did a fist pump when I saw she had cranberry relish. For some reason I just love that shit, and when I saw it there it struck me that I hadn't grabbed any at the store. She also had some food beeping in the microwave, all done and ready to eat. It was some day old spaghetti with a meat sauce. I didn't realize I was hungry until I popped the button to open the microwave, but holy shit it hit me then. I snagged a fork from the drawer and ate the whole plate standing in front of the sink. Yay mom!

I quickly did the whole room clearing deal to make sure the rest of the house was safe, and I saw a half empty banana box on the floor of her closet. Probably a leftover box from the move into here a few months ago. I would also like to make a short aside here and point out how useful and sturdy banana boxes are. Anyone who reads this, if you need a good, sturdy box, go for the banana box, it's reliable, and has handles.

I dumped her shit out, took the box into the kitchen and just took everything. I emptied all her canned goods and her freezer as well. She had 10 of those frozen dinner meals, which I thought was pretty cool. (ironically, I had one of them for dinner earlier) Anyway, once I had the box filled with all her stuff, I knew I had to get out quick. If there were two zombies outside in this hallway alone, God only knows how many others there might be. I guess it makes sense that older people might've died ahead of the curve for normal deaths. Heart attacks from stress, strokes, or even just a natural death would've introduced a zombie to the building here and if the older folks were nearby, it's not like they can run well to get away. Plus they are not as able in defending themselves, so really, it's like fish in a barrel for zombies.

I figured I would be best served by clearing my exit out of the building, then taking the box out. If I was jumped holding the box I might drop it, cutting down on my reaction time as well as possible busting my banana box, and frankly, banana boxes are just too damn good to risk losing it. Lol. Oh Christ I just farted and it smells like pure evil. Fucking frozen dinner is giving me gas. Otis just got up and walked up the stairs to get away from me. I am awesome. I gotta crack a window, brb.

Much better. Anyway I checked the eyehole in the door and it looked clear. I slowly opened it, and peered out in both directions, Sig at the ready. It looked clear in both directions, and it was also quiet. I propped the door open wide enough to push the box through with my foot, and I stepped out into the hall. Mom's body was still face down where she fell on top of me. Both the zombie bodies were still where they went down when I dropped them as well. Good shooting I guess on my part.

I brought the Sig up, and started my slow and smooth gait down the corridor. I had 20 feet or so to go straight to the four way intersection, then a left to head out to the lobby area with the nurse's station in it. I made the first 20 feet clean with no contact, but when I took the left I nearly shit myself. Not like the farts I'm dropping tonight, I mean legit underwear filling fecal slippage. The nurse's station looked like a motherfucking butcher's table. One of the nurses was slumped in the chair behind the counter, head all the way back with one of the elderly residents just going to town on her neck. You could clearly hear the gristle popping in the dead dude's mouth as he chewed his way through her throat. Horrible. I noticed that she was wearing the same style of shirt and pants as the woman who got decapitated outside my condo earlier that day. That confirmation kind of felt good.

Laying on the floor in the middle of the lobby was a younger guy, probably mid 20's and dressed athletically. He was face down and two more of the older folk zombies were lying on top of him, eating away. It was just gross. The smell alone, even from a solid 15 feet away was sickening. Entrails have a nasty smell. Earthy, a little like vomit as well, with some poo stench mixed in. Add to that the coppery tinge from all the blood and it's enough to turn any appetite. Certainly almost made me hurl the spaghetti I just ate. Of course as soon as got within 15 feet or so the zombies either smelled me or saw me. I don't think they can smell, so I think they saw me or maybe heard me.

The one already standing eating the nurse's neck was the closest, and quickest to respond. I took a few steps in his general direction and squeezed off two rounds at his head. I remember the first round hit him squarely in the neck and punched a dark hole right where his Adam's apple was. The second hit him in the nose, and he went down immediately. The other two zombies were pretty much jerked into motion from the sound of the gunshots. They were more or less in a prone position though, and being older, they were slow to get up. Finishing them was easy. A few steps closer, and two 9mm shots put them down for good. I did a quick survey, saw nothing else between me and the glass exit doors, and decided to go back for my haul. Here's where I made my first few major mistakes of the day.

I grabbed the box, stuck the Sig back in the holster, and started a slow creep back to the lobby. Hallway was clear for me, just like the first time, but as soon as I made the corner heading out the lobby I was nearly knocked over by the fucking nurse who had her neck eaten apart. I totally forgot to put one in her head before walking away. Somewhat fortunately, the banana box was between me and her when she kinda stumbled against it, and I was saved. I took a few steps back, dropped the box as gently as I could, drew the pistol and popped one in her forehead. She fell so hard that her head nearly came disconnected from her spine. Really jarring visuals, seriously, the image frequently haunts me.

By that point I realized there was another un-dealt with body in the lobby. The kid. This guy was younger too, so he would likely be quicker and stronger than these older folks. Not that the nurse was old, but she was kind of a big girl, and not that young.

I made the corner again, this time leaving the box behind so I could deal with the kid. As soon as I took the turn at the four way I could see he was getting to his feet. Coming up slowly, like he was a sore athlete doing push-ups. It was nasty though, because his guts were coming apart underneath him. I made a snap decision to shoot him before he fully got to his feet. I took a few quick jogging steps at him, and drew a bead on the back of his head as he was halfway up. Of course that was when I realized my second great mistake. The gun clicked dry. I was like two feet from this fucking zombie, and my gun was empty.

Tired now. I'll finish after my trip to the store tomorrow.

-Adrian

October 13th

The best laid plans of mice and men right? I hate my fucking life.

Alright so the maintenance dump truck I grabbed started fine, no problem. I gathered up my gas cans, the Sig, the shotgun, and my short sword. It's the smallest high quality sword I own, and if possible, I would rather use that first. However, driving with a sword sheathed on your hip is really awkward. I totally can see why a cop would take a nightstick off their belt when driving. I wound up just tossing it on the seat beside me.

So I was up early to get down there. About 8am. I'm pretty fortunate in that my girlfriend bought me one of those self winding watches that always stay running as long as you're moving. You know I bet there are a shitload of these watches that are gonna run forever on the arms of zombies. How weird is that?

So I grabbed a good sized bite to eat (frozen bagel with jelly, can of beans, and two glasses of OJ from concentrate) and set off down the road to the gas station. The campus is pretty high in altitude relative to the valley we're situated next to. We're almost on a plateau really. What that means is our road (well, I guess it's just MY road now) is pretty steep going downhill, and has a few ups and downs. The truck made it about two miles before it started hiccupping and coughing, and came to a halt. I pulled over after the power steering died (which if you've never done it is a pretty herculean task)

Turned the key off, tried to start it, and it tried real hard, but just sputtered and died. Lather, rinse, repeat a few times, and still a dead truck. So I had to make a decision, walk back and scrap the trip? Or walk back, get truck #1, and do it with that one. I'd be missing out on a lot of fuel doing that way, but at the very least it'd be a recon mission. I decided to do that. I got out into the cold morning air and immediately felt some burning fury and frustration. This shit always seems to happen to me. Always the crap that should NEVER go wrong, goes wrong. I should've expected this shit.

I started a slow jog. I had 2 miles, mostly uphill, and I didn't want to gas out on this unnecessary and unexpected jog. I paced myself, and everything was fine until I got to the nice cape home that's about a half mile from campus. It was on the right side of the road, set back about 50 feet with a long, curved driveway. It had lovely crème color siding and a very nice veranda connecting the garage to the main house. It also had two zombies meandering in the yard , one in the wilting center flower garden, and one right in front of the garage. I only noticed them because I happened to stop jogging right next to the house and glanced absently sideways. Had I not stopped, I would've jogged right past them. Well they sure as shit noticed me. When I finally took them in, they were both shuffling with their stiff, clumsy walk at me, arms sweeping, feet dragging.

My cursory examination of them pegged them as a couple. Probably the snooty people who owned this 300k house here in the hills. The guy had a sweater vest for Christ's sake. In can only imagine the prick he was in life. Fashion notwithstanding, they were a threat, and they were moving pretty good. Their yard tilted to the road and I think they were building steam coming downhill at me. Course maybe I was just scared shitless. I brought up the shotgun, racked up a shell, and was about to drop mom, when I realized I really didn't want to waste rounds, or make noise. I slung the shotgun once I figured I had time to use the sword (which I'd put on my belt when I left the truck). I drew the sword, and entered into an old fashioned ass whupping. Zombies don't block or dodge anything, so it's not a fair fight if you just keep your spacing. They have no sense of self preservation. I took off her right arm with a backswing at the elbow, sending her into a wobbling tailspin. Once she stumbled to a stable upright position, I snapped the sword two-handed right into her neck.

Now let me clear something up for un-initiated: beheading someone isn't easy. There's a lot of muscle, cartilage, bone, sinew and jazz in the neck, and unless you have a heavy duty axe, or big sword, it's fucking work to chop a head off. Certainly not like in the movies where a cavalier swing send the head flying and a gout of blood fountaining from the neck. It goes without saying I didn't get it on the first swipe. However my strike was pretty high on the neck, and it crushed her jaw completely, as well as knocking her to the ground. She landed face down, and I curb stomped her head from behind. She twitched a few times, and I moved away to address Wally. (I was assuming at some point I would find the zombie Beaver shortly)

Wally was a good five feet away when I came down with both hands on the base of his neck, where it meets the shoulder. The sword sunk in a solid six inches, and lodged in the top of the ribcage I think. It didn't kill him, but it gave me a solid handle on his movement. I used the grip of the sword to twist him down onto his back, where I kicked his head repeatedly until he stopped moving. Once I felt reasonably safe, I got the sword free, and stabbed him the eye. I know, this shit is grody, but I'm recording history for posterity, so fuck you if you're sensitive and offended.

Wally and June were down. I gave the area a once over and saw it was clear, and I also saw their garage door was open. Inside said garage was a gigantor pickup truck. A Tundra, gunmetal grey. I slid into the garage quietly, making sure that it was empty, and checked the truck. Quarter tank, keys in the ignition. I gave it a quick once over, and then reached inside to start it. It turned over immediately, and sounded smooth. No hiccups. Smooth.

Fuck walking back for truck #1. This would work, and I'd make do. I took the sword off, hopped in, adjusted the seat, and backed out. In the rear view mirror I caught a brief glimpse of a kid running out behind the truck, and I jerked the brakes. I heard a thunking noise, and my heart dropped. I just hit a kid. After killing the kid's undead parents. Fuck my life. I was exhausted, frustrated, and suddenly racked with tremendous guilt. I powered the window down and leaned out to look back. I saw a little girl, maybe 10 years old laying splayed out behind the truck. I dropped my head on the window frame and my mouth dried up. I looked again though and the kid had sat back up, and was coming to her feet. It didn't take much for me to figure out she had been a zombie awhile. Her cheek was missing, teeth showing through, and her skin was a super alabaster color. I was actually relieved to see she was a zombie. I threw the truck into reverse again, and lined up the tires to run her over.

There was a bump, a crunch, and a giant stain left behind in the driveway. With a clear conscience, I drove down the road, off to my original destination. I stopped at the original truck and grabbed the gas cans before heading all the way down the hill. The road was just as clear of cars as it has always been, but there were quite a few tree branches down in the road. Rather than clear them out of the way, I just drove carefully around them. I didn't want to clean the road out too much for two reasons. First, it is shit a zombie can trip up on. That's saying something too. These fuckers can get entirely bamboozled by simple obstacles like that. I once watched a zombie walk straight forward for 15 minutes stuck in a playground swing. Damn swing was up around its armpits and it just kept going forward. Probably still there right now. And secondly, any survivors might think a cleared out road leads to salvation, and I wasn't sure I wanted roommates just yet. Call me selfish if you want, but I'm fucking pragmatic so suck it.

I crept up to the stop sign around the corner from the gas station. Old habits die hard and I came to my complete stop. Mostly just to check out the surroundings, but traffic safety has always been a pet peeve of mine too. I could clearly see movement inside the two houses across the street from the gas station. It was slow movement, deliberate and a little clumsy. Pretty sure it was zombies. I counted at least 6 different shapes moving in the windows. I figured they were stuck inside and wouldn't be a problem. I slipped into the main road and drove the last 100 feet at about 5 miles an hour. The gas station lot was clear, and the two open garage bays were void of movement. There was a body half under a car on a lift, but it looked pretty ravaged as I pulled up to the pump.

I work like the military in situations like this. Clear the building first, then do your work. I hopped out, sheathed up the sword as I kept an eye out, and headed up the few steps into the front doors of the station. This station was a mom and pop shop, not a chain, and it looked like a house more than a franchise style square building. I pushed the door open slowly, and took a sniff. Always trust your nose. I've learned that. Dead bodies and zombies smell wretched, especially if they're in an enclosed space for a long time. The interior of the gas station actually smelled pretty good. It smelled a little moldy maybe, dusty for sure, but no rot in the air at all. I stepped in once I felt comfortable.

I move with purpose. I'm quick, assertive, and have good violence of action. (look that phrase up, it's good shit if you don't know what it means) I cleared the main store area, which consisted of 4 chest high aisles, and the back room, which was just a glorified janitor's closet. There was one exit in the back room area, but it led upstairs to the apartment above. I didn't feel the need to go up there at the moment so I left it shut. No power was on. I checked the cooler doors and immediately wished I hadn't. The milk inside had gone rancid, and the stench was overwhelming. I actually panicked for a second because it was almost the same as a ripe Zombie. It wasn't though, all was safe for the moment.

I immediately grabbed a handful of plastic bags from behind the counter and started filling them with everything I could see. My main items of note were pretty fucking outstanding. Soda, chips, and candy. I hadn't had shit like this since the world ended, and it was long since overdue. Energy drinks, coffee cans, sealed juices so stocked up with preservatives they were good until the next apocalypse, and a whole bunch more of the good old canned sustenance. I filled four bags at a time and made a trip to the truck, setting them gently in the back. Once I had filled the bed of the Tundra with bags, I searched for the keys to open the pumps. Nada. I looked for a solid 15 minutes but found jack shit. Eventually I saw the body outside in the garage again and figured I'd check the pockets.

I felt pretty safe checking the corpse because the head was crushed by some parts that had fallen off the car. Looked like the whole ass end of the car had come loose and crushed him. He was also pretty fresh compared to the bodies I've seen from the first of the zombie days. I wonder now if he was trying to fix the car to mount an escape?

Anyway, he had the keys in his pocket, and it only took a minute or two to get the pump door open, and get the manual handle set in it. It only took me three rotations to get fuel coming out the nozzle. Like an asshat though, I didn't put the truck on the right side for the gas cap. I filled the four gas cans though, and then pulled a quick U-turn, switching the truck around. As soon as I pulled into the pump again and got out, I heard the car coming.

Frankly, I panicked. Hide? Just stand there? Get the gun ready? My decision was made for me though when the car crested the little hill and drove by me. They stomped on their brakes though, and stopped the car right in the road. It was an import station wagon. Volvo? Subaru? I don't remember right at the moment. A woman was driving, and a young guy was in the passenger seat. The car sat still in the road for a solid minute before the dude got out of the passenger side. He had a big scruffy nap of hair that looked like a badly trimmed beard that ran into an afro, and he was wearing a heavy flannel shirt and jeans. Reminded me of a hippy crossed with a logger. Funny stuff.

He hopped out of the car and just stood there, looking at me. I waved slowly, and rested my hand on the Sig at my waist. I could see he had a shotgun inside the car, set in the doorframe and within easy reach. I forget exactly what he said after our moment of awkward silence, but it was something like this:

"Uh, hey dude, you okay? You need help?"

And I said, "I'm fine man, thanks. You two okay?" He seemed genuinely concerned, so my guard came down a little. After I said that, he replied:

"There's actually three of us, we've got our son too, he's only 3." I remember vividly him looking in the backseat of the car, and I could kinda see a car seat. "Do you have any food? We need food for him, we've been looking but we're low on bullets, and it's hard to get into stores that way, you know?"

I took my time answering him. "this place is cleared out,

it's safe." I thumbed at the gas station behind me, "I actually left a bunch of baby food in there too. I've got some stuff in the truck here you can have too, just hang on and I'll dig it out." I carefully watched his response to that. And honestly, he started to tear up and smile ear to ear.

He could barely get it out, but he muttered something like, "oh my God, thank you so much man." That made me feel good. I rooted around in the truck, emptied a bag, and refilled it with stuff I knew I had plenty of back at the school. I also felt good because turning the truck around faced me in the opposite direction of the road I would be heading towards when I left. It's a small detail, but it might point them in the wrong direction. As I did this, the guy asked politely if he could go in the shop, and I nodded. I kept my facing so I could see him, and his wife, who was turned in her seat to watch the events unfold.

About the same time I got done repacking a good sized bag for them he came out with two bags himself. I handed the bag to him, nodded, wished him good luck, and his lip trembled in response. He had tears streaming down into his face. It was then I noticed how filthy and skinny he was. Gaunt almost. He backed away, put the food in his car, got in, and they drove away.

I gave it a minute to digest everything, then got the pump running and filled the Tundra. According to the pump I put about 20 gallons in the truck. Pretty good haul for a Plan C. I checked the pump's tank capacity numbers and it looked like there was over three thousand gallons of fuel left in the two tanks. Plenty to go me quite some time, the whole winter at the very least.

I did a quick last second check of the garage and found a 5 gallon fuel tank. Score right? I walked it out to the pump and immediately my stomach dropped. The wagon was back, and mom was outside it, coming across the road straight at me, handgun raised in my general direction. She looked... loony.

Nonverbal aggression commonly escalates things.

Threatening posture, physical motion, all that stuff. I just slowly lowered my arms to my side as non-threateningly as I could, and let her come to me. I could see she was pretty detached from reality, and was crying just like her husband was just minutes earlier.

Her hands were shaking something fierce as she brought the gun to my chest level and stopped at the back of my new truck.

"We need more food, and gas, and water too. I don't want to shoot you but I'll do it for my son. We can't go on being nice anymore I'm so sorry." She got the sorry out as more of a guttural choke than a word. I could tell what she was trying to say though. You could see her pleading with her eyes. I forget exactly what I said at that point, but it was reassuring her that there was plenty of food and water, as well as food, and I was more than willing to share it.

She motioned for her husband to come out, and he did. You could feel the fear coming off him though. He clearly wanted no part of armed robbery and it was palpable. He gave her a wide berth as he reached into the truck and grabbed two of my bags of groceries. I pointed out two that I knew had good food in them. He nodded frighteningly in thanks to me as his wife continued to shake with fear and anxiety.

I stayed as calm as I could but things got worse when she started yelling at him to grab more. I knew I could go without the stuff, so I wasn't about to get into a gunfight with a young mother and father over some candy bars. However, the young man was willing to argue with her over it. They started screaming and crying and she started gesturing wildly, trying to get the point to him that they were going to die if they didn't take all of my newfound food. It was about that point I saw the zombie across the street moving towards their open car door, and their little kid.

Sternly, not loud, but certainly audible, I simply said "zombie." Her gun went off. I don't know if the sound of my voice did it or if she was trying to shoot the zombie or what, but her pistol went off. Her husband dropped like a rock, clutching his chest. The plastic bags filled with food dropped at his side, and tipped over. She wailed at a thousand decibels and dropped on top of him screaming she was sorry. I took a few steps to my left, got a clean angle on the corpse walking towards her car, and fired a single round, splitting its face in two. It fell in the road a few steps from her open car door. Dimly, I could hear the kid start to cry inside the car.

I put the Sig away and went to the guy to attend to him. Immediately I regretted not bringing a first aid kit. I tried calming her down but in the end I had to shove her off of him to check his situation. For being a total shit-show with a gun, she hit him dead square in the left lung. I could hear his chest gurgling when I put my ear to it, and his entry wound was starting to bubble and froth outward. His breathing was becoming more and more labored, and his mouth was filling with blood. He had a hole in his lung, and he would die. He would have no last words.

"You gotta get out of here. He won't make it, and he'll try and kill you when he comes back."

She sobbed, staring at me like I wasn't even there. I took action and loaded the bags of groceries her husband had dropped into the back seat of their car. Like I said, I didn't need it, I just wanted it. I did glance at the little guy in the car seat though. Despite the fact that he was screaming in fear, he was a handsome baby. If they survived, he'd be a good looking boy, suitable to proud of. She was sobbing still, but her breathing was controlled. I picked up her pistol and glanced around. No more zombies visible.

I got her up off the ground, brushed her hair back to clear her eyes, and looked her straight up, "I'll take care of him, now you need to go take care of your son." She nodded weakly in response, and walked back to her car. I dropped the clip in the pistol, ejected the round into my hand, loaded it back into the clip quickly, flicked the safety on, and handed it to her as she shut her door.

"I'm sorry." She said.

"Me too."

And the woman and her 3 year old handsome boy drove off. Once I felt comfortable about them being far enough off, I walked back over to her fallen husband. He was just starting the twitches that come right before the reanimation. I slid the sword out and sunk it in one of the eyes that not minutes before were crying in gratitude for the small good deed I'd done for him and his family.

I never got their names.

-Adrian

October 18th

It bothers me a great deal that I had to watch a wife kill her husband so I could get a fucking candy bar. The state of affairs of this shitty ass world now has my head in shambles.

It's Monday. The weather blows. It's cold, rainy, and raw. Typical fall weather for around here. I am still "recovering" from my jaunt to the gas station on Wednesday. Physically I was unharmed, despite running into three full on zombies, one lunatic wife, and one freshly attempting to reanimate body. I went maybe 6 miles roundtrip and I ran into all that. What the fuck is downtown like? Baghdad of the Living Dead?

Christ's sake. I got back Wednesday at like 1 in the afternoon I think. I didn't check my watch exactly. Got the Tundra to the dorm, backed it right up to the door as close as I could, and got the groceries inside. I took the gas cans down to the basement where the generator is and left most of them in an adjacent room. Outside chance the generator blows up I didn't want gas cans nearby. I also took one of the gas cans down to the maintenance shed so that just in case all the gasoline wasn't in one place. Always have a Plan B, right?

The rest of that day I basically vegetated. Damn near grew roots. I was so fucking pissed I could barely see straight. I had this awesome habit when I was younger of punching things when I lost my temper. I couldn't even tell you how many times my older brother and my Dad had to patch the drywall in our house growing up. Fist holes in walls were available wholesale when I was going through puberty. I was almost that mad that day.

I found solace in candy. Don't judge me. I have a hardcore sweet tooth and this was the first chocolate I'd had in months. I didn't think to grab any on any of my trips out or on "that day" so I was pretty stoked to have some finally. I gorged and ate three candy bars. Sugar joy alleviated my tension. Otis too, he always knows when I'm down.

The days leading up to today have been pretty quiet. Thursday when I woke up I was kind of sore, which is pretty normal for a day after the one I just had. Despite not getting hurt really when you're all adrenalized you can sometimes hurt yourself a little just being in a fight. I think I swung the sword so powerfully I actually strained my shoulders. So I took four ibuprofen and a break and read a few books out of the library all weekend. Our library here is the majority of the second floor of the main school house. There's about 16 classrooms in it, 8 on the first floor and 8 more on the third. Second floor is all library though.

I need to be really practical right now though, so my readings are more or less limited to trying to pick up usable skills. I stuck to gardening and agricultural texts this weekend. I know I need to plant the seeds I got, but frankly I don't know shit about farming. After this weekend's reading, I now know shit about farming. Not much about it, but some. I did read this neat book about growing stuff in your apartment so you could have fresh produce in the city, and I desperately want to put that into action. If I can score a few bags of potting soil and the pots to go with it I think I can get some stuff growing here in the dorm over the winter.

But, it's been five days since I last touched this journal, Mr. Journal, and I think I still have a lot of story left to put down in the annals of history, such as it is. The last part I remember I had talked about was when I was at my mother's place, and my gun clicked dry.

I had walked up behind the younger Zombie that was face down but getting up, leaving his entrails on the floor as he did so. I was close enough that I was really almost at his feet when the gun clicked empty. I can totally remember that sharp pang of fear hitting me square in the pit of my stomach. What. The. Fuck.

I backpedalled a few feet and watched in horror as the kid kind of rolled over and started to come at me. I looked around the lobby to see if there were any weapons, but there was nothing visible. I took another couple steps back, and thought about how having the Glock would've been so much better. The Glock I wanted had a higher magazine capacity, and I would've been good to go.

Phil to the motherfucking rescue.

I reached into my pants cargo pocket on the left side and grabbed the spare mag Phil hooked me up with earlier that day. I dropped the empty and slid the full one in, and thumbed the slide forward. Calmly and with relative precision, I snapped two rounds at the undead mess coming at me. First round sailed a little high and hit it in the back, but the second round split his forehead clean. His brains flew out the exit wound and covered his back with bloody grey poop. My heart was fucking pounding hard, so hard it actually hurt a little. I can recall the uncomfortable doubt of wondering whether or not I was having a heart attack. I wasn't though, panic attack maybe.

Once I gathered myself and got my heart to slow down some I grabbed my empty clip off the floor and went back carefully to grab my banana box. All was clear this time, and I got the fuck out. I tossed the banana box in the back seat and got in. Once I got the door locked I snagged a box of

9mm and reloaded my empty clip. I also filled up the chamber and the two rounds I shot out of the new clip. I hate to admit it, but that ass Phil totally saved my bacon with that second clip.

Phil, if you're out there, I take back all the bad things I've ever said about you. You have earned your passage to heaven in my book, sir.

Still on my agenda was checking on my friends. The rest of my family was long since out of the question. Dad had been dead for some time, my older brother Caleb lived right in the city, and my younger sister Rebecca was away at college, which was on the other side of the city. No chance for a rescue for either of them, at least not that day. I guess it's ironic that I actually thought about the logistics of driving all the way through the city to get to Rebecca, but not 45 minutes to find Cassie. I don't even know what to say about that. I guess I'm a total fucking scumbag.

Anyway, earlier I mentioned that I wanted to check in on Steve, my coworker buddy, and my two friends John and Dorothy. It was getting dark at this point though, and I really wanted to get a move on. I knew for one that Steve was probably either A) doing just fine, or B) not home anyway, so I knew, or at least had a good feeling I wouldn't be long at his place. I switched my destination order immediately. I think it was about 6:30 or so by that point, and it was half dark. I had until maybe 7 or so before I'd be in the dark. I left my mother's place, moving a little faster than the speed limit and headed past the school. The school parking lot was still packed. I didn't know why then, and I still don't know why now, but my bet was that there was some kind of parent teacher conference that night, or a basketball game or something. The kids would have been out of school for hours by that point so it didn't make sense that this was a rush of parents getting their kids. I couldn't get involved anyway. I almost got sideswiped by some prick in a Prius though as I drove by the exit. It was close, but no damage done.

I hit Main Street, and headed straight east the 8 miles to John and Dorothy's place. Now I said it was out of town, and it is. Their place is a few hundred feet down a side road off of a fairly well traveled state route. It's rural, pleasant, and was a bitch to get to. The roads were packed big time that day, and everyone was *flying*. I got passed at least 20 times on a solid yellow during the trip. No middle fingers given my way though, which was a pleasant change of pace from the prick earlier in the giant truck.

I got off the main route without getting the car wrecked and turned onto the street John and Dorothy lived on. No traffic here, just trees and darkness, as the sun had fully set by now. Now before I go any further I should mention my buddy John was a bit of a gun-nut. That's being fairly mild. He was ex-Army, just like me, (I did 4 years, he did 8) but he came from a long and storied lineage of deer hunters. He spent far more money getting his hunting rifles geared up than he did on his cars. Funny that he drove a $900 pickup truck with a $3,000 hunting rifle in the back window. Only in America I guess. Good times. Classy fella though, he just really enjoyed firearms and spending time in the woods with them.

I turned left super slow into their driveway and came to a stop about 15 feet from their garage door. Lights were on in the living room, but I didn't see anyone. John's truck wasn't visible, and Dorothy's little beater car was nowhere to be seen either. I let myself out of the car and made sure I had the Sig and the spare clip on me. No sword though, shit was crazy enough without me marching into their place with it. I knocked on the door they used as the front, which was on the breezeway that attached the garage to the house. More of a mudroom really than a breezeway.

I waited a full minute while looking into the window next to me. It looked into their living room, and with the light on inside I could see everything. No one came to the door, so I tried the knob, and it was unlocked. Remember earlier how I said to trust your nose? As soon as I opened the door I got a whiff of something awful, something bloody and dead or dying. I drew the pistol out of instinct, and walked slowly into the mudroom. Stretching across the floor from the back door opposite my door to the interior door heading into the house was a crimson streak of blood. It wasn't a huge swath of blood, but it came from a serious bleeding injury. A bit of dread hit me, I can remember it clearly. I hoped it wasn't either John or Dorothy, or especially their 4 year old Danielle. Shit if that kid died I think I would go loony on the spot.

The door heading inside was ajar, and I used the muzzle of the pistol to push it open fully. The streak of blood continued through the living room, past the central fireplace, and down the hall. It looked like it ended right at the bathroom door halfway down their hallway. I decided then and there to clear the house as normal. I went room to room carefully, cautiously, using standard room clearing military procedure. Living room and kitchen were both clear, both closets were empty, but when I cleared the bathroom I saw where the blood was coming from. Before I went in to examine more fully I cleared the bathroom at the end of the hall and crept upstairs to clear the other two bedrooms. The house was totally empty. I noticed in both of the bedrooms where they slept the bureau drawers were pulled out and gone through. Clothes were also missing from the closets.

I returned to the bathroom and the source of the blood. In the tub, dead as a doornail, was their family dog Dwayne. John loved Dwayne Wade and named his dog after him. I can't fault him, Dwayne (the dog, not the basketball player) was his homeboy just like Otis was mine. Can't be hatin.

Honestly I was relieved. I had started to think the streak came from their kid Danielle and when I knew it wasn't, I was so relieved. I did however remember that John kept his gun safe downstairs. I flicked the lights on, and went down to clear the basement. Everything was kosher though, and I found the safe door open. All the guns were gone. However, he did leave behind two packages of gun kit cloth, which is disposable stuff, and I knew I would eventually need more, and he also left behind two full boxes of 12 gauge double ought. That was 20 more shotgun shells for me. Huzzah.

I checked the basement for anything I could take, and found little. There were some tools, which I already could get, and some cleaning supplies, but those would be in major motherfucking abundance at the school, so I skipped the basement. In the kitchen upstairs though, I found about ten cans of food they left behind as well as a few boxes of crackers and bags of chips. God bless John and his obsessive love for Cool Ranch Doritos. I was now hood rich with 4 bags.

I did get a scare though when I looked out the window above the sink. In the backyard, barely visible in the light shining out of the window I could see a person standing near the back fence. They were just standing there, and I can remember feeling really creeped out. I mean, who the fuck just stands in someone's backyard? Dorothy have a stalker or something? I figured I would look into it. I gathered my shit in a few brown paper bags Dorothy had under the counter and carefully exited the house going to my car. All clear. I tossed the stuff in the back, and grabbed the Mossberg.

Rather than go through the mudroom area, I opted for walking around the garage outside. It was getting chilly now that the sun had been down and gone for a bit, but it wasn't cold at all. I kept the gauge at my shoulder, and peeked slowly around the back corner of the garage. In profile, lit without any glare from inside the window, it clearly was a dead guy. Well, mostly dead. One of the freshly risen.

I crept across the backyard very quietly, and made it to within about 12 feet of the zombie, but I accidentally punted one of Danielle's toys right at the fucking Zombie. I think it was a little plastic play set for a farm or something. Weebles went everywhere as the barn silo bricked off the dead guy's head.

Hey if anything, I'm funny.

The zombie pervert turned abruptly and made a lunge in my direction. I popped off three shots in rapid succession at him and ended his ass quickly. Note to the uninitiated: Aiming with a shotgun is a relative thing. It's like horseshoes, close is frequently good enough. One of the three shots hit him in the neck I think because his head just vaporized off his shoulders. I got a bit of warm spray to the face, which made me retch a little. I grabbed a shirt or something off the laundry line in the yard to wipe my face. Grossness anywhere else I think I can cope with, but keep the gore from my mouth, seriously, it's fucking nasty, and completely un-fucking necessary.

Filth off my face I made my exit, stage right. I'm not sure, but I think that zombie must've killed Dwayne. (the dog, not the basketball player) Makes sense at least. I have no idea where he came from of course, nor will I ever, but I find myself trying to make sense of this shit as time passes. I do have a LOT of spare time to kill. The mind wanders.

So that was John and Dorothy's place. Empty save for a few bits of food, some extra shotgun shells, one pervert zombie, and a dead dog.

Next stop: Steve's place.

More on that cluster fuck in the next entry Mr. Journal. Stay safe.

-Adrian

October 20th

I've been laughing about this since I left off on the journal a couple days ago. After the quasi-debacle at John and Dorothy's I left for my friend Steve's place. Steve actually lived near where I lived in town. It was more or less downtown a little closer to the center than my place, so I was worried about the condition of the world there. How shitty would downtown be? I would soon find out.

Aside from the story: Tuesday was solid, nothing happened here on campus, and today was good too. It's still kinda damp and cold out, but the rain has subsided. Feels like it's getting a little warmer out.

So the drive to Steve's place was something like 6 miles from John and Dorothy's place. I got back on the state route heading towards town and was sort of surprised at the lack of traffic. Well, the lack of traffic heading in the direction I was going. Cars headed east were practically tailgating at 80 miles per hour but heading west it was dead. That stands to reason though as heading east dumped them onto the interstate which would take them either to the more populated areas or up north where it's pretty sparsely populated. I ran the stop sign at the end of their street btw, which kinda bothers me to this day. Foolish risk really.

The drive to Steve's apartment was smooth. No traffic accidents, no bullshit. One of the things that I actually had to laugh about was I finally figured out to turn off the goddamn CD I had playing and turn off the radio. Don't get me wrong, I had been kind of enjoying my end of the world day to the soundtrack of Eminem, but I needed info now. I listen to the radio so infrequently it just didn't occur to me that I had a media option to listen to. When I did listen to the radio, I usually listened to NPR, so when I switched, that's what I got.

I forget the exact details, but the radio reports were really bad. I guess things had gotten dramatically worse since I had last watched the boob tube or checked the internet. Hospitals were flooded during the day with people who were sick or injured, or who thought they were sick. Of course it took some hours to get things sorted out, and in the meantime, lots and lots of people got bitten or killed outright. That spread the disease. With the medical infrastructure totally fucked within 8 hours, things went from bad to worse. In a non-stressful environment there are shit-tons of car accidents, work accidents, home accidents

69

etc. Imagine how many extra accidents happened that day, and in many cases from the sounds of it, no ambulances arrived to help? And if they did come, they probably took you to an epicenter of the plague or whatever you want to call this.

If you haven't figured it out by now Mr. Journal, shit was terrible by this point. Little to no medical care to be had anywhere. Hospitals and clinics were unsafe, as were the body collection areas they tried to set up. NPR said something like 5,000 plus cases of bite attacks were reported in New York State that afternoon alone. Can you imagine the fallout there? It had to be exponential.

I listened intently the whole drive to Steve's place. I was really hoping to find him there. Not only to make sure he was safe and good to go, but also I was hoping to drag him along to the school as a fellow "survivor." He's a helluva guy to have around. If only for comedic purposes.

Downtown was amazingly sedate. Very few cars moving around at this point and a lot of darkness. The street lights were still on, and all the businesses were still lit, but I think those all operate on automatic lights. That or whoever was there went "peace-out" and left everything on. What was dark though were the house lights. A lot of the houses were boarded up, and a lot were probably empty. I also imagine a lot had their lights off to avoid attracting any attention. The thought of all the people huddled up in the dark was fucking creepy.

Steve's place is in one of the handfuls of small apartment complexes in town. We have weird ordinances here that prevent apartment buildings over two stories, so there aren't many. We do have lots of old multi-family homes instead. Anyway, Steve's place consisted of 4 brick and shingle buildings, arranged in a square with a central parking lot just off a street that's perpendicular to Main Street.

Each building had a single entrance with a central hall and stairway linking all four apartments. Steve's place was on the second floor of the building closest to the street.

Honestly, if Steve could block off and secure the central doors on the first floor, his place would be sweet to hole up in. Pretty secure.

When I pulled in I scanned the parking lot for movement. It was well lit, and I could see maybe a half dozen folks putting shit in their cars frantically. Seemed pretty safe all things considered. I pulled right up to the curb in front of his place and got out. I took the shotgun with me.

I hit the buzzer for Steve's place but there was no answer. I hit it again and waited another minute or two, but zilch. This was normal for Steve. Steve's couch was his close, close friend and often you had to text him to get him to answer his buzzer. His priorities were a little different than most you could say. He always figured fuck the doorbell, everyone he knew that was coming over would text him anyway. Random doorbells were probably Jehovah's Witnesses, or girl scouts trying to sell a product that wasn't a piece of ass. Hence: no interest, and thus no answer of the door.

Pretty luckily though, one of his neighbors, a cute chick that I think he originally moved into the building to try and fuck came out just then. She blew right past me like I was a fucking lamp. No eye contact, no hello, nada. Women. End of the world and I can't even get a phone number. I wonder if Steve ever got to fuck her? Seems like a little bit of a waste if he didn't.

Anyway I slipped inside after she left and went upstairs to his place. I found a note taped to his door, carefully handwritten with a little smiley at the end of it. I kept it, and here it is, in all its glory. (Spelling and grammar errors are original, and all courtesy of Steve.)

To whom it may concern,

If you are reading this you are either concerned for my well being or are about to loot my house. If the latter be the case have at, I left my broken laptop on top of my bed and that's about as good as its gona get for you. If you fall under the categories of being concerned for my well being have no worries, I'm on top of my game.

I've always wanted to have the playing field leveled and for better or worse this whole end of the world thing has done just that. So I figure while everyone else is panicking or hiding or just shitting there pants I'm going to go get the Benz I always wanted. I'll be occasionally coming back into town to check on my parents at the "Davis Family Compound." Who would have thought that my father's ludicrous paranoia would have set him in the perfect position to survive the end of the world? I am never going to hear the end of it from him.

Anyway since cell service is gone I finally have a reasonable excuse to use a CB Radio and can be reached on channel ten around noon everyday if you are in my vicinity.

Much Love

-Steve

Lols.
Off to the school I went.

-Adrian

October 25th

10 fun zombie facts for the uninitiated!

1) Zombies are almost entirely silent save for the noise they make while shuffling around. Use your vision and sense of smell to notice them!

2) While slow moving, they never seem to tire. Running and frequently taking right angles seems to allow you to escape them. They do NOT corner well. Great on the flats though.

3) Only wounds that damage the brain seem to drop them for good. Aim for the head or neck with your firearms or melee weapons. Remember, circling a single zombie works well. They turn around for shit.

4) They are weaker than you, and are unable to pull themselves up. If you can change elevation, they usually cannot continue their pursuit. This also works if you can trip them. They frequently lay there for seconds trying to figure shit out, and then it takes them time to get upright. Plenty of time to either kill them or flee.

5) Zombies appear to have excellent hearing. They are attracted to movement as well so if you can be quiet, and stay very still, there is a good chance they will not notice you!

6) Zombies only eat the flesh of their victims so long as they are moving around. Once the person is dead and stops moving, the zombies stop eating, and pursue their next victim. Watched this happen several times now, and I'm not sure what the deal is.

7) Zombies do not bleed. They ooze a thick, blood like goo.

8) Zombies trip on just about anything in their way. If you can put obstacles in their way, most of them cannot wrap their decaying heads around how to get past it quickly. Eventually they will figure it out, but if you can get out of their line of sight and out of their hearing range, they'll give

up, and meander elsewhere.

9) It seems like they tend to hang out wherever it is that they died. Some wander about, especially if they hear or see something go by. What this means though, is that where people died there are huge concentrations of the undead. Hospitals are like irradiated zones for danger.

10) Lastly but not least, zombies don't seem to be decaying at a normal rate. Not sure why, but it seems like once reanimated if they stay that way for any substantial length of time, say a week or more, they just kinda mummify. If you kill a freshly risen body though, it decays as normal. I think the Zombification factor may build up some form of preservation effect. Not a scientist, just taking a stab in the dark.

-Adrian

October 27ᵗʰ

What a weird day. It's hot out, and it's almost November. The thermometer on the tree outside says it is 72 degrees. Normally not what you would consider hot but the humidity is really uncomfortable. I am really missing air conditioning right now.

Today is Wednesday. My last meaningful entry was last Wednesday, so I've been slacking. Of course I only set out to put occasionally entries into you Mr. Journal, but I guess I've been enjoying getting all these memories out. Well, that and putting down some of the everyday details I am experiencing here on campus. It's actually been helpful in keeping myself more organized I must say. I definitely have been more cognizant of the passage of time, amongst other things. Not sure what I feel like talking about right now really. I know I've got a lot left to write about in terms of the trip to get to the school here "that day" but I am not sure I feel like writing about that. Maybe. Let's take a "stream of consciousness" approach and see what my fingers type out. Maybe I'll get there.

This past week has been uneventful. The weather has been shitty since my last entry so I've been both down in the dumps as well as unmotivated to do much. Otis has reaped the benefits of me being inside though. He's gotten a pretty excessive amount of attention this week. I haven't achieved shit around campus otherwise. I do two patrols a day now where I walk around the buildings and check the bridge to make sure no zombies or stragglers are wandering about. All week I saw nothing. I really think this was a great choice to hole up in, even if I almost died hardcore trying to get it safe to live in.

Ah fuck it, you win, I'll tell more of that story.

Alrighty then! I think it was around 7:45 or so when I finally got out of Steve's place and headed out of town to the school here. As I said before the houses were all dark, and the roads had calmed themselves down to a nearly empty point. I made good time down the side streets and finally out to the outskirts of town towards the school. I did make one last quick pit stop at the second to last convenience store going out of town. (not the one I just got the gas from, one a few miles away from that one.)

I hit the gas pump and topped off my tank. Fortunately the automated atm charging dealie at the pump was still working so I didn't have to go inside. The clerk watched me with intent worry the whole time I was pumping. She was just a little girl really, maybe 18 years old. She kept her eyes peeled on the road the whole time, and she scrammed when a car pulled in for her. I think I might've weirded her out because the whole time I pumped I held the shotgun and stood vigilant. What a different world just a few hours of nightmare can create right?

So once topped off I got back in and skedaddled. I passed

a few more cars than would be considered normal on the road that leads directly to the school here. You can always tell when there's a shift change because the employees and parents are always coming and going at the same time. It's like a school of fish, moving in concert at all times. This time though it was all expensive snooty cars booking it out. Easy guess was that the rich parents who shipped their kids off to the school were picking them up to take them away. I couldn't make out all the plates in the dark, but a few I did see were from out of state.

So up until that point my assumption had been that campus would be a quiet place, where I could set up shop pretty easily that night. I could not have been much more wrong. I remember crossing the bridge to get into campus and saw half a dozen cars parked at the admissions house. In the little yard I could see maybe ten folks all gesturing frantically, clearly agitated and alarmed. I pulled my car over, grabbed my sword and .22 and got out to check out the situation.

Amy, one of the admissions women was trying to calm down about 8 parents. I took a roundabout path to come up sort of behind her so I could not only back her up, but so I could also hear better what was going on. It was hysterical. I guess these parents couldn't find their kids. Anyone who has ever worked at a school, especially a private school knows that missing kids are a big deal. I was listening intently while scanning the campus surroundings. Everything was a nightmare. I could see at handful of cars all clearly crashed into random places. A few crashed into the sides of buildings, a few into guardrails, and a few into parked cars. Not sure what caused the crashes but you can use your imagination to figure that out.

I could see other cars zipping through the campus getting the fuck out as fast as they could, nearly hitting other cars and some students and staff doing the same thing. It was a solid minute though of silence before I realized that everyone had stopped talking and was staring at me. Amy had turned to face me and the parents were giving me the stink eye. Rich fuckers.

Amy's comment got a laugh out of me. "What the fuck happened to you?" I remember just shaking my head confused at her. I had no idea what she was talking about. She was kind enough to point out my current blood soaked clothing and generally disheveled appearance. I remember looking down and being shocked at my own appearance. I was fucking covered in zombie goo. I had streaks of blood all over my sweatshirt, my jeans, and apparently my face. I hadn't seen myself in a mirror all day. You know, in retrospect, it might've been the fact that I looked like a blood-soaked, shotgun toting maniac that the girl at the gas station was weirded out. Live and learn I guess.

I shook my head at her and told her it wasn't very good out there. I think I told her I had had a "long day." The parents look mortified, and Amy not much different. She filled me in as the parents started to build up speed and fervor in their yelling again. From what she had gathered school had started as normal that day. (incidentally, "that day" was a Wednesday) As the first few hours went on, school officials realized shit was going down, and entered into lockdown mode. The kids were sealed into a few of their classrooms with their teachers, and the campus was more or less shut down. Locking the students into classrooms caused a few problems that were unexpected. A few of our kids were diabetic, and had insulin reactions or "sugar attacks" as my grandfather used to call them. One of our kids had epilepsy, and apparently he had a seizure due to missing some meds. These problems just compounded everything making it a very rough place to be.

Some staff just plain old walked the fuck out. Can you blame them? If I were working that day I would've been gone in a heartbeat. Parents started calling and streaming into the campus, causing total havoc. Most just kicked in random doors looking for their kids. Apparently there had been many altercations throughout the afternoon between staff and parents, as well as parents and parents, and in three cases, someone had been hurt seriously. As in, would probably die. There was no emergency response to any of their 911 calls. I knew why.

One of the parents arrived armed with a weapon only an hour prior and was "taking it into his hands" to rescue the kids. This guy seemed to be the one causing most of the trouble at the present. The parents were worried he would hurt more people. There was still one more pivotal fuck up to this story.

The eight parents here were trying to pick up eight kids that were still in a classroom, locked down on the top floor of the main classroom building. Amy told me that our resident off-beat English teacher Mrs. Goodell had sealed the door shut, barred it, and wasn't allowing ANYONE in. Our intrepid armed hero-parent was currently on his way to said classroom to, and this is a direct quote from Amy to: "fix this bitch."

I think it goes without saying that someone who would say something like that is generally the kind of person who does less "fixing of bitches," and more, "totally fucking up of things." Amy also said that she had heard multiple gun shots over the last 20 minutes or so heading in the general direction of the school house. No one there knew what to do.

Well Mr. Journal... I do not think of myself as a hero. It is my distinct belief that courage is not the lack of fear, but the will and fortitude to do what is necessary in spite of that fear. That night, I knew I had to make the campus safe or I could be totally fucked over by this guy.

I told Amy and the parents to get safe inside a car, or the admissions building, and that I would take care of it.

I was off to "fix that bitch."

-Adrian

Phil's Story

Growing old is no fun. Ask anyone who has done a lot of it, and you'll find that out. Once you get to a certain age you stop building up that head of steam that youth gives you, and you wind up starting to sputter out. The moments where you sputter out tend to come pretty regularly too. They come after a long day at work, one when you've spent too much time on your feet. Or they come to you when you've spent a little too much time horsing around with your two grandkids, who you adore more than life itself. For Phil Stevens his moments came most often and most regularly when he woke up in the morning.

Phil was 58 years old, and looked every moment of it. His hair was grey enough that you couldn't call it black anymore, but just black enough that it looked disheveled no matter what he did to it. His wife Marcy had been on his ass for two years now about buying some of that "greekian formula" as she called it to get it back to at least one color, but Phil didn't give a shit anymore. He just wanted to go to work, come home for a decent dinner, if possible play with his grandkids, and watch football on Sunday. Everything else was peanuts.

Phil's creaking back tormented him all the way to the bathroom in his small house where he downed a handful of arthritis pills. By the time he'd gotten done washing his crotch and feet the pills were kicking in, and he started to feel like today could be a pretty good day. After toweling off, applying deodorant to pits and balls, he put on his trusty

Moore's Sporting Goods polo shirt, and his khaki pants. His work uniform for the past 16 years.

His empty tummy and his nose told him that Marcy had the bacon and eggs ready and waiting, so after he got his shoes on, he shuffled his way into the kitchen and sat down to eat. Marcy was a big fan of The Morning Shows on all the big networks, so Phil and her put a small television set on the counter so she could watch them while she made breakfast every morning. Creatures of habit, these two. Phil grunted appreciatively at Marcy, spooned a thick wad of salsa on his scrambled eggs, and dug in.

Marcy paid Phil no attention while he ate, which was unusual. Normally she sat down with him and ate her eggs beside him. (always sunny side up on toast) But today she leant over the counter and was glued to the morning show she had on.

"Marcy? What's so interestin' you letting your eggs get all cold for?" Phil spooned another mouthful of eggs in as he finished talking.

"Phil I think something is wrong out there." She didn't even turn to him say it. That wasn't like her at all.

"Well could you move so your husband can see what's so wrong?" He absently slid a whole piece of bacon into his mouth as he gestured for her to move aside. Marcy obliged immediately, still without taking her eyes off the television. She turned the volume knob on the old set up so Phil could hear it.

"So reports are now telling us that overnight in about 80 to 100 locations there were very violent attacks by people who appeared to be on some form of sedatives, or perhaps sick with some form of rabies. Authorities are unsure what the root is of this strange occurrence, but the global nature of the attacks has authorities on alert everywhere." The perfectly dressed and primped morning show host said in his mild baritone voice.

The other host, this one a far too artificially beautiful blonde lady chimed in and added, "Well Chuck, reports from Bangkok, Chicago, London, St. Petersburg, Bogota, and Sydney are all the same. These people are reaching a near-death catatonic state, and then suddenly becoming violent, biting and scratching anyone near them. It's almost like one of those terrible zombie movies that have been so popular on late night television lately." She giggled on the last delivery. The male news guy smiled awkwardly and played along with her joke.

"Authorities here in the United States are advising all people to be attentive to anyone acting suspicious, especially anyone who appears to fall asleep, or go into a trance. The Department of Homeland Security is investigating what exactly is causing this, but the CDC is now circulating information that it's likely a form of virus. Perhaps some form of worldwide biological attack by extremists."

"Bullshit. It's Al-Qaeda." Phil mumbled angrily. "Ain't no fucking bird flu." He scraped the last bit of egg off his plate and downed the last mouthful of his black coffee.

"I don't know Phil, it's on all the stations. I think this could be real serious." She finally tore her eyes off the television set and looked at him worriedly. Her hazel eyes could say more in one glance than an hour of her talking. Phil paused the rant he about to give and swallowed it. He'd be a good husband and worry along with her.

Phil put his dishes in the sink and gathered his wife of 35 years up in a bear hug, "Well you just stay here in the house all day like normal, and I'll go to the shop, and have a normal day there, and tonight we'll start a fire in the fireplace, and that'll be the end of it. Okay?" He kissed her warmly on the forehead. Her body relaxed a bit against his, pushing his potbelly in a little.

"Okay baby." She smiled up at him and they kissed each other goodbye.

*****

Phil and Marcy's house was about three quarters of a mile down the same street that Phil's place of work was. This meant he didn't drive to work ever, and it meant he got to fire up one of his cigarettes without driving her up a wall. She'd quit years ago when they found out they were going to be grandparents. It was a warm morning, a good June day. Phil didn't feel like it was going to get too hot either, which was always nice.   Warm but not hot and humid. To hell with humidity Phil always said.

Moore's Sporting Goods was the only real gun shop in town. Of course three towns over there was a Walmart, and a couple sporting good stores, but Moore's was small town owned and small town operated and you couldn't beat that. In fact, Moore's was opened by the Chief of Police 20 years ago, and his son was Chief of Police right now too. Two generations of locals, proud to serve the hunting and outdoors needs of its residents.

Moore's was still locked up when Phil got there, but he let himself in with the key. He was 15 minutes early, as he always was, and beat everyone there. He trudged himself inside, turned off the security alarm before it called the cops as he always did, and started getting the shop ready.

Soon as Phil had the window shades up and the register turned on the rest of his work buddies rolled in. Mr. Moore himself was next, dressed just the same as Phil, though he came with his .45 on his hip in a holster. No one would ever rob his store, at least not without killing him first. Phil didn't strap his piece on until he got there, which he presently did. Bobby, Mike and Ben all rolled in right after that. No matter how much Mr. Moore yelled at them they just couldn't seem to beat him there in the morning. Phil always suspected that Mr. Moore would just wake up 5 minutes earlier anyway if they did, just to make sure he had something to yell at them about. Part of Mr. Moore's charm Phil always thought.

"Gentlemen, gather around." Mr. Moore said as all his men poured themselves cups of the coffee Phil had brewed earlier. They stopped bullshitting and quieted down.

"If you all have seen the news, there's some weird shit happening out there today. I suspect this might be like 9/11 again. So we need to be ready. Phil, how's our inventory looking? We got a lot of spare firearms in stock? What about ammunition?" Mr. Moore was all business, serious as a rattlesnake.

Phil thought about it for a few seconds before replying, "Well, we got normal shelf stock, plus we got that order of extra Ruger and Mossberg stuff in the gun vaults in the back. No extra pistols really. Ammunition is normal. Next week we got the first batches of the hunting season supply coming in though."

"Hm. Well if it's at all like 9/11 we'll be sold out of shotguns and rifles by dinnertime. Don't forget to run background checks and make sure that anyone who buys a pistol along with another gun doesn't walk out with the damn thing. Waiting period, remember guys?" Mr. Moore stared intently at Mike, who had sold two pistols to customers over the past year and let them walk out with them the same day. A really big no-no. Mr. Moore had managed to hide the incidents, and they'd gotten lucky, but he couldn't risk losing his gun license. Mike kept his eyes rooted firmly on the floor while Mr. Moore made his point.

"Alright boys. Let's have a good day. Bobby and Mike why don't you get all the new guns in the vault prepped up, and get some extra gun cleaning kits and supplies out there on display. Let's try to move all those goddamn boots I ordered by accident last month too. Thanks men." Mr. Moore nodded and headed back to his office.

The guys all exchanged looks with Mike, who finally looked up. They all laughed briefly, sharing in Mike's shame. After that they patted him on the back, and went to work.

Mr. Moore called the day almost perfectly. No sooner than when the men left from their little meeting, customers began coming in. It was always the same kind of people who came in on days like this. Phil had seen it happen countless times over his 16 years. People tend to get nervous when bad things happen. They think that whatever bad thing has happened, or is happening, is going to happen to them too. As Americans, purchasing a firearm is a constitutionally approved way to alleviate anxiety, so that's what some people do. It's always the indoors folks that do it though. The hunters don't, they don't have to. They already own guns. The veterans are the same. They either own a gun already, or don't freak out when bad things happen.

The customers that come in on days like this are the people who've never shot a gun before. Bankers, IT nerds, psychologists, moms afraid for their kids, you know the type. The pocket protector posse. They're the people who make a rushed decision that having a gun is now necessary because the world has changed so much overnight. Phil thought these people were idiots, but if they had cash, or a credit card, he's sell them bazookas if he had them in stock.

Normally Phil and Mike ran the gun counter but Mike was currently banished with Bobby in the backroom. That left Ben to help Phil, and he wasn't ready for the constant stream of customers. By noon Phil pulled Mike back to the counter, and by one Mr. Moore was up front as well. They had Bobby stand at the door holding an empty shotgun to make sure none of the panicked customers did anything stupid. By 2pm though, Mr. Moore had had enough of the crowd, and called his son to send a patrol car over.

Phil was up to his neck in uneducated gun buyers for so long he forgot to eat lunch. He had dealt with assholes who didn't know about the wait for pistols, and he dealt with the assholes who wanted the biggest hand cannon magnums money could buy. He'd dealt with the moms, holding their babies and toddlers while they "tested the feel" on a .38 special. He'd also watched as one baby threw up on a $800 Benelli shotgun. Italian walnut goddamit, all fucked up.

He was hungry, sweaty, and frankly getting a little scared as things got busier and busier. The crowd did get a little more courteous after the officer showed up though, and when Bobby came back inside to help, Phil got a break to eat the frozen dinner he had in the fridge. Of course he took it out to the counter to eat it, and fortunately they had a little break in the flow of customers at the same time.

The four men all took a seat wherever they could find one, and hung their heads in exhaustion. So much state paperwork filled out, guns handed over, and ammunition boxes sold, and believe or not, Mike had managed to sell four pair of boots to one worried housewife that was afraid her family's footwear wouldn't survive this outbreak of the bird flu. The cop came inside at about the same time, and Phil noticed it was Officer McGreevy, the town's largest cop. McGreevy nodded to Mr. Moore, and gave a little wave and a nod to the others.

"Danny, what is all this bullshit? Is this shit for real?" Mr. Moore asked him as he took a bite out of a Danish.

"Well sir, I can assure you this is no hoax." McGreevy rested his thumbs in his belt and kicked absently at the dirt on the floor. The men exchanged amused glances.

"Elaborate son." Mr. Moore chewed his Danish.

McGreevy was icy in his delivery, "well we got the call from the State Police early, early this morning that this was legit. We even heard from the FBI and got a few calls from the state health department too. Apparently State Police have blockades on all the interstates and routes coming in. They're stopping and turning around everyone that's sick, especially those folks that are bitten or scratched. I guess a few of the blockades have seen some pretty bad shit too. Few cars ramming through the cruisers, a couple of officer involved shootings. Shit is terrible Mr. Moore. Ain't no joke."

The men all had to remember to breathe after hearing that. Murmuring of all forms of curses were uttered, and the quiet was only disturbed by the cop's radio going off, "McGreevy come in, this is Chief Moore."

McGreevy reached up and thumbed his radio transceiver on his collar, "go for McGreevy."

"Hey is my father there? Can you go to him?" The Chief

said over the walkie.

"I'm in his presence Chief, anything you say him and his guys will hear." A few more customers came in just then and Mike and Ben got up to take care of them. Mr. Moore moved closer to the officer to hear his son.

"Dad, I just got the call from the FBI and the ATF that we have the local authority to suspend firearm background checks. What do you think of that?" The Chief's voice was filled with doubt, Phil could hear it straight through the walkie.

Mr. Moore scratched his balding head and furrowed his brow, "shit son I don't know. Is this all that bad? We need to put that many guns out on the streets today?"

"Dad the FBI just called and said that some of the larger hospitals in major metro areas are now quarantine zones. I guess Los Angeles is under martial law already. Apparently down south in Mexico City the military is doing purges of the ghettos it's so bad. I guess there are thousands of these sickos attacking randomly all over the world."

Mr. Moore exhaled, and rubbed his face. The customers who just entered had stopped asking about guns, and were listening intently to the conversation. The men, Mr. Moore included sat quietly for a bit. "Son, we're the only shop in town. We can be judges of character. If we think someone can buy a gun without the check, then we'll let 'em. If we think they're shady, then they go through the process as normal. Sound good?"

The radio was silent for a few seconds, then it squawked, "that'd be great Dad. Be safe there you guys. McGreevy, if you see anyone that's bit, you put bracelets on them immediately, you understand? State Police have authorized that if an officer sees a wounded person and they don't respond to immediate verbal commands, we are to put them down, understand?"

McGreevy looked at the people around him, suddenly even more somber and serious than before. Absently, he scratched his smooth scalp. The officer thumbed his radio once more, "Roger that Chief. Put them down if uncooperative."

"Uncooperative and hurt, they have to be visibly hurt, otherwise follow normal protocol."

"Roger that."

*****

That was at 2pm. Mr. Moore had Bobby write up some signs telling folks that they could only buy a few guns, and Bobby used his faintly superior magic marker skills to make a few signs to put up. At 3pm the store picked up dramatically again. Apparently the two or three large businesses in town had dismissed their entire workforces to go home and make preparations for whatever the night would bring. From Phil's perspective it seemed like every person in town was coming in there to give him a hard time, and to try and buy a gun after that.

At just shy of 4pm Mr. Moore told his men to let the folks start taking pistols home with them if they bought them. Further, Mr. Moore said that if the people who had pistols on hold from earlier in the day didn't come and get them by 5, to put those guns back on the shelf to sell again. He said he had a bad feeling about this. Mike brought out a radio and turned it on so they could listen to the reports coming in. News from all over kept getting worse and worse. Occasionally Officer McGreevy would poke his head inside and tell the men about another shoot out somewhere in the state. There were lots of gun stores being robbed, grocery store fights, and car accidents. People apparently forgot how to drive and act like humans in the span of 6 hours. Terrible world we live in Phil thought to himself.

At about 4pm things started to slow again. The mob at the counter was only two or three people deep by then, and finally it slowed to a trickle. Phil noticed this one character when he came in immediately, but was surprised after he kept his eyes on him. He was a tall dude, little over six feet. Hooded sweatshirt and jeans, and had a strong look about him. Like he'd take no shit from anyone today. Phil was sure he'd be the one to rob them, but he just stayed in line, kept his eyes peeled on the door, and everyone around him, and was a model citizen. Phil wasn't sure quite what to make of him when he motioned for him to come up to the counter.

"What flavor of destruction can I get for you today sir?" Phil asked, trying to stay somewhat positive.

"Well I need one rifle, one shotgun, and one pistol if possible." The big man said politely to Phil.

Phil nodded, "What would you like young man?"

"Well if you still have any, I'd like a Glock handgun, preferably one of the 9mm's with a 17 round mag, or one of the .40 cal models. I'd also like, uh," he looked at the racks behind Phil, searching for what he wanted, "a 12 or 16 gauge pump or semi-auto, and a .22 rifle. Preferably one that uses a clip if possible."

Phil nodded knowingly. He immediately started liking the big fella. He knew enough about weapons that he knew what he was asking for, and he seemed confidant in doing it, and just struck Phil as someone who'd also use them appropriately. Phil nodded, sent out an "ayup." And went to gather the man's order.

Phil checked for the Glock, but they were out. Instead he grabbed a few of the Sig-Sauer pistols, which were top grade firearms to show the guy. Phil came back and told him the bad news.

"Son we're flat out of the Glocks, all models, those went pretty early I think. We do have some Sig's left over. One 9mm and one .40 cal. Either of those work for you?"

The younger man nodded, "Yeah, the 9mm is fine."

"Terrific, I'll grab the rest of what you need. You care what models or anything?" Phil asked him.

"Use your best judgment. I trust you guys."

Phil smiled at him, and went to get the rest of what he

asked for. He grabbed the Mossberg Tactical .22, which was a clone of the M-16 and M-4 rifles the Army used, and a shotgun he felt the guy would like, another Mossberg, the Model 535 ATS. Both were high quality, and would be put to good use by the guy. Phil was confident. When he returned to the counter with the man's order, he had piled up some supplies to go along with his guns.

"Ammunition? How much you think you'll be needing?" Phil asked as he laid the guns down on the counter.

"All of it?" The guy joked. Phil and he shared a little laugh.

"Tell you what son, I think I can spare you 4 boxes of .22, 10 boxes of the 9, and 4 boxes of the shotgun shells. Will that work?" Phil started getting the boxes out from under the counter before the other man answered.

"It'll have to do I guess. If I need more than that I guess we're in a lot more trouble than we realize." He smiled and looked warily out the door. Phil could tell this man's head was screwed on straight. He watched the exits, kept his hands free, had his knees bent just slightly so he wasn't flat footed. Clearly someone with some time served in the military.

"Young man I'm gonna give you the hook up here. I've got some spare magazines for the rifle and the pistol if you're interested. Two each." Phil waited for his response before taking those out from under the counter.

The big man's eyes lit up like it was Christmas morning, "Hell yes I'll take them."

Phil nodded again and grabbed the clips, "this everything?"

"Yeah I think so, for now at least." The man pulled his wallet out and took a credit card from inside and got it ready to hand to Phil.

As Phil wrote up the receipt for everything he looked at the state and federal paperwork normally required for all the weapons. He shook his head to himself and decided it wasn't needed for this sale.

"So what's the news, has it gotten worse or better?" The big man leaned on the glass counter and asked.

"Well," Phil took the credit card and swiped it, "McGreevy out there keeps giving us updates. Guess it's pretty bad out there, but it sounds like the Staties are doing a good job of keeping it under control. He just said a few minutes ago that the only people attacking other people are from out of state so far. People who have been bitten or something. Seems like it's only spreading slowly up in this neck of the woods. Might get lucky with all this." Phil handed the man his card back. He noticed the name was Adrian M. Ring on the card. The receipt printed shortly after and the man signed it for Phil.

"Well Mr. Ring, you use these carefully, and be safe. Have a great day." Phil said to the guy.

"Thanks Phil. I appreciate it. Your name tag is crooked by the way." He pointed and smiled at the name tag Phil had long since stopped giving a shit about. Phil huffed a little laugh and dismissed it. They exchanged one last nod, and the man gathered his stuff and left.

The store finally had a lull right then. Gratefully Phil sat down on the stool behind the counter and took stock of the store's heavily depleted inventory. They had less than a dozen shotguns and rifles left for sale, and only perhaps a dozen pistols left. Most of those were of the "pea shooter" variety though. Derringers used mostly for show, or target pistols. Phil chuckled quietly thinking about how they'd probably be closing up shop today due to there being nothing left to sell to anyone.

Phil rested his eyes for a minute and opened them again when he heard a car screech into the parking lot. It pulled up so close and so fast to McGreevy's cruiser that it damn near hit him. He could see through the door that the car had out of state plates. McGreevy barked out a few commands to the driver, and backed away. The driver got himself out of the car, and started towards the entrance of the store. McGreevy moved himself between the man and the door, and drew his service weapon.

Phil moved to the end of the counter near the door and put his hand on the revolver he kept holstered on his hip. Bob and Mike were also behind the counter, but sped around it towards the door to get a better look at what was happening outside.

Phil could see clearly that sitting in the passenger side of the car there was a young kid, maybe 12 or 13 years old. He was absolutely mortified at what was happening. Phil knew it was the driver's son immediately. McGreevy leveled his weapon at the chest of the driver and yelled for him to freeze again. The driver was sliding along the front fender of the car, leaning heavily, like he was drunk. He slid one hand along the hood absently as he moved, like his arm was dead weight. That was when Phil noticed the crimson stain spreading out from the man's forearm. His bluish white shirt sleeve had a menacing red stain on it.

Phil couldn't see well enough at his age to see if the man was frothing at the mouth, or if he was clearly out of control, but McGreevy could. The Officer's service weapon barked angrily a few times, and the driver immediately went flat on his face like a sack of mail. Mike and Bob grabbed their guns and bolted out the door. Phil just stood there behind the counter. He'd seen this before, back in Vietnam, and had seen enough already. He didn't need to see any more dead bodies.

A screeching of brakes down the street echoed shortly after the gunshot. Another car, this one a grey import sedan sped in reverse, returning to the Moore's parking lot. Phil could see through the window enough that he made out that it was Adrian, the man who just left. Apparently he was returning to see what had happened. The muffled screams of the adolescent boy in the car were starting to get louder when Mike and Bob started hooting and hollering.

McGreevy took a few steps closer to the fallen body of the out of state driver, and put one more round into the back of his head. Phil could see Adrian and the Officer exchanged

CHRIS PHILBROOK

glances before he drove off. That was the last time he saw the Adrian guy.

McGreevy called in the ambulance immediately, and notified the Chief. The rest of the Moore's staff helped McGreevy with the kid. He was hysterical, and they got him as far away from the scene as they could, which turned out to be Mr. Moore's office. Luckily, Mr. Moore had a talent for dealing with kids, and especially the hysterical ones. It didn't hurt that he had another Danish in his desk either. Just minutes later the ambulance pulled into the parking lot with the Chief's cruiser in tow.

It took almost an hour to get everything figured out. It took another five minutes for everything to go to hell after that. The young boy, whose name turned out to be David, had just arrived in town from out of state, where he and his family lived. As he told it, in slight hysterics, his 8 year old younger brother had gotten rushed to the hospital in his hometown during lunch at school. Apparently he had been choking on something, and they were unable to clear his airway in time. He suffered some form of brain damage, and as David put it, "he had become a veggie burger."

David's mother and father made the decision just hours ago to pull the plug on their son and donate his organs to other needy, sick children. So with doctor supervision, they removed David's little brother from life support, and shortly thereafter, his little heart stopped beating.

David said he wasn't sure what exactly happened then, but his mother and father were crying a lot, and were holding his little brother when something bad happened. His mother was hurt, bitten badly by his little brother in the neck. McGreevy, the Chief, and the paramedics surmised that it was an arterial spray, probably caused by a bite to the neck. She bled out all over the hospital room, and died within seconds. While trying to save his wife, David's father was bitten in the arm by his dead son too.

David said that his father backhanded the little boy as hard as he could, and the two of them left the room, slamming the door behind them. Phil cringed as the details were spilled out by the young boy. He was far too young to have witnessed such horror.

David described through tears that the hospital had become a nightmare. Staff was leaving because it was too dangerous, some patients were dying from whatever conditions that brought them there, and more and more ambulances kept showing up with hurt and dying people from all over. The little boy said that within minutes of his brother dying, there were dozens of the sick, attacking more and more of the living.

He said his grandparents lived here in town, and his father got them out of the hospital, fighting off more than ten of the rampaging monsters that seemed to multiple faster than possible. The father and son got to their car and escaped north on side roads to here. David said about 30 minutes into the drive his father started to not feel well. His bite wouldn't stop bleeding no matter how much pressure David put on it in the car. He also said his father started to get sleepy, and was sweating like he was running a marathon. They stopped here so they could get a gun and a first aid kit. His father was scared of the hospitals now.

Everyone in the office was floored by the story the child shared. The silence was awkward, and palpable. No one knew what to say to each other, let alone to the child. David yawned though, and took off the baseball jacket he was wearing, and a paramedic broke the silence.

"David what's that blood on your shoulder?" The young female paramedic asked as she pointed to the kid's collar. He had a small dark brown stain right in the middle of the shoulder and the neck.

"Oh it's nothing, when we were escaping I got bit by one of the nurses that got sick, I'm fine though." David yawned again and wiped his brow, which was now covered in a thin film of sweat. Everyone else in the room shifted back, away from the kid. The Chief moved his body slightly, putting it between the kid and the entrance to the hall.

"Wha…" David tried to ask what was wrong, but the word half fell out of his mouth, and he collapsed face first out of the chair, straight to the floor. The two paramedics yelled for space, and the Moore's employees quickly exited the room as they got to work. The two police officers stayed inside, gathering equipment and handing it off to the paramedics. All of the other men gathered in the hall just outside the room, trying to watch what was happening.

The two paramedics worked feverishly to figure out what was happening to little boy. They checked his vitals and tore his shirt off to get a better look at the bite on his shoulder. Once the wound was exposed everyone gasped. The bite mark was very deep, and was surrounded by an angry red halo of infection. The flesh was swollen and was turning a slight shade of grayish blue right at the edge of the teeth marks. A very unhealthy wound indeed.

Within a minute the two emergency technicians were performing CPR on the limp boy. They pumped his chest vigorously while squeezing an air bulb connected to a plastic mask on his face, trying to get life back into his tortured little body. The boy's arms and legs jumped with every powerful chest compression. They struggled for nearly ten minutes before they slumped to the floor next to his dead body, defeated. The male paramedic's eyes welled with tears, and soon after, everyone was rubbing their eyes, and all were in shock from what had just happened. The Chief excused himself out of the room, unable to contain his emotions. Not 20 minutes ago this young boy was talking, had emotions, and was alive and well. Now he was on the floor dead, his life gone.

The whole group of people assembled was in shock. No one spoke at all, at least not until David started to twitch. Both paramedics jumped into action and wiped their eyes clear of tears. Phil's heart leapt out of his mouth as he felt a sudden burst of hope. All he could think of was his two grandkids out there somewhere, and about how he hoped nothing like this would ever happen to them.

The two paramedics started to take David's vitals and get an oxygen feed on his nose. His little frame went from twitching to still again in seconds. The two paramedics hovered over his chest, confused. Then his eyes snapped open, and all hell broke loose. David's dead eyes focused on the woman EMT right above his head, and he snapped up at her, biting the underside of her arm viciously. A gout of blood sprayed all over David and the floor of the office as she leapt away, clutching her arm. As soon as that happened the other paramedic grabbed David by the shoulder and pinned him to the floor, but his wrist was too close to the kid's face, and David turned his head and chomped down on him.

His little teeth dug into the wrist until blood flowed freely, and the medic had to yank away. This turned out to be a terrible mistake though, as when he yanked away David's teeth stayed firm, and a giant chunk of the wrist came free from his arm, severing tendons and veins. He fell onto his back holding his bleeding arm, blood vessels exposed, screaming, and started to go into shock.

The Moore's employees were flat out dumbfounded. Their entire world had been turned on its head in mere minutes. As they stood slack-jawed the little teenager sat himself up and crawled across the office floor to the frozen medic with the bleeding wrist. With no compassion, no malice, and no emotion whatsoever, he bit the arm again, ripping another chunk out. It was as if he were a machine, slowly, silently consuming the meat in front of him. The paramedic tipped over, slipping even further into shock as he was eaten alive one child sized bite at a time.

The lady bitten in the arm who had tried to resuscitate David shoved her way past the Moore's men, screaming for them to get out of her way. She took off at full speed down the hall and out into the store. They could vaguely hear the bells ringing on the door as she left. Eventually, the shock of what was happening was shattered when a gun went off.

Phil had quietly drawn his revolver and shot David in

the side. His little frame was tossed violently against the corner of Mr. Moore's desk from the impact of the heavy slug. His back snapped in two as he was bent around the edge of the desk. He crumpled in a heap on the floor.

"Jesus Phil it was a fucking kid!" Mike screamed.

Mr. Moore yelled back in Phil's defense, "Shut the fuck up Mike. That kid was sick, and he woulda eaten you just as soon as he got done with the guy in there." Mike shook his head in disbelief.

"Sir, you know I love you, but I am the fuck out of here. I gotta get my parents and my girlfriend, and my dog, and head up to our hunting cabin, this shit ain't funny anymore." Bobby said, looking desperate. Mr. Moore nodded, and Bobby was gone out the front immediately. He passed the Chief who had run back inside, gun drawn.

Mr. Moore walked slowly into his office, and knelt over the prone form of the paramedic. He checked his neck for a pulse, but shook his head. There was no pulse to be found, and now they had a dead paramedic to add to their growing list of casualties.

Mr. Moore looked up to his son the Chief and shook his head in total disbelief. You could read the expression as plain as day.

"This can't be happening."

Suddenly Mr. Moore's face twisted in pain, and he let out a yelp and grabbed at his ankle. From behind him, the corpse of little David had taken a bite out of his Achilles tendon. Mr. Moore tilted forward and fell on his side, scrambling as best as he could to get away from the wrecked body of the boy. The Chef stepped into the room, and he and McGreevy began firing at the child. The racket was deafening in the hall. Officer and Chief emptied their weapons into the little boy, sending his body flipping back and forth all the way into the corner of the office until it came to rest propped up at an odd angle against a file cabinet.

Phil's ears were ringing loudly as the two men ended

their barrage on the boy. Mike started to mumble quietly, shaking his head. All he could manage, over and over, was, "no.. no.. no.." Eventually he turned, and walked out of the store. Ben looked around the room, and without waiting for any acknowledgment, walked out following Mike.

Mr. Moore in the meantime had started to let slip a string of profanities that would make a drunken sailor blush. The Chief and Officer McGreevy went to his aid as Phil just tried to regain his hearing. He holstered his revolver and rubbed his temples in a vain attempt to repair his beaten eardrums.

"Dad are you okay?" Chief Moore knelt beside his elderly father, checking his leg. McGreevy thumbed his walkie again and started to send out the call for additional medical personnel. No one was answering.

"What the hell is happening?" Mr. Moore said through clenched teeth. He exhaled powerfully, frustrated and in pain.

"I don't know Dad, but we're having more ambulances come, and they'll take you to the hospital, we'll get this sorted out." The Chief was starting to panic, his voice was cracking.

"Nope. Doesn't work that does it son?" Mr. Moore shook his head, wincing in pain. "Those bites are all it takes. Look at what happened here, right here, right now. That boy was bitten and he now he's bitten me and that that man there." He poked a finger over at the slumped form of the dead paramedic. "He'll be trying to eat you before we know it, and then I will too."

The Chief's eyes were spilling tears down his cheeks, "That's bullshit Dad, nonsense, help is coming." He shook his head defiantly against his Dad.

"Only help I'm getting now is a bullet to my temple. Who's doing it for me?" Mr. Moore winced again in pain and made a conscious effort to make eye contact with the three other men remaining in the room. McGreevy shook his head in a clear no, stood up, and walked out of the room. He wanted no part of this.

The Chief was sobbing now. He buried his face in his father's chest and hugged him awkwardly. Looking over his son's shoulder he locked gazes with Phil. Phil knew what had to happen. Mr. Moore nodded ever so slightly, and hugged his son back for the last time.

After a moment or two, Mr. Moore said, "Alright, tell your Mother I love her, and you take care of her now. You get your ass home and take care of Stacey and your boy. To hell with the town now, you take care of them." Mr. Moore's voice cracked at the end. He saw the writing on the wall, felt his clock ticking down.

All the Chief could choke out was a meek, "okay." He stood up and walked out of the office, pausing only to put a hand reassuringly on Phil's shoulder. They looked at each other briefly, then the Chief walked past him and out. Phil could hear him starting to sob again as he passed the counter and exited the shop.

The two longtime friends just sat still where they were. Neither man looked at each other while they separately contemplated the situation. From the side of the office where the paramedic's body was, came a scratching noise. Both men looked over in unison and saw that he was twitching.

"Shit that's fast." Mr. Moore said in a disinterested monotone.

"Ayut." Phil muttered, eyes intently on the convulsing medic. After a few seconds the twitching stopped, and his eyes popped open, fixated on the fallen gun store owner. The undead medic began the slow crawl across the office to get at his prey. He was stopped short.

Without missing a beat Phil drew his revolver again and put a .357 round straight into his ear. His head blew wide open and painted the side of the desk a thousand shades of red and pink. Chunks of brain slid slowly down, mixed in with streaks of blood and clear cranial fluid. Mr. Moore watched with no emotion, and nodded his approval.

"Nice shot."

"Thanks Boss."

"Okay then."

"Yep. Anything you need me to do?"

Mr. Moore squirreled his face up in thought. He thought long and hard about it, but eventually shook his head no.

"Okay. I'm gonna grab some stuff here, and head back to Marcy, if that's ok?" Phil hadn't moved an inch since he shot the paramedic.

"Phil buddy you are gonna blow my head off in a minute. You don't have to ask me for any permission to do shit." Mr. Moore smiled.

"I know Boss. I guess I'll see you soon." Phil's lip trembled as he steeled himself for what he was about to do.

"Not too soon brother. You take care now." Mr. Moore closed his eyes.

Phil raised the revolver and aimed at his longtime friend. He kept it there for too long though, and had to lower it. Finally he choked down a sob, and raised it again.

It was the loudest gunshot Phil had ever heard.

*****

After he gathered himself and stopped crying Phil went back out into the store. He grabbed two of the remaining pistols, several boxes of ammunition, and threw on a hunting vest. He peeked outside to find the ambulance still parked in the lot, but the Chief's cruiser and McGreevy's cruiser both long gone. For the first time all day the parking lot was essentially empty. Since the ambulance arrived, no customers had come, so the store was empty.

Phil turned off the coffee pot, locked all the gun safes, then unlocked all the gun safes, and walked out. He decided that if anyone needed a gun now, it was better to leave the safes unlocked. Not like he needed any more weapons really. He still had a few more at the house if it came to it. Out of habit the aging gun store clerk almost set the alarm on the door, but caught himself. Not much sense in doing that either he thought.

It had gotten pretty warm outside, and the sun was beating down pretty good on his walk home. He kept a good eye out as he walked the vacant sidewalk back. He didn't want to get jumped by anyone, especially after surviving what just happened at Moore's. His whole walk home he tried to think of ways to tell his wife that the nightmare was here already. He tried to think of a way to tell his wife how he'd just blown his best friend's head clean off, and shot a paramedic too. He was never clever with words though, and by the time he got home he still didn't have any idea what to say to her.

As he walked up the steps to his front door he noticed a few dark brown splotches on the concrete. Blood. Phil's back yelled out in protest as he bent down to touch it. Gooey. Almost dry.

He started to worry. The old man with the perpetually disheveled hair let himself into the front door, and drew his handgun again. The door stopped short of opening fully though, and he stumbled a bit, bumping his head on the door. He took a step back and realized the door had hit a human foot.

Laying in a heap in the hallway was the body of the female paramedic that David had bitten earlier. Her body here explained why the ambulance was still in the Moore's parking lot. Heading off in a trail towards the kitchen was a series of blood splatters. Long streaks of blood were on the wall. Phil's nose caught a whiff of an unfamiliar smell in his house: cigarettes. He holstered the revolver, and walked into the kitchen.

Sitting in the same spot he had occupied for breakfast earlier that morning was Marcy. Her back was to him but he could see an ashtray on the table in front of her. Her left hand held a cigarette and she absently flicked the ash into the tray. She was fixated on the television set, which was blaring out the emergency warning. Phil's mind couldn't focus on that, he was too intently tracking the blood spatters that led straight to the floor beside his wife. His beloved Marcy.

"Marcy baby, what's happened?" Phil asked quietly.

Immediately his wife leapt out of her seat, stomping the cigarette out in the tray, caught red handed. "Nuh.. nothing Phil, nothing at all." When she turned Phil could see she had a large bandage on her other arm. It was dark red with blood seeping through it. A trickle was running down to the wrist as she faced him.

Phil looked over his shoulder at the body of the paramedic, then back to his wife's arm. He looked up at her eyes. The same eyes that could always say more than then a thousand words could. They said everything he needed to know.

Phil closed his eyes for a second, then opened them and sat down in the chair that Marcy usually sat in at the table. He fished his pack of cigarettes out of his pocket and fired one up with the lighter Marcy had on the table. He motioned for Marcy to join him. She giggled a little and sat down next to him. Phil picked the butt up she'd just put out in the tray and gave it back to her. She put it to her mouth and he lit it for her. She took a long drag.

"Thought you quit these?" Phil asked with the cigarette in his mouth.

"Seemed like a good time to start again." She raised her arm and showed him the bloody wrapping on her forearm.

Phil looked long and hard at it. He knew it was a bite. Her eyes were still talking to him.

"Well. How was work?" She inhaled deeply, enjoying the sensation she'd deprived herself of years ago.

"Busy." Phil blew a smoke ring out, sending it across the room.

"That's good." She exhaled her smoke out, and watched it drift up to the ceiling.

Phil took the revolver out of the holster on his hip and clicked the cylinder out. Still had enough shots to do it. He clicked the cylinder shut and sat it down on the table next to the ashtray, right in between he and Marcy. She took another drag and looked at the silver gun on the table, with its long barrel, full of grace, strength, and violence.

"Phil I love you." She looked at him again with those eyes. Those bright hazel eyes. Phil noticed her brow was starting to bead with sweat.

"Marcy I will always love you." His voice broke and he sucked in a deep breath. Tears were streaming down both of their cheeks now. Phil hefted the revolver up and looked at it, contemplated it.

He did it as fast as he could, before his brain could tell him not to do it. As it turned out, that was the loudest gunshot he'd ever heard.

Phil sobbed at his kitchen table until he finished his cigarette. Once he put it out he got down on the linoleum floor next to his wife Marcy, and kissed what was left of her face. He cried a little more, and put the muzzle of the gun under his chin.

Phil never heard how loud the gunshot was that took his own life.

October 31st

Happy Halloween Mr. Journal.

It's weird. I'm sitting here in the afternoon of October 31st, aka Halloween, and there isn't a single iota of me that wishes things were normal today. Is it wrong of me to think that way? I guess the little kid inside me is kind of stoked that there isn't anyone around to tell me what to do. I don't have to go to work tonight, I don't have any bills to pay anymore, and I can eat more or less whatever I want, whenever I want. Of course if I eat whatever I want, whenever I want, I will run out of food very quickly. It's like a one person, adult Lord of the Flies here.

That's not entirely true. I love kids, and I love giving out candy on Halloween to see the kids in their cool costumes. I can remember this one kid a few years ago that came to our door dressed in a green dragon costume. He had this plastic cybernetic arm on one hand as well, and after he said "trick or treat" he presented his cybernetic arm to me proudly and belched out, "I AM A ROBOT DRAGON!"

Priceless.

That kid, I miss. I never saw him again to my knowledge, but I hope that kid is okay. For the sake of all future robot dragons.

Tonight, I miss Cassie. She always liked dressing up on Slut-o-ween and I miss the trampy outfits. They led to good sex. I don't think I miss the sex yet though. Just being with her. As long as I don't reminisce I'm okay. When I start to think about things that we did together, or things that happened between the two of us, I get emotional. Gotta keep off that subject as much as I can to try and stay together.

So it's Halloween, and I sit here at the dorm kitchen table, gas generator humming in the basement, laptop plugged in, all alone save for Otis my cat, a world filled with flesh eating zombies, and starving survivors of the

106

apocalypse. Granted, things could be better, but I'm not starving, I'm warm, and I'm holed up in a pretty safe place I think. Enhance the positives someone once told me.

Daily update portion of the diary: Weather is cool, seasonably so, but not cold. It's been damp and drizzly since my last entry. Incidentally, I have come to fucking HATE fog. I mentioned that I do two checks on the campus every day to check for stragglers or zombies. Fog makes that patrol amazingly difficult. Vision is almost totally hampered, and I can't hear shit through the fog. It really scares me about snowstorms in winter later on. Anyone who's been outside while it's snowing knows the dead silence caused by the falling snow, and I can't imagine it'll make my life any fucking easier. Fuck mother nature, fuck her in her foggy, stupid ass.

Luckily I haven't encountered anything in the past few foggy days. Well to be more technically accurate, I haven't noticed that I've encountered anything. For all I know I walked right by a horde of the undead bastards every time I stepped outside and just don't know it. Whatever I guess. From the inside of Hall E here, everything is quiet, and I feel pretty safe tonight. Safe enough to eat one of my candy bars.

Safe enough to write at length about my first night here on campus. I like to call that night "Night of the Living Dead Private School Students." You'll see why.

So I arrived on campus to a disorganized mess. Amy, one of the admissions chicks, had filled me in on the day's events on campus which were all bad. They had locked down classrooms, paranoid and or crazy parents, car accidents, one seizure, staff running away screaming, one diabetic reaction, a few assaults, etc etc. Not a safe place to be and it was where I had chosen to make my nest to ride this thing out. You could say with relative safety that I had some doubt at that moment. I mean, I could walk right then and there. Just fucking get back in my car, and go somewhere else. Kick in the door of some rural farmhouse and board that shit up. Aka Plan B, turtle it up somewhere else.

CHRIS PHILBROOK

But noooooo. I stick to my guns. I never walk away from a fight I think I can win. And strangely enough, I think I can win just about every fight. Cassie said my confidence bordered on arrogance. I think it turned her on.

So after checking in with Amy and the eight paranoid parents trying to find their children, I decided to go find the crazy ass parent that was going to go "rescue" the kids from Mrs. Goodell's classroom. I thanked Amy and tried to reassure the parents right before I told them to stay in the admissions house. I needed more firepower. I had grabbed the pistol and the .22, but this struck me a shotgun kind of situation. I went back to the car, switched the rifle for the gauge, and started to head south towards the main classroom building. Just as I headed that way, I heard the distinct sound of gunfire coming from inside the building. Not good right?

I picked up some speed and got to the front of the building. All of our doors are either glass industrial doors, or steel fire doors. The school had the glass kind. I looked through, yanked the door open, and headed inside. The halls were lit by the emergency lights that are on at night normally. They're on a timer and kick on automatically at 8pm. Two lights are in each major hallway, one at each end, flooding towards the center of the corridor. They aren't the brightest bulbs in the building, but they suitably keep it lit. That's not a joke or a pun about the students or staff or anything, I'm actually talking about the lights there.

So the school building is square and three floors. Classrooms were on each side of the central hallway with some offices in the front and back. The staircase was in the middle of the hall, on the left side. I remember feeling very out of place here. Normally I'm never in the main classroom building. I work (read: worked) in the residential program at night, so there's no reason to be in that building. It was weird just being in there, let alone being in there specifically to find a gun-toting lunatic, and to liberate eight kids being held captive by a granola crunching English teacher.

108

Weirdness abounds.

I combat-cleared the lower floor in 4 minutes. I did it silently so as not to arouse any suspicion, or to let the dude upstairs know I was here. The bottom floor was all clear. You could tell from the clutter in the classrooms that it had been a bad day. The rooms smelled… sweaty. Plus the kid's book bags were tossed about, and there were snack food wrappers all over the place. You could tell they had been holed up in the rooms for awhile earlier. Right as I was getting to the back office for the guidance counselors, I heard some yelling coming from upstairs. It was distant, coming from the third floor.

I couldn't afford to move much faster though. My safety would be at risk. That's a debate you have a lot in situations like that. You weigh your safety with the potential outcomes and at some point you realize that your safety is not worth any potential outcome. I was willing to go in the building to try and rescue the kids, but I wasn't willing to die for them. Not today at least. I wanted to survive this.

I remember tripping slightly going up the stairs. One of those times when your toe catches the lip of a stair. I didn't fall, but I did put a hand down to catch myself. I made it to the 2nd floor after that with no problem. The second floor is largely wide open, save for the bookcases in the library. There are some floor to ceiling support posts, but otherwise, its bookcases and tables. I swept down the aisles in between the bookcases and quickly made sure the floor was clear of students, staff, and the undead.

I made it back to the main staircase and took the steps up to the 3rd floor a little more carefully. I could hear a man yelling, but couldn't make out exactly what was being said. I could also just barely hear someone else talking, but it was really muffled, like they were in a closet or something. I made my way to the top of the stairs and lay down on my belly. I slid my body up the last couple feet and poked my head into the hall at floor level. People generally don't look for threats at floor level. It's a pretty safe way to check out a situation around a corner. (Although I don't know if this would work on the undead. Caveat emptor)

Backlit by one of the emergency floodlights I could make out a guy, about six feet tall, holding a gun and looking into the small window of the classroom at the end of the hall. Classroom doors are sturdy fire class doors with the small rectangular window with the chicken wire glass in it. Strong doors for sure. He was banging on the door pretty solidly in between trying to look through the window. I took it in for a bit, then slowly got to my feet and came out into the hallway.

"Freeze!" I barked out like a cop. I hoped his reaction would be instant compliance. Luckily, he froze. I think I told him to identify himself, and without turning or moving an inch, he said he was "Dan Haggerty." I knew his kid; Dale. Jock, prick, womanizer, prized football talent. Huge sense of entitlement. I was just fucking thrilled to meet the guy that spawned that MTV castoff. He sputtered out a few sentences and I pieced together that his son was in the room, and that "something was wrong with the teacher."

That struck a chord.

I told him to calm down, that I was staff, and I was here to help. He turned and looked at me and even in the shitty light of the emergency lamps I could see he went pale. Evidently my appearance was... disturbing. I remember forcing a chuckle to lighten the moment up a bit. He laughed with me after I told him things were "messy out there." Even after we sort of had our bonding moment, you could see he was pained. You could also see he had a huge shotgun, and a handgun stuck in the waistband of his Dockers. I asked him what the problem was.

To sum up, Mrs. Goodell had secured her classroom according to safety procedures. To keep the kids occupied all day, she had turned on the television in the classroom, and had them watch the news networks to learn about this "historic" day. Not sure that was a good idea. From what I gathered from Dan, a couple of the kids started to panic, eventually freaked out, and together with a few of the calm students, they had restrained them. That was hours ago. In the meantime, Mrs Goodell had put some cloth over the small window to obscure the view into the corner classroom.

Mrs. Goodell was concerned for the health of the two restrained kids. One was a boy, one a girl. Dan explained that apparently the kids had gone limp in their restraints hours ago, but had started to move again, and were struggling against the hob-cobbled bonds. That line totally set me off. First they went limp, then "woke up" and were struggling? Immediately I was sure they had died, and were now reanimated.

I motioned for Dan to get away and let me try and talk to her. I rapped on the window and yelled in to her that it was me, and I was here to help. I could hear some of the kids whimpering through the door, and even heard one yell out my name. I had pretty good relationships with a few of the kids in the dorm. I could hear the tension in their voices straight through the door.

After a maybe a minute I saw the cloth get pulled back a bit and Mrs. Goodell's face appear. Like I said she was a bit off-beat. She was about 5 feet even, a bit chunky, and had a giant poofy afro puff of grey hair. Her black rimmed glasses looked straight out of the 60's, and she generally dressed like she was headed to Woodstock. Amusing lady to talk to for sure. Not that night though. Her eyes were bloodshot, and she was pasty white from stress. I remember when she appeared she didn't say anything, she just looked at me silently through the door. I could tell from the look in her eye things were bad inside the room. She mouthed and pointed that Dan had to leave for her to talk, so I asked Dan for some privacy. As soon as he was 20 feet away or so, she finally whispered to me.

"The Haggerty boy was one of the kids who had to be restrained Adrian." I can remember everything she said word for word. "He's dead Adrian, I didn't mean to, the kids didn't mean to, but he was so strong we had to tie him down

111

extra tight. Except now he's not really dead anymore, and we've got him in the closet, but I think he's free now, and we don't know what to do Adrian. I don't want to lose my job, and I don't want his Dad to find out his son is dead, and-" I cut her off.

"Erica," that was her first name, "I'm sure everything that has happened was an accident or was absolutely necessary. A lot of people have been hurt today by accidents and things are not good everywhere. We need to stick together right now, and these kids need to get to their parents. Can we at least get the kids who are being safe out, and down to their parents so they can go home? We'll deal with the two tied up kids afterwards?" I said it all as quietly as I could. I didn't want to alert Dan that his kid was one of the two that were restrained, and likely dead.

Mrs. Goodell swallowed and nodded, "Keep him away." I nodded at her and asked for a moment. She waited as I walked down the hall to the armed father.

I'll never forget this discussion either. The banality of it in retrospect haunts me.

"Dan, in order for her to let the kids out, you need to be safe, and stay away from the classroom, okay?"

His response was a little sullen, introspective even, "Yeah, yeah. I get it. I suppose if it were MY kid in there I wouldn't want you guys to let them out with a guy with a gun the hall right?" He sort of laughed, realizing the absurdity of it all.

"Exactly. Can you hang back here at the stairs for me while we get the kids out? There are still two that need to be calmed down before they can be let out, okay?" I remember he nodded emphatically.

I walked back to the classroom and nodded to Mrs. Goodell. She turned, addressed the class quickly, letting them know what was up. They absolutely leapt off their desks and chairs to get out. I can't blame them either, they had been locked up in there since morning. It was now nearly nine.

Once they were up and calmed down enough to exit safely, she unlocked the door, and they started streaming out. I didn't notice that Dan had made his way right back up behind me. As soon as the first kid was through the door, he shoved me out of the way, and pushed past the exiting students and into the classroom.

Chaos ensued. The kids all backed away, deeper into the room. They knew who it was. Father and son looked too familiar. One of the girls at the end of the line in the classroom started sobbing, and simply pointed at the closet door next to Mrs. Goodell's desk. Most of the kids were paralyzed as I entered the room and started to physically shove the kids out the door. Mrs. Goodell herself put her body in the path of the kids and Mr. Haggerty. Valiant really.

Dan ripped the closet door open and saw his son for the first time that day, and for the last time in his life. Dale was standing, freed from the make shift bonds that had held him most of the day. My bet is he suffocated, or maybe had a heart attack or seizure. Who knows. But he was dead for sure, really dead. And he was a foot away from his Dad. Dan had no chance or ability to defend himself from his son. Dan's breath escaped him, the look of shock and pain on his face was epic.

Dale lunged at him and bit him savagely on the shoulder. I remember Dan letting out a low howl in pain as he had a chunk torn from him. Everything else happened so fast. I was almost frozen, watching, and had stopped pushing the kids out. Mrs. Goodell had just gone stone faced witnessing the events unfold. Dan backpedaled away from his son, clutched his shoulder, and turned to the rest of us.

All he said was, "You fucking bitch." He really choked it out through a mess of pain. Must've taken tremendous effort to say it. Then he started shooting. I only saw his first two shots. Shot number one went at his son Dale, hitting him center mass, and throwing him back inside the closet. Shot number two went right at Erica, hitting her flush, and hitting a bunch of the kids. Remember folks, close with a shotgun is usually good enough. As soon as I saw him wheeling towards the kids I dove away. I don't know exactly what happened next. Well, I don't know what happened while I was unconscious. I've pieced it together a little since that night, but essentially when I dove, I just went on pure instinct, I didn't look where I was going. It would seem that I went headfirst into a desk and took the corner right to the temple.

I don't know how long I was out, but it wasn't that long. Five minutes? Easily the luckiest five minutes of my life. As I came to I remember just blinking a few times, and realizing my head was throbbing like I'd been hit with a jackhammer. I stayed very still, as I could hear some movement in the room with me. Scratching, chewing, slurping. The floodlights were not giving me a lot of light to see by, so I was a little off kilter. Being blind is no fucking fun. See: hatred for fog.

I rolled over slowly and my eyes adjusted to the level of light. I could see bodies all over the front of the classroom where the kids had been, and where Erica and Dan had been standing. Some of the bodies were down, clearly down, and a few of them were either sitting up, or moving to stand up. I counted four kids, plus the two bodies of the adults. I reached around slowly for the shotgun but couldn't find it. Plan B was the pistol, which I drew as slowly as I could. I knew I had to get out of the room. Third floor window wasn't a jumping option, and this room didn't have a fire escape. Across the hall was Dr. Potter's classroom, which did have a fire escape. It was also empty, so that was viable.

I very slowly sat up and assessed things. This was one of the moments where I really learned and appreciated how quiet these fucking things were. I was in a room that was for all intents and purposes filled with the motherfuckers and I could barely hear anything. Four kids were dead in the room and getting back up to do the whole "undead thing" that was all the rage today. Erica was dead too, nearly blown in half by Dan's shotgun blast. She was starting to sit up presently. Well, as much as someone bisected by a shotgun can at least. Dan and Dale were nowhere to be found. I could hear struggling coming from the closet, which had to be the second student restrained earlier.

I lifted the pistol, drew a bead on the kid closet to me, and shot. She flung sideways on top of another kid. Erica turned towards me immediately, as did the other zombies. I started shooting from the hip as fast as I could squeeze the trigger. I shot until the slide locked back and the gun clicked empty. In retrospect, it was a huge waste of ammunition. I don't even know how many I killed with my spray and pray tactics, but it caused enough commotion and sent their bodies around enough for me to bolt out of the room. I didn't find the shotgun when I jumped up, so I was down to just the pistol. Once in the hall I found three more kids. They were dead too. Well, dead-ish. Dale was there as well, finishing a meal of one of his classmates. He found me much more interesting though, and came at me. Luckily the hall was pretty wide, and I just side stepped him and the other two and bolted for the stairway.

I fucking FLEW down those stairs. Two or three at a time in giant leaps. I got to the ground floor in maybe 20 seconds. I blasted my way out through the glass doors and reloaded the pistol, which was empty. I had the presence of mind to slip the empty clip into my cargo pocket too, go me. By then the throbbing in my head was starting to fade, which was about the only good thing that had happened to me in some time.

I hoofed it back towards my car as fast as I could go. That too turned out to be a pretty shitty idea. The couple of kids who had actually made it out of the classroom went there too, and they were both badly wounded I guess. They made it to the admissions office, and made things much worse. I think they bled out from shotgun wounds. That or they were bitten by Dale on their way out. Either way the two kids had died, had come back, and had killed more people here. As I stopped my run towards admissions I nearly got ran over by one of the parent's leaving the campus at top speed. I could hear them screaming in grief as they drove by.

I could see several of the zombies feasting in the yard of the admissions house. There was at least half a dozen dead there now, and my car was right there next to them. My other gun was in the car, as well as the extra 9mm ammo. I did a quick check around campus and in the dim light of the few street lamps we have, I could see more shambling forms headed my way. It was more of the dead from earlier in the day, congregating to the noise.

I needed a place to hole up for the night. Shit at that point I needed a place to hole up for five minutes to catch my damn breath. At that point I had no idea where anyone was, or where to go. My plan had crashed and fucking burned all in a heartbeat. Fuck Dan Haggerty.

I started jogging towards some of the maintenance buildings, away from the bulk of the zombies I saw moving my way. I went into my pocket for my facilities keys and that's when I realized they were gone. I found them much later in Mrs. Goodell's classroom, but for the moment, I was sans-keys.

Anything else God? Getting pretty sick of these pop-quizzes here dude. Way to test faith bro.

I remember getting really pissed, and actually screaming out "What the fuck?!" I'll grant you that wasn't a good idea at all, but I was really angry and pissed, and was starting to feel a little helpless. I started jogging again, this time around the back of the maintenance buildings near the water. I didn't see anything of use. I did however see a ladder laying on the ground behind the last out building. I remember looking, and saw the back of the admissions building. Admissions had a steeply sloped roof for the main structure, but an addition they put on two years ago was almost flat roofed. It took me a minute or two, but I got the ladder free of some shit on it, and ran with it to the admissions house. My heart was pounding bad.

Zombies aren't smart at all. They can't plan ahead. The

ones in the yard not minutes before had followed me all the way around all the maintenance buildings and were now coming up behind me, leaving the yard empty again. I leaned the ladder against admissions, and started to run around to my now largely wide open car, but I saw a bunch of the kids from the school house coming right at me. Ten feet away from my car at most. Scrap that idea.

I spun, realized that the zombies following me from around the out buildings were damn near on top of me and dashed for the ladder. I climbed like never before. Despite moving like my life actually depended on it, several of my kids actually got close enough to grab my pants legs as I pulled myself up higher. I kicked at them to get them off my ankles. I scrambled to the top, rolled onto the roof, and wrestled the ladder away from the growing throng of zombie children and parents gathering at the base of the admissions house.

I think it was half past nine or so by then, maybe even ten, and I was hungry, kind of cold, mildly concussed, surrounded by dozens of quietly hungry zombies, trapped in the dark on a rooftop with 15 rounds of 9mm ammo, a sword, and no keys to get inside anywhere.

And that was just the beginning of the worst night of my life.

More later.

-Adrian

November 2010

November 2nd

Mr. Journal, where were we?

Ah, yes. Rooftop on the admissions building. Worst night of my fucking life. Yeah about that… So let's refresh the page eh? I had gone into the classrooms, and found Dan Haggerty on the third floor trying to "communicate" with Mrs. Goodell. Once I got him away a bit, Mrs. Goodell revealed to me that Haggerty's son had died, had become a zombie, and was locked in a supply closet inside the classroom.

Once we got everything calm, Goodell opened the door to clear her students out, Haggerty surprised us, and burst in trying to find his son. He found him, got bit by him, and retaliated in a totally sensible fashion by blasting his son, Mrs. Goodell, and several of the students with a 12 gauge. I was knocked out cold when I dove for cover.

On returning to the land of the awake (and living dead) I discovered I was surrounded by fucking zombies. I lost track of my shotgun, but using my Sig I had managed to shoot my way out of the classroom before the zombies killed me. Complete shit luck that they didn't take a nibble when I was passed out. I got the fuck out of the classroom, and bolted back across campus to admissions where I found yet another degenerating situation. Two of the kids wounded in the classroom incident (or perhaps bitten while I was out cold) had made it to the admissions house, promptly died, sat back up, bit their parents and a few staff members, and spread this disease even further.

During that scramble I realized my keys were history, I had a minor mental breakdown, found a ladder, and climbed on top of the admissions building after running for my life for a few minutes. I only made it onto the admissions roof by the slimmest of margins too, zombie kids, parents and staff all clawing at my feet as I climbed the ladder. I'm lucky I didn't lose a sneaker on my way up.

So that's where I realized that maybe, juuuuuust maybe,

I had made a mistake. Perhaps a "minor" error in judgment. I distinctly remember flopping down, facing up at the stars on that clear June 23rd. "That day." I think that's actually the first time I've said the actual day all this shit went down. It's weird that it's taken me this long to actually put a date to the "that day." That Wednesday, June 23rd.

Anyway. I took a minute or two to gather myself and assess my new situation. I had enough space on the roof to lay down comfortably. (assuming of course you find laying on asphalt shingles comfortable) I had 15 rounds in my pistol, and my sword. My car was locked, and my keys were incognito. I hadn't eaten in hours, and I had no water. Otis, my devoted and handsome cat was still locked firmly away in his carryall in my car as well. He hadn't eaten in hours either, and also had no water. I peeked over the edge and did a quick assessment of the walking dead hanging out and got really depressed. Where I had pulled up the ladder there were at least two dozen zombies. Couldn't barely hear them either, creepy as shit. The only noise you could hear was a few cars running in the parking lots nearby, the sound of the water lapping at the shore nearby, and a faint scratching at the siding of the house. Ever heard a bunch of people slowly scraping their nails on wood in the dark? Ever hear the same thing only by undead just a few feet away that are aching to eat the meat off your bones? Creepy doesn't even come close to touching it.

What to do, right? I was fucked. I couldn't see well enough to really feel comfortable in trying to get off the roof. I couldn't get to the other side of the building either as the roof was far too sloped to risk trying a crossing. I had zombies on all sides and little to no options even if I did get off the roof. I decided to wait for daylight. I would be hungry, but at least then I could see.

Many things happened that night. There was still a small number of staff, parents, and students on campus. I saw several of them escape, driving at breakneck speeds over the bridge. I even tried to flag them down, jumping up and down, screaming, waving, but it was all to no avail. I thought at several times I would be able to get off the roof when they left, as some of the zombies started to follow their cars, but they came back too quickly to risk it. I spent long stretches that night just trying to be quiet, observing the zombies. I learned a lot that night watching them, and I've put it to good use since then too.

Lowlight of the cool night up there was when the last car came on campus. It was another parent coming for their child. I don't know what kid, or who the parents were, but I remember vividly how they died. Their sedan crossed the bridge cautiously at about midnight, creeping along. I was already starving by then. They crept up to the admissions house and I remember jumping up and waving at them. They didn't see me. The car came to a stop, and mom and dad got out of it, and walked carefully up to the door. I didn't want to holler at them as I felt I had just gotten the zombies below to forget about me, so I was trying to do a "loud whisper" if that makes any sense. They didn't hear me.

The dad was older, probably mid 50's, with grey hair, and had an aluminum baseball bat. Mom was much younger, struck me as sort of a trophy wife, but you could tell she wasn't a gold-digger. I don't know how exactly I knew that, but I could tell she was emotionally invested in the dude and the kid she came for. She looked... concerned I guess. They tried the door, but it was locked. Had they kept quiet, I think they would've been fine, but one of them said something to the other, and the zombies below me heard.

It didn't take long for them to shuffle around the corner of the building, and as soon as I saw the zombies moving I started to yell. I screamed at them to get back inside their car and get the hell out. The woman did turn and start moving, but hero dad decided to beat some ass with that fucking bat. Lemme tell you right now: bats are not that effective. I mean, if you're a rugged person, and can swing it like a pro, yeah sure, you can split some wigs, but not this guy. He clocked several of the zombies pretty good but didn't get any head shots in. I kept yelling to hit them in the head, but he didn't change tactics in time. He kept hitting them in the sides and the arms and as you can imagine, it had no effect. It was as useful as trying to beat a tree into falling over. They swarmed him pretty quickly and collapsed on top of him. I could hear him scream as they ripped him apart one bite at a time.

MILFy had made her way back into the car. Passenger side, where she started this fiasco. She must've dropped her purse though because she didn't start the car. Daddy Rich probably had his keys on him as well, so she was just as stuck as I was. Half of the zombies shuffled over after eating the dad and listlessly scratched at the windows of the car. I don't know if a zombie has the strength to break auto glass. I suspect a big one could, but I didn't get my answer that night. The other half of the zombies came back to the admissions building and returned to their incessant scratching, trying to get up at me and my skin again.

That's how things settled for an hour or so. If I got right up to the edge of the roof nearest the road I could watch MILFy in her car without being seen by the undead below. She cried a lot. The more I sat there, the more I started to realize she was really beautiful, and how sad everything was for her. It's like the fantasy that's always better than reality I think. I wondered what her family life was like, I thought about which of the students her kid was. I fantasized about how the kid would hate how hot his mom was, and how hot his friends thought she was, and how much he would've hated that. It was how I passed the time for that hour. I really felt like I got to know her.

I was totally shocked when she opened the car door and got out. It was obviously suicide. I think she came to the conclusion that she had no more life left to live, and she just gave up. Can you blame her? One of the students, one of the nerdy ones killed her. She just tilted her head back against the door frame of the car and he ripped her throat out, right where the Adam's apple would've been. She died pretty quickly, never put up an ounce of fight either. Her mind was made up the moment she got out.

I hated to see her die like that, but you have to respect the will it must've taken to do what she did. I'm not condoning suicide Mr. Journal, but there is some sense in what she did, after what just happened to her and her family. I was genuinely sad to see her go. I actually was hoping to talk to her after we got to safety. Maybe in a way I was trying to rescue her like I didn't rescue Cassie. I felt really miserable after that woman from the car died. I felt even more miserable after her body got back up, and started meandering around, looking for something to eat. Namely, something like me.

The rest of the night was spent laying as silently as possible on the roof of admissions. Eventually everyone who was capable of leaving campus was history, and I was left alone with no help anywhere to be found. My stomach was growling like you can't imagine, and I was really thirsty. At about the time of dawn when the eastern horizon takes on that faint bluish tinge I remember I felt a little bit of optimism. Maybe I would make it. I had fallen in and out of sleep a few times that night, and I don't remember my dreams. I do know when I saw that horizon I was achy and my back was killing me. When I launched myself away from my mom at her elderly home earlier I really smashed my back against the wall. Falling asleep on the roof did me no damn favors. So I got up to stretch.

I walked around my little roof world and re-assessed things. About ten zombies had walked off. I was happy to notice that when I shifted my weight, and heard a loud crack under the shingles. I nearly dented my head when it dawned on me how retarded I was. I knelt down, and noise be damned, starting ripping up shingles. Below the shingles was plain plywood. It was a gamble, but I felt the house inside was empty, and if I could get through the roof and got inside, I would be one step closer to safety.

I had no hammer, but the sword would work as a lever pretty good to pry up a sheet of the plywood. As quietly as I could, which wasn't very quiet at all, I pried up one edge of a sheet of plywood, and got it torn up. That was loud though, and by the time I had the wood up, I was fully surrounded by even more zombies than before. The crowd on the ground below was at least 3 or 4 zombies deep now, and surrounding half the building. Below the plywood was the ceiling, which was drywall. A few good hacks with the sword though, and I cleared a space conveniently right above a desk. I started making noise inside the building to draw attention, but nothing came. I dropped down into the office, and proceeded to clear the house and check the doors. Empty, and locked, respectively. The zombies were gathering outside en masse though, so I needed to work quickly.

As I said, the campus doors are strong, so that was going in my favor. Windows though were not. I had just watched a handful of the dead try and break car glass with no success, but regular window glass is a different animal all together. I needed to get into a room with more security. Luckily one of the back offices had only one small window, and had a strong interior door. I checked one more thing before I began my plan for escape: the refrigerator. The staff fridge had two lunches from the day prior still in it, as well as some bottled water, and I started eating the crappy little sandwiches and gulping water as fast as I could. Reminds me of my military days. Eat as much as you can, as fast as you can and worry about digestion later. I didn't know when my next meal was coming.

New plan was this: make a shitload of noise on one side of the admissions building, then run into my secure room after drawing them in. I would have to be really quick, or really clever to get the majority of them inside the building with me. Open the small window, escape to a hopefully clearer exterior, get into my car somehow, get the rifle and more ammo for the pistol, (possibly retrieve the shotgun as well, but that really seemed like reaching at that moment) and start doing some serious yard work on these fucking undead. No rest for the wicked.

I implemented plan "day after that day" immediately. Well that's not entirely true. I kept a small chunk of turkey from one sandwich for Otis. He needed something to eat badly, and I do not want anyone to think I don't take good care of my cat.

Love that guy.

Talk to you soon Mr. Journal.

-Adrian

DARK RECOLLECTIONS

Crime/Incident Report

Case # DRM062310-01

Month June **Day** 23 **Year** 2010 **Day of Week** Weds.
Time approx 1625

Code section or description of incident Officer involved fatal shooting.

Location of Incident Moore's Sporting Goods, 1421 Riverside Way

Victim or witness name Daniel Roger McGreevy
Address: 14 Wilbur Street

Phone: 4995553459 **Ht** 6ft 5 in **Wt** 265 lbs **Sex** male **Eyes** Green **Hair** None

Race Caucasian

ID type: Badge# 114 **ID#** 114. Issued March 8th, 2004

Relation to victim/subject None, arresting officer

Addt'l information (vehicle) City police cruise 06

 # witnesses of crime/incident 6 direct witnesses, 1 more on scene that heard incident, 1 more witness who returned to scene directly following.

Names of witnesses and relevant info regarding
Direct witnesses are as follows; 1. Off. Daniel McGreevy, 2. Mike Desmaris, 3. Robert Zewicki, 4. Benjamin Barnes, 5. David Johns(son of deceased), and 6. Phillip Thompkins. Indirect witness inside business was 7. Gerald Moore, CoP, retired. Witnesses 2, 3, 4, 6 and 7 are all employees of Moore's Sporting Goods. Witness 8 left scene before statement could be retrieved. Filing Officer recognized witness as Adrian Ring.

Place of attack (if applicable) Parking lot of Moore's Sporting Goods, north side. Directly in front of customer entrance.

Weapon used (if applicable) Filing Officer discharged his service weapon twice at suspect. Weapon is a Glock 21, identified as property of City Police Department, weapon ID# 22161

Suspect arrested Y/N? Suspect was DOS.

Suspect name Paul Matthew Johns **Address:** 11 Oak Ridge Blvd, Mount Temple

Phone: 6705554141 **Ht** 5ft 7in **Wt** 145 lbs **Sex** male **Eyes** brown **Hair** lt. brown

Race Caucasian

ID type: OOS Driver's license **ID#** DL06JSP41280

Addt'l information (vehicle) 2009 Nissan Maxima XLE. Burgundy/wine. OOS tags 14198S

Physical description of subject Subject exited vehicle wearing a light blue dress shirt, and corduroy pants. Subject had a large blood stain spreading on his right forearm, appeared sweaty, in pain and confused. His hair was disheveled as was his general appearance. On closer inspection he was found to be covered in fine mists of blood, similar to those found on attackers using blunt force trauma.

Evidence collected at scene relevant to prosecution No evidence was collected at the scene of the incident. Directly following the shooting ambulances arrived, and the son (David Johns) entered into some form of seizure/shock. He became physically aggressive and attacked witnesses as well as responding EMT's. The scene was cleared after that. Evidence collection would have resulted almost certainly in Officer injury.

Narrative AO was stationed at Moore's Sporting Goods
for the day to ensure customer safety due to concerns
regarding attacks on the general populace by sick/
infected citizens. Store owner made the request to
Chief Moore and instructed AO to station there.

Majority of early afternoon was spent maintaining
basic order in parking lot, and keeping a visible
presence to deter crimes against the business and its
employees. AO neither witnessed nor intervened in any
criminal activity. During afternoon Chief of Police
Moore instructed AO that any citizen that appeared
injured, and did not respond intelligently should be
handled with extreme caution. The CoP advised that
deadly force was authorized if the AO felt that
safety was a concern, and if the injured was
unresponsive to verbal commands.

At approximately 1625 the suspect arrived in Moore's
parking lot driving at excessive speeds, and
recklessly. Suspect pulled into parking In such a
dangerous fashion his vehicle nearly struck City
Cruiser #06, as well as the AO. AO then backed away,
drew his service weapon and instructed driver to exit
the vehicle with his hands raised. At this time the
AO noticed the subject had a passenger in the front
passenger seat of the vehicle. Passenger was later
identified as David Johns, the suspect's son.

The suspect exited the vehicle, and started walking
towards the AO, ignoring all verbal commands. Behind
the AO the Moore's Employees were getting dangerously
close to the unresponsive suspect. AO knew that the
employees were legally armed, and wanted to take
control of the situation before it escalated into a
multi-person firefight.

AO then visually confirmed that the suspect had an
injury. The right hand sleeve at the forearm location
was covered in fresh red blood, and appeared to be a
bite wound. At that point the AO decided that being
bitten as well as unresponsive combined with directly
approaching the AO ignoring all Officer commands

authorized deadly force given the prior instructions by the CoP.

The Officer cleared his lines of fire to ensure the passenger was safe and that the subject had no one behind him that could be hit by any rounds missing and/or passing through. Once cleared, the Officer discharged his service weapon five times into the center mass of the subject, whereupon he collapsed in the parking lot, directly in front of suspect's vehicle. The Officer observed the subject for some time, and identified that the subject was dead.

After ensuring the subject was dead, the AO made the decision to shoot the subject one additional time in the head to fully ensure death. With media reports and police reports earlier in the day instructing those in danger to shoot or damage the brain, the AO wanted to ensure further public safety and took the extra step. This course of action later proved invaluable, as the son David Johns was bitten, entered into some form of seizure/shock, and became violent. It is quite possible that the suspect would've done the same thing were he not shot in the head.

AO notified Emergency Reponse Units and the CoP, who responded almost immediately.

Charges filed or to be filed: Threatening an Officer, Assaulting an Peace Officer, Resisting Arrest, Reckless Operation, Endangering the Welfare of a Child.

Additional Notes not related to incident (if any) AO McGreevy is leaving town. I am gathering all my things and heading three towns over to my mother's home. You can reach me there if needed. Assuming we even do an investigation any further. I think the state internal affairs department is going to be a little swamped with all these attacks. Good luck to whoever reads this, and God bless.

November 4ᵗʰ

Hey Mr. Journal! How's life? Mine is fucking phenomenal! OMG! I almost totally, like, fucking died today! LOLZ! That's super l33t!

Sigh. Sarcasm font off.

Vigilance, and attention to detail. I used to preach that shit at work all the time, my whole frigging like. Attention to detail. Attention to detail. Vigilance. I cannot cut corners anytime I am out of Hall E anymore. I am so furious at myself right now I can barely type.

In fact, fuck this. I have to calm down.

-Adrian

November 4ᵗʰ (2ⁿᵈ entry)

Much better now.

Let me dial this back a little bit and rehash why I was so pissed off and all 'roid ragey earlier at myself. I went to the campus cafeteria this afternoon to get some canned food to move it here to Hall E. I was running low on a few different things, was jonesing for a bit of variety, and I haven't yet moved all the supplies into here so it was a pretty standard food run. We're talking a hundred yards from door to door.

I've checked campus twice a day for weeks now I think making sure nothing is here. I mean shit, why would anything be here anyway? I make little to no noise, I stay inside as much as possible, I give those motherfuckers no reason at all to come up here. Apparently I need to re-think my whole vision of how and why these things move about. Because one of them made his way onto campus, and all the way into the frigging cafeteria.

So I always do my errands during daylight hours. As you

132

may have gleaned from my prior entries here Mr. Journal, I do not operate at night. Clever guy that I am, I use the campus maintenance four wheeler to get around when I need to move a lot of things. It has a little trailer that can be hooked up to it which makes moving heavy things, or lots of little things a lot faster and safer. Plus if shit hits the fan I can peace-out like a girl scout and regroup somewhere safer.

I keep the ATV 10 paces from the door of Hall E for convenience. Hopped on, fired it up, and motored over to the cafeteria at a leisurely pace. Now when I do my little patrols I always bring the Sig, one of the swords, and the bow. I use them in the exact opposite order listed should something happen. As I said, I believe noise is really bad, and draws them in. The bow and sword are both silent, so it suits me and my plan.

Today was no different. I rolled over to the cafeteria, parked at the kitchen door, which is on the side, as opposed to the main entrance the kids would've used during school hours. Staff never used the main doors at night, as we primarily would be going there to raid the fridges to feed ourselves. SOP as they say.

Hopped off the quad, grabbed my banana box out of the trailer, unlocked the kitchen door, and moved in like any other day. Now right inside the kitchen door you entered a short hall and there is the walk in cooler, and walk in freezer. Opposite those two doors in the hall was the area we used to call "they honey hole." Where they kept staff only food. All the good shit basically. It meant all the food I needed was within 15 feet of the back door. Now the electricity has long since been off in this building, and that means the cooler and freezer are offline. Now if you've ever had your electricity go off for any time, you probably know that frequently the fridge can get pretty warm all on its own. Especially after any food inside it begins rotting. The freezer stayed cold for quite some time, which was awesome, but the cooler was basically a total loss within a week. Fresh veggies didn't keep, rotted, warmed the cooler, lather rinse repeat.

So I walked into honey hole and started my shopping spree. I filled up the banana box, and brought it outside. Transferred everything into the trailer and brought it inside again. By the way, if you're curious, yes, it's THAT banana box. Same one, still kicking like kung fu. I'm telling you if you're not on the banana box team, get on it now.

So I went back inside for a second food run, and filled the box again. I continued humming the Linkin Park song I had stuck in my head, and casually turned to bring load two out. When I turned, I bumped into the goddamn zombie.

Have you ever, truly been scared? I don't mean like when you watch a freaky movie that makes you not want the lights off at night, I mean like when someone catches you off guard, and your heart leaps into your throat? You get that immediate single POUND of the heart, and the sudden surge of adrenaline? Usually about one second later whoever scared you is laughing because of the look on your face, and then you either smack the shit out of them for scaring you, or you're laughing with them… You know what I'm talking about, right?

This was like that. Sans the laughter. I nearly had a heart attack on the spot, and immediately went on the defensive. I was already in the corner of the pantry so I had nowhere to go, and this thing was already pressing against the banana box which weighed a solid 50 pounds by that time. (It was filled with cans.) Only way to get rid of it was to drop it, which would put it right on my foot, or shove it at the zombie.

The zombie was so close he had the initiative. Now they aren't fast, but they can lunge like a fucking pro when they have you like that. This guy was on me like white on rice. He sort of came down with both hands and knocked the box free right onto my feet. Fortunately it landed on my feet and not my toes. It hurt like a bitch, but as we all know, toe pain is the worst. Foot pain is much more tolerable.

Now the box falling on my feet sent me backwards and I hit the wall pretty hard. The frigging zombie kinda fell onto me, and bit me pretty good.

Yeah I know. I said the B word. Curtains for Adrian, right? No way, no how Mr. Journal. Adrian gets lucky again. The zombie sunk every last tooth into the collar of the fleece jacket I had on. The fucker's weight on me took me all the way to the ground. Cornered, on the floor, with a zombie on top of me, biting the fuck out of my collar.

God hell he smelt to high heaven. I flat out do not know how I didn't smell him coming. Maybe I was used to the smell of the wretched freezer in the kitchen and just tuned it out? I don't know. Any way I look at it way I'm a fucking idiot.

Soooo.. panic time. I've got a few years of Jiu-Jitsu and Karate under my belt, so I am fairly good in a scrap. Not a ninja mind you, but I could give a ninja a fucking hell of a bloody nose if one tangled with me. I think I gave the zombie a sweeping elbow right to the jaw and dislodged him from my coat. He didn't fly off me, but it got his mouth off me, and shifted his weight enough so I could slide my hips sideways, and get a leg under his body. I kicked out and up, and tossed him like a fucking ragdoll about three feet.

I used the wall and scrambled to my feet while the dead guy got back up. I didn't want to waste a bullet so I yanked the sword out, and sunk it into his rotting melon head with an overhead swipe. His head came apart like an eggshell filled with rotting cauliflower. Goddamn horrid. If I couldn't smell him before that, I sure as shit could then. It was horrible. I almost puked but choked it down.

After a few dry heaves I checked the whole building and cleared it. Empty. All the doors were shut too, which mean this guy had been here all along and I missed him when I cleared it months ago, or he had the mental ability to PULL OPEN A DOOR! Fuck me. I've never seen one that smart. Usually when presented with a door that doesn't push open, they just press against it until something gets their attention elsewhere.

This changes things. I'm really hoping that it was

scenario A, and I'm just an idiot that made a mistake. Because if it's scenario B, then I need to really rethink where dangerous places are. I haven't locked any of the campus buildings that have doors that pull out, or have knobs, or latches. They haven't figured any of that out any time I've been observing them.

Fucking-A man.

Tomorrow, I am going to every building here on campus, and locking the doors. That really irks the shit out of me too. I don't want to have to fumble with keys if I'm in a situation. I've seen it so many times it's a goddamn cliché. Right up there with cars not starting when the killer is chasing you, and that the pretty girl ALWAYS falls when being chased. Fumbling with keys. Awesome. Can't wait for that to happen. Mark my words Mr. Journal, it WILL happen. I know my luck.

Okay Mr. Journal, moral of this story is attention to detail, and vigilance. Until all the buildings are fully locked, I clear every single one of them as if I was expecting a zombie to be inside. Further, any time I am moving anywhere outside of Hall E, I will increase my vigilance, and stop humming.

Furthermore, every room must pass the sniff test.

In other good news, the zombie had $350 in his wallet. That'll come in handy.

Sigh.

-Adrian

November 6ᵗʰ

The campus has been locked down. Took me all of yesterday to check every unlocked building fully, but it's done. I didn't find anything in any of those buildings, which doesn't prove or disprove anything. I hate this not knowing bullshit. I wish the radio would spark up and say something one of these days. It's been silent for a very long time. I only turn it on at night for an hour or two just in case now.

I honestly don't think I'm ever going to get any answers to the big questions. All I can hope to do is get enough info from my own observations around here to form enough of an intelligent opinion to make good choices. The consequences for making a single bad choice could be staggering, that's obvious enough, but there's fuck all I can do about it.

That's not entirely true. I could try and find more people. Hooking up with more folks who have survived this long might be a good thing. After all, they have to be reasonably able and intelligent to have made it, and that's got to be a good thing. Plus they might have information that will improve my situation. It's not like I don't have a ton of space up here. I could easily house 150 people here without giving up one inch of my own space. Feeding them would be a problem though.

Shrug. Food for thought.

Yesterday and today thus far have been pretty mundane since the scare of a lifetime in the kitchen. The clearing of the buildings turned out to be a pointless pain in the ass, as opposed to a dangerous string of encounters. I'll grant you it felt dangerous as hell, and reminded me of kicking in doors in Iraq, but it turned out to be nothing. Thank God for the little things I guess.

I figured I'd use this entry to reminisce over the day that I started to clear this joint out. June 24th was the date as I recall. A rough day in my history book. Mr. Journal I think the last thing I talked about was how I hacked my way inside the admissions building via the roof, and finally got some food. I scarfed down a couple sandwiches and a bottle or three of water out of the little staff fridge.

I found a good office that had a single window, and a strong door, and the plan was to make a shitload of noise at the entrance to the building, somehow get them to come in to said building, scramble to the office, and theoretically trap the majority of the zombie horde surrounding the building inside the above mentioned building. All of this while simultaneously avoiding being devoured by my former students, co-workers, and random family members. Genius right? I'm sure you can predict how foolproof the plan turned out to be.

So over the night I became positive that these things went to noise like moths to flame. Every time I stayed silent, they started to drift off, anytime there was a noise, they moved towards it. I knew I needed a noisemaker. In Amy's little office I knew she had one of those little radio/CD players on a file cabinet. I grabbed it, moved it to the office I planned on falling back to, plugged it in, and cranked it to 10.

Noisemaker established and ready to make noise, I went to the lobby area and started banging on the windows and hollering. It reminded me so much of that scene in one Romero zombie movie where the guys are yelling in the department store trying to get the zombies to come to the window. I mean freakishly the same. Enough that I actually found myself laughing just like them. I mean it was laughter or tears at this stage. No sense crying at this point.

I ripped the curtains down to increase visibility as well. It seemed to work almost instantly. That side of admissions had remained pretty empty of the dead since MILFy and husband got killed, and within seconds of yanking the curtains, the windows were full of zombies, three deep out into the yard. They pressed against the glass desperately, mouths opening and closing reflexively, filthy hands leaving streaks of brown and red blood and flesh. One of the windows cracked loudly under the pressure and I got the answer to my glass question.

I did have a huge moment of genius right then though. I grabbed the curtains and stuffed them under the back edge of the front door. Enough blockage to trip them up when they opened the door, which might give me enough time to safely get to the office I had set up. I remember psyching myself up real quick before the glass broke again, and I cracked the door open.

The door surged inward maybe 4 or 5 inches immediately, and the curtains hung it up perfectly. I didn't wait to gauge any further success and got the fuck back to the office. I remember hearing the door creak further open as I slammed the office door shut behind me. Within seconds they were pressing against the interior door, and it started to rattle and vibrate in the door jam. I had no idea how long it would hold against them. My heart was throbbing up into my neck I was so jacked on adrenaline. My mouth was bone dry. Man what a rush.

I hit play on the CD player to fully set my trap, and Lady Gaga burst forth. A little bit of me died right then. I'm not saying she sucks or anything, I just think she's a tad bit overplayed. Flavor of the month if you will. That's not a pun regarding her likely fate as zombie food somewhere out there either.

You know actually I take that back, I really do think she sucks. Sorry to offend you Mr. Journal, but I have got stick to my guns on this.

So I pushed the desk over against the door as best I could, but the closest I could get it was about 3 or 4 inches. There was a bookcase and a fire extinguisher on the walls that prevented me from getting it flush. Hopefully if the door gave in the desk would trip them up. I yelled at the top of my lungs along with Lady Gaga for the better part of a song before I started to get a bad feeling for the door's integrity, and my nerves. I peeked out the small window, saw it was clear behind the building, and slid it open quietly.

I'll tell you this: hearing that door rattle so violently with all those zombies just on the other side was creepy as old man balls. Mind you, they make no noise (the zombies, I can't vouch for old man balls), so it was just the violent shaking of the door in the frame with a slowly building rotten stench behind it. There was no audible malice on the other side. Just this… sinister, silent hunger. Freaky shit.

Plan was this at that point: escape via window, slip around in a wide circle to my car (if it was clear enough) get my .22 and some 9mm ammo, and then find a decent place to start killing zombies. I know, shitty plan right? This is really all improv Mr. Journal.

The windows we have were all replaced a few years back with brand new energy efficient ones so it slid up smoothly and silently. I poked my head out quickly to double check it was clear, and then basically dove out. I came up jogging. I remember realizing that it was much warmer now and much brighter too as the sun was coming up. Late June can be hot as hell here, and it was definitely going to turn hot later. You can always tell when it is really warm that early.

I started jogging as quietly as I could around the building and behind the maintenance building thirty feet or so away. I could see a few zombies still surging mindlessly towards the door, so I knew my plan was working at least somewhat. I slid around the back of that maintenance building and came around it with my head real low to the ground so I could get a clear look at the front of admissions. I think there were maybe 8 zombies still outside the building, and with the dawn light coming in from behind me I could see the lobby area was packed to the gills. Wall to wall dead people.

For a second I entertained the idea of just setting the building on fire to kill them, but the more I thought about it, the more I realized that the one thing that scared me more than a zombie coming after me, was a zombie that was set on fire coming after me. I shit canned that idea promptly. So from where I was on the corner of the maintenance building it was clear in all directions for at least 30 yards. I couldn't see anything in any direction actually, aside from the handful of zombies at the admissions door. Smooth sailing to my car. Now remember here. I had lost my keys earlier that night. So no car keys. I would have to break a window and deal with the fallout fast. I couldn't remember where I had left the rifle in the car either. Figure that out when I got there right?

Low, loping run with the sword drawn. I crossed the distance pretty quickly, and didn't draw attention. I checked the car through the driver's window, and stayed low so a few other cars obscured me from the house and the zombies in front of it. I took the sword and using the handle, cracked my car's driver side window. I stopped cold and waited, watching the zombies to see if they heard it, but apparently Lady Gaga fucking fascinates them. I really should do some kind of testing to see if they are attracted to different music. Might pass the time.

I popped the door lock and swung the car door open. Immediately Otis started meowing and purring desperately from the back seat. I got the chunk of turkey out of my pocket and tossed it into his carryall and grabbed the rifle, which was on the seat. I checked to make sure it was loaded, grabbed the spare clip for it, and snagged a box of 9mm and a box of .22 cal. I did another check around me, saw it was clear, and reloaded the spare clip for the Sig. Otis needed a safer place for the moment, so I hit the trunk release, picked his thing up and set him down in the back amongst all the stuff I'd grabbed earlier. Right on top of the crap in the trunk I saw the grocery bag that had the energy bars I got at the store the day prior and snagged a few of those as well. I clicked the trunk closed as quietly as I could.

Armed and dangerous right? When you learn how to kill people in the military one of the most important things is a good view of your battlefield. High vantage points give you a clearer view of targets, shows you avenues of approach, and gives you more time to make your shots. I knew with the .22 I had range across most of campus, but I needed a good spot to set up that was safe to shoot from, had a good view of what I was shooting at, and yet was still easy to escape from.

The tallest building on campus was the school house. Three floors. I immediately thought of Dr. Potter's classroom across from Mrs. Goodell's on the third floor. It was empty yesterday, was probably still empty, and had the fire escape should the room get assaulted and I was overwhelmed. Hopefully the way up to the classroom was more or less clear.

I was off. Otis was safe in the trunk, I had the rifle, my pistol, the spare clips for each, and hopefully enough ammo to last. That's such a vague term right? Long enough to last for?.... The day? Enough to last until they were all dead? I dunno. I scampered across the campus towards the school house staying as low as I could, and made my way through the same glass doors I had the night earlier.

I shouldered the .22 and cleared the first floor again. I should point this out now so folks can visualize it better. The rifle I got off of Phil was a very fine weapon. It's a Mossberg rifle called the Tactical .22 It looks an awful lot like the M4 rifle that's standard issue to US troops. The clip is a lot smaller, just 10 rounds, but you get the idea. I felt good using it, it felt familiar.

The second floor was squeaky clean as well. There were a lot of blood smears on the stairs, and in the foot path where people would go up and down the stairs, but it was clear. I didn't run into anything until I started up the stairs to the third floor. I saw Dale first, and didn't hesitate. He was covered in blood, and his entire face was smeared red from gorging on someone. He was about six steps above me in the stairwell, and I leveled the iron sights on his forehead, and popped him once. The crack of the .22 was damn near deafening in the stairwell. The bullet hit him low, going in under the jaw. His head whipped back, then he tilted face first and tumbled full force down the steps. His head split open on the steps and I had to juke sideways to dodge his body.

Time was a factor now. I was making noise that could be heard over the music. I ascended the stairs as fast as I could while keeping the rifle aimed steadily at head level. As if on cue, students started rounded the corner at the top of the steps, coming right at me. I stayed calm, remembered my training. Fire, evaluate. Fire, evaluate.

I am a good shot.

I waded through the handful of zombie corpses and moved down the hallway towards Mrs. Goodell's room again. Hall was clear, but I found one more zombie in her room. It was the girl who had been tied up with Dale the day before. She was clearly dead, but I still recognized her as Dale's girlfriend. One of the new underclassman this year. Pretty, impressionable. She was struggling meekly against the bonds the teacher and kids had put her in. I can remember exactly the blank stare her whitish eyes gave me when we locked gazes. There was nothing there. Dead eyes. The moment someone dies and their life fades away, you can actually watch the life go. There's no way to describe it really. A lot of veterans know what I'm talking about here. Not a fun look at all, and she had it.

I drew the sword and finished her. Couldn't afford to waste any more of the .22 ammo. When I turned around I saw my shotgun on the floor under a desk, and my keys right next to it. I snagged them both and slipped into the hall. It was still clear so I let myself into Dr. Potter's room, and shut the door behind me.

It was time to clean house.

Talk to you soon Mr. Journal.

-Adrian

November 8th

Hello and good day Mr. Journal. Today is a reasonably good day. I find myself feeling a little chilly, but my spirits are pretty good all things considered. I have decided to make another supplies run down to the gas station. My fuel stores are doing well but I've consumed enough to warrant another trip. I also found a giant heavy duty plastic barrel which is rated to hold gasoline during one of my patrols of campus. It was stuck behind one of the athletics sheds down near the football field.

Ironically, this school did not have a football team. We didn't have enough students to field a team. We did have a pretty good basketball and soccer team though. Our girl's athletics was excellent as well. It was one of the reasons why we drew so many female students here. Great prep school for college sports.

So anyway I got the barrel back to the center of campus and I've got it cleaned out. The maintenance area had one of the rotary style oil pumps that fit on top of it so when I fill it, I can crank out as much fuel as needed. Sad thing is that once filled, I will not be able to move the damn thing. I'll have to fill it one batch of gas cans at a time. I think I will siphon off all the fuel in the cars around campus into it first. It's a 55 gallon barrel, and I figure I can completely fill it with just the fuel tanks in the cars.

Now I once had a mechanic tell me gas taken out of a car's fuel tank was dirty and unusable. I don't know enough about fuel or cars to know if that's true or not, but I'm going to filter the fuel before I put it in the big barrel. Fyi the barrel is blue, so I've taken to calling it "my boy Blue." Heh. I'll start the siphoning and filtration tomorrow, and once I have a better idea of when I need to hit the gas station I'll get a plan together. I also need to look into getting that wood stove asap to more adequately solve the heating issue.

So much to do. I guess that's another reason to try and gather some other people up here. They could be doing some of this shit too. The case continues to build for looking out to find others. No decisions yet though. I've got it pretty good and I want to make damn sure I don't fuck myself over.

Otis is well. I think he's enjoying this thoroughly. He gets to crawl up into my ass to stay warm at night, there is a steady procession of mice to for him to play with while I'm busy, and he gets my undivided attention. He'd always get jealous when Cassie and I were affectionate. Man I miss her. I dream about her a lot. I can't remember most of the specifics in the dreams, I just remember she was in them, and that they were good dreams. Sigh. More guilt. Time may heal all wounds, but this guilt may kill me first. It's a slow bleed.

But today is not a day to vent. I have my emotions under control for a change, and I'm feeling like recanting some history. I need to speed this up too, as the longer and longer I wait to document everything that's happened to me, the harder it is for me to remember what the hell has happened. On good nights when I write in here it all comes back in a flood. On the senility nights I sit here wondering what the hell I did in certain situations. I backtrack and change things when I get them out of order all the time. Good thing I have nothing but time to edit my own stories right? Forgive me Mr. Journal, I am far from perfect.

Day after "that day." According to where I left off in the last journal entry I had just reached the top floor of the main school building, and had shut myself into Dr. Potter's classroom. It smelled funny in there, that much I recall pretty easily. There was a musty odor of sweat and old books that was just kind of gross. Dr. Potter was our English department head, as well as the instructor for Mythology, Greek history, and all that jazz. He had a ton of old books on shelves in there. All the classics.

The room was still clear, as was his staff closet in the corner. That turned out to be a goldmine as well. Dr. Potter was.... a fairly round person, and that's being generous. He had a thing for snacking and his closet was full of cups of soup, fruit bars, granola bars, and bottled water. If anything, I was thankful for that.

Dr. Potter's desk was a heavy oak number, and I pushed it against the door the longer way so the length of the desk stuck out into the room. More effort required to move it inwards that way should the door get collapsed in. I needed a good sniping position. That classroom is a corner room, and it had a great view of the portion of campus that admissions was. Out one side it could clearly see Hall A as well as one of the school office houses. The windows on the other side of the room had visibility to the lake, and could see two maintenance buildings. The small brick industrial buildings where I got the ladder the prior night from in fact.

I pushed the desks out of the way and left one desk, and one chair cornered and set back about 5 feet from the window. One of the cardinal laws of sniping is you never let the barrel show. Always recess yourself into your hide so there is no glare, and no muzzle flash visible. Zombies didn't strike me as being able to look for either of those intelligently, but setting myself back put me mostly out of sight, which was useful. I pulled another desk over and set up my ammo, and spare clips so I could quickly reload, which I also did right then. I had 10 shots, then a clip change, then 10 shots, then reload both. I wouldn't touch the Sig until I was desperate.

Right then was when I realized that I was missing something. Phil (my man at Moore's Sporting Goods that hooked me up with my guns and ammo) had sold me TWO spare clips for both of these guns. I currently only had one spare clip. I remember laughing at myself because sitting in a plastic bag somewhere in my car were the two extra clips that I flat out forgot to load in my hurries earlier that day and the day before. Sad... just sad. Oh well, at least I had one spare clip.

So I set myself up in the chair, leaning over the first desk as a stand, wished I had bought a scope for the .22, and started shooting zombies. Sniping is both an intensely personal act, and at the same time, one of complete remoteness. I am not near my targets, but because I aim so intently to kill, and I observe the target prior to, and after the shot, it is very intense. This wasn't. I think my emotions had just switched off by that point that day. I was exhausted, tired, and frankly sort of thrilled to have the upper hand finally. I put the front sights on the head of the first zombie, lined up the rear sights, exhaled slowly, and gently squeezed the trigger. I did this slowly and methodically for some time. Within a few minutes I had shot all of the zombies outside admissions easily. It was only perhaps 75 yards, which isn't a tough shot in calm winds. Only a few misses, and only a few penetration failures.

While I was reloading, I saw perhaps another dozen zombies moving about in the general campus area by looking out other windows. I remember seeing quite a few zombies banging on the back door of the staff office house, which raised my suspicion that there were still people alive in there. I didn't see anyone in there over the night, but that didn't mean anything. I resolved to check that building first.

Once I had killed every visible zombie outside on the campus, I was in a bit of a pickle. Inside admissions there was a solid 20 to 30 zombies if not more still trying desperately to get into the office where the Lady Gaga CD was blaring. I could still hear it faintly all the way in the classroom. I couldn't get them to leave, and I sure as shit wasn't going to go down there and start shooting them up close.

I had plenty of daylight to work with, was solidly holed up, had food and water, and when I checked the hall, there were no zombies coming at the door. My immediate hope was that when the CD ended, the zombies would shuffle back outside, giving me more clear shots. It had been about 45 minutes anyway, so I would know shortly. I gobbled down a granola bar and just a few minutes later heard Gaga go silent. I waited in the shooter's pose, leaning over the desk for several minutes more before they started coming out the door. I got so excited I missed my first few shots down at them.

So the pros of the situation I already listed. The cons were a short list, but they were motherfuckers. Now that Gaga was done doing her thing, they could clearly hear me. Even if they couldn't see me they were coming towards me. I

147

remember hoping the glass doors downstairs would hold up if I couldn't shoot them all in time.

As I said before though, I am good shot. And, despite being moving targets, they are not elusive targets. In sniping talk you are never "outnumbered." Instead we used to call that a "target-rich environment." I calmed myself down, and started aiming and shooting like a professional.

I had to stop though when I saw the woman from the night prior. MILFy. She looked really ragged in the daylight. I'm not talking beer-goggles here, I mean the nerdy zombie that killed her the night before had done some work on her. Her face was all bitten up, her nose mostly gone, and some of her hair had been ripped out, leaving huge swathes of bloody scalp showing. I think she'd been bitten a bunch on her arms and legs too, as she was just covered in blood. I think I apologized to her, and then I put one through the hole in her nose. She crumpled down to the ground, and I moved on to the zombie behind her.

I shot the nerdy kid shortly after I shot her, and I shot her husband not long after that. He was much worse off than she was. He was tripping himself up on his own guts. Apparently they'd been ripped out of him during his failed death struggle with his bat. Sad really. The last one I killed from my sniping position was Amy. I always liked her too. She was just pretty enough that you could imagine falling in love with her. She had a great personality too. Warm, kind, funny.

I killed her just like the others. From a distance it wasn't quite real yet though, but it was real as hell when I started cleaning later.

So for the moment, once I had killed the slow bleed of zombies trickling out of the admissions building, there was no movement anywhere. I hung out for 20 more minutes, and actually fell asleep for a bit. Technically it was more of a "blacked out from exhaustion." I think I was out for 2 hours, but I'm not sure. I wound up waking up when I heard one of the cars parked in front of admissions take off like a bat out of hell. Some luxury import moving like a bullet. Lol. They clipped the side of a huge SUV and blew out the tire on it before speeding away. I think there were 3 or 4 people in the car when it left. Don't know for sure.

I was pretty refreshed from getting some actual sleep. Felt like a million bucks. I checked the campus, which was all clear, checked the hallway, also clear, and made my decision to head over to the staff office house to see why all those zombies were banging on the door earlier.

Only a few more neat tales to tell about the clearing out of the campus Mr. Journal. Exciting eh? After that I think I have a few other good stories to tell about my time after that, but still before the first journal entry. Stuff like how I got more food from the grocery store. What a fricking nightmare. Plus how I got my .30-06 when I returned to Moore's. I'm just about ready to tell that story.

Moral of today's story Mr. Journal: Never underestimate the staggering drawing power of Lady Gaga on zombies.

Until we meet again Senior Journal.

-Adrian

November 10th

I am very tired today quite literally from sucking hose. Siphoning gas is a horrible process that tastes terrible, is surprisingly exhausting, and has left me with little to no interest in writing tonight. However, I feel guilty for not writing anything at all, so I wrote this. Thus Mr. Journal, I give you:

10 things I miss the most right now
(in no particular order)

1.) I miss meat. Like, a legitimately well grilled steak, or a

149

pork chop. I haven't had fresh meat since… I don't know when. And you know what? I miss bread too. I need to figure out how to bake bread.

2.) I miss sports. I used to love watching basketball, football, and baseball on tv. I miss that a lot. I miss competition! Being alone fucking sucks.

3.) I miss my bed. We had a great frigging bed at home. I have half a mind to go get the damn thing and get it up here. The student bed I'm using is new, but it's shitty for my back.

4.) I miss my friends. A lot. I miss joking around, and getting picked on, and picking on them.. man. I hope they're all okay.

5.) I miss Cassie. Oddly enough though, I do not miss sex. I'm so tired all the time I wouldn't even have the energy to get my dick wet even if I wanted to.

6.) I miss internet pornography. (reasons withheld to preserve the illusion that I am a decent human being)

7.) I miss Chinese food. General's chicken, lo mein, spring rolls, crab rangoons. Jesus I would straight up fist a horde of zombies for some decent Chinese takeout.

8.) I miss shopping. I really miss going out for the day on a weekend with Cassie and just going to the stores we liked to see if a new movie was out, or a new CD, or if we needed a new shirt, or a comic book or something. I miss getting out.

9.) I miss being able to wear shorts and pants without a belt. I don't go anywhere anymore without a sword, and my Sig on a belt. I miss sweatpants and gym shorts. I know that may sound stupid, but at any moment in time, I need to be able to get up, and get the fuck out. Dress appropriately.

10.) I miss the kids here at the school. They were always a source of endless entertainment. So young and naïve, but still open to the world. As we get older we seem to forget about all the wonder the world holds.

Well.... What wonder the world used to have.

-Adrian

November 11th

Good morning. Mr. Journal, it is Veteran's Day today. I noticed it just a few minutes ago when I looked at the calendar after I got out of the shower. I think from now on I'm going to be hyper aware of holidays because of their previous significance.

You know, I'm also making a pretty big assumption that you're an American Mr. Journal. I mean, it's completely possible that you're from somewhere else. Shit, you might even be an alien. Martian or Venusian. Or from one of the moons of Jupiter. How cool would that be? You could also be an illegal alien, which doesn't really bother me anymore. There aren't a lot of job opportunities out there to be stolen, so no skin off my back.

I digress. I wanted to put a short entry in this morning to reflect on the idea that these holidays are "still happening." I mean, if we have a holiday, and there's no one celebrating it, does the holiday mean anything? Wrap your head around the meaning behind that.

Thinking about the fact that it's Veteran's Day here in America got me thinking even more about the situation the world is in. Here in America, and in most of the "western" world, and by "western" I guess I mean any country with healthcare, infrastructure, safety etc. We are much better suited to dealing with the aftermath of this, then say a place like Somalia, or Nigeria, or the Congo, or Iraq. Imagine how fucked they are now? I mean shit was bad when I was in Iraq, and there were no goddamn zombies then. It's probably better now though, now that I think about it. Less IED's and VBIED's. Zombies are an entirely different breed of insurgent.

Holy train of thought Batman! Thinking about Iraq got me back on the thought of it being Veteran's Day. Can you imagine how fucked up it would be to be a current member of the military when all this went down? I mean a deployed member of the military? Fuck, we have tens of thousands of troops in Afghanistan and Iraq fighting. That's not even taking into account all the servicemen and women who are stationed in all our overseas bases.

Germany, Japan, Italy, Turkey, Guam, Uzbekistan, Cuba, England, Kuwait, Saudi Arabia, Qatar, the list goes on and on. I don't know if that's evidence of imperialism or whatever, but my point here today is that all the people who volunteered to serve their nation are now stuck wherever it is they were last deployed to.

They're cut off from their families, at risk of death, lonely all the time, frequently stressed out, armed 24/7, and in constant danger. You know Mr. Journal, that's exactly how it was before this all started. That's the life of a person who volunteers to serve.

I enlisted when I was a kid because my dad served, and my grandfather served. It made me feel like I could finally measure up to my dad if I could do what he did. I'm glad I served. It was hellish at times, thought I was going to die a few times, but in the end it's something I can be proud of. I can vote and know that I am invested in my country, and no one can take away the fact that I sacrificed my personal time, my professional time, and put my life on the line to give my fellow citizens a chance at a better life.

Serving in the military is an underappreciated sacrifice

Mr. Journal. People don't understand how much it tears families apart, and how much loneliness and separation it puts on the table. You lose years of your life to the military and to politics, not to mention the sad rate of pay many of them deal with.

I'm ranting now. I guess I am single handedly attempting to celebrate Veteran's Day all by myself. So let me try and end this on a more positive note:

Celebrate those people who give their time, energy, and possibly their lives to sustain your freedoms and safety. Regardless of the political motivations of whatever administration is in charge of your country at any given time, we need to make sure the people who are ready to protect us at all times are rewarded with our gratitude. Sometimes the only way to ensure peace is to be ready to inflict harm on those who would take it from you.

One of the best quotes I've ever read goes something like this;

"We sleep safely at night because rough men stand ready to visit violence on those who would harm us."

Fellow Veterans, American and otherwise, friend and foe, living and dead, I salute you.

Busy day today, lots to do.

-Adrian

November 12th

Greetings and such. It's been a hellishly exhausting string of days here Mr. Journal. Getting sick of doing everything alone. The campus itself doesn't require a ton of maintenance, but the day to day things that I have to do for

153

myself takes up a ridiculous amount of time. I still do two patrols a day which take half an hour or more each, plus prepping three meals a day for myself, as well as moving all the fuel around for the gas generator downstairs.

Every time I fire my weapons they get cleaned, and even if I don't fire them, I clean them once a week anyway. I do my own laundry every couple of days here. Luckily the school had artesian wells that run on electric pumps that work as long as my generator is going. So as long as I have the generator going, I have running water, and if I wait until morning when I'm about to turn off the generator, the hot water tank has heated up, and I get a hot shower. I am so profoundly thankful for regular hot showers.

That's not all the work either Mr. Journal. I clean obsessively almost every day. I can't risk vermin or the sickness they bring, and even though Otis is the fucking MAN when it comes to killing mice, I'm scared they might bring something in that'll give me dysentery or something like that. I have no doctors to go to, and very little medicine to take, so maintaining my health is a big deal.

I also force myself to read a lot. There's just so much I don't know how to do still. If my car breaks down... it's broken. I have zero fucking mechanical skills. I am learning more about growing my own food, but when I do start growing it, I'll have to tend it, harvest it, and more than likely, I'll have to figure out how to can it too.

The real frigging irony is I just described the life of a house wife during the great western expansion of the 1800's. Too funny. I am a frontier mom now. Oh how the mighty have fallen.

Enough bitching. I'm sure you're sick of hearing me go on and on about how tough my life is anyway. So the last I left it with you I was planning another trip down to the gas station down the street where I went before. I think that was on the 8th or so. I spent the 9th and 10th running around campus with my 2 gallon gas cans siphoning fuel from the cars I know I'll never use. For example, sub compacts. Their fuel efficiency doesn't mean shit really because they can't hold much for gear or salvage or stuff like that, and I can't run over anything in them. I'll share my story about running over zombies some other day. I assure you it's amusing, and will turn you away from sub compacts in the post-apocalypse market. I highly suggest upgrading to something with decent ground clearance.

So to make sure I wasn't siphoning any crap out from the car gas tanks, I filtered the gas through some rags into my boy Blue. (that's the big ass blue barrel I found) Gotta be careful with fumes though, as I really don't want to set myself on fire. Not only are there no doctors around, but no one has picked up 911 in forever. So I've been extra cautious.

So after emptying enough cars to fill Blue to about three quarters full I decided that was enough, and I drained out the Tundra I stole (read: salvaged) from that cape on my last trip. It was solid, basically brand new, and had a huge tank I could fill again. (Not to mention some serious ground clearance) I managed to siphon it down to about one eighth of a tank, which meant I'd get something like 26 gallons or so. I also emptied the 5 gas cans I have, so I can theoretically get 25 gallons or so in the truck, plus 13 gallons in the cans. Quite a bit. I'm thinking that'll fill blue right up to the top. I wish I'd found another blue barrel so I could stockpile more up here, but that's probably reaching considering I still have hot water. Don't want to be too greedy right?

So by the end of the day on the 10th my siphoning was done. After I made the early morning entry on the 11th, I couldn't figure out a reason why I should put it off, and gathered my crap to go down. I figured the same shit I brought with me before would be good, so I grabbed the gauge, the sword, and the Sig as usual. This time I was a little more intelligent and grabbed my first aid kit too. See? I can learn!

The weather has been kind of fucked up. Feels like

155

winter is coming a little early. We had a straight up wintry typhoon blow through here the other day. Sleet, snow, freezing rain, you name it and it fell from the sky. Dropped down to 20F the last few nights too, which has formed up some pretty good ice on the smooth surfaces that the sun doesn't hit during the day. It's made my morning patrols a little treacherous. Almost ate shit several times on the sidewalk.

Anyway before I left I bundled myself up a little heavier than I did the time prior. One thing I forgot to grab in my rush on "that day" was a heavier jacket for cold weather. Heaviest thing I brought from home that day was a hoodie. Not exactly survival gear. Lucky for me, Dr. Potter's winter jacket was in his staff closet, and once I gave it a good wash it was close enough in size to fit me. I'm not anywhere near as fat as he was, but I am a pretty big guy. Shoulders wise it has always been a bitch to find shirts that aren't stretched on me funny. My sleeves are always too short. I was fortunate Dr. Potter had the coat in his closet. Sucked that it was covered in goop from the shootout in the classroom, but beggars can't be choosers.

I bundled up, grabbed my shit, and headed down the road. There was way more trees down in the road this time. So many down in fact I had to turn back and get the little chainsaw from the grounds keeping shed. As much as I absolutely loathe making noise, it was needed to get through. I had to stop three times to cut trees out of the way in just the few miles from school to the station. I didn't see any activity anywhere during my stops, and I didn't pass any zombies that I saw on the drive either.

So I crept up to the stop sign just like last time, and scoped the joint out. I could see from where I was the body of the young dad near the gas pumps as well as the feet of the dead mechanic I saw before. I waited a solid minute or two before I decided it was safe, and pulled the truck up to the pumps again. This time I pulled the truck in the right way so I didn't have to park it twice.

Same place, same methods. I cleared the garage first, made sure it was empty, and then cleared the store again. Once again, all clear. I did a quick visual inspection and saw pretty much all the stuff that I left there was still there. There were some missing items, like the baby food jars, but I knew the guy had taken some stuff that day. Then I pumped my gas. Truck first, then the small cans. I paid extra special attention to the road this time in the event a car came, but none did. I also was a clever bastard and took the manual crank off the pump. No one would be able to access the gas without it. Heh.

So after that I slipped back into the store and gathered up everything else that I could. Most of it was total shit. However, on the outside chance I needed car fresheners, I figured it was better to be safe than sorry. The biggest haul I got out of there was beer. I didn't grab any on my first trip, so I grabbed ALL of it this time. I like beer. I just need to make sure I don't get sad some night and drink it all and streak through campus butt nekkid and get eaten alive. Moderation, right? Oh! I also grabbed motor oil, WD40 and some things of dry gas.

I did however decide to check the back room where I found the locked door last time. I had assumed that it led upstairs to an office or apartment, and I wasn't interested in checking it out last time so I left it be. Now was as good a time as any to check it out.

Turns out it was locked, and locked pretty damn good at that. Solid deadbolt on a solid door. Luckily I brought the 12 gauge master key. I leveled the Mossberg at the spot where the deadbolt would've met the frame and squeezed a round off. Ka boom! Loud as hell inside that closet. My ears were ringing so bad I thought I'd shot a church bell not a door. The deadbolt did give way to the shotgun round though, which was to be expected. However, I nearly shit myself when the door swung open and a fucking zombie fell down the stairs on the other side and on top of me.

Fortunately the shotgun blast must've gotten him a little

bit through the door, because once the door opened, he went down in a pile and only fell on me by happenstance. He smelled horrible. It was an old man, and even in my struggle to crawl and kick him off I instantly recognized him as the guy who owned the station. His momentum falling on top of me sent his rotting body sidewise so we were lying in sort of a t shape with him across my legs. I kicked him so that he was off me and I pinned his neck to the metal racking in the closet with my foot. I put the shotgun right to his face as he wordlessly tried to chew at my shoe. I looked away and pulled the trigger. His head was vaporized by the blast but his body twitched for a few seconds more.

Once I caught my breath I totally made a resolution: all locked doors that were going to be opened in this manner would have an additional step added to the process. One shotgun round through the door, at chest level. It'd blast any zombies back, plus make a hole for me to see what was going on inside. Reconnaissance by buckshot.

I peeled myself off the floor, opened the door with the barrel of the shotgun, and headed up the stairs to the apartment slowly. Remember the sniff test thing? Place smelled terrible. I knew something bad had happened long before I got to the top of the stairs. I actually had to leave the stairwell and go back down into the store to get a rag to tie around my face, the smell was so bad. I headed up after that and it was still just bearable.

The stairwell opened into a single big room at the top. To one side of the stairs was a small kitchen, and opposite that was a little living room. There were three doors all shut going off those two rooms. In the living room I could clearly see a desiccated woman's body on the couch. Most of the head was missing, only a few clumps of grey hair left, so I felt comfortable with it being dead. Must've been his wife. You could clearly tell too that the stench was coming from that direction.

The door off the kitchen was slightly ajar when I got to it, and I pushed it open with the shotgun and revealed the bathroom. Several pill bottles were on the sink counter and I saw that one of them was a sleeping pill bottle. It was empty. Bathroom was clear of danger.

The two other doors were shut but not locked. I listened intently before opening them and they were silent. I couldn't smell anything over the stench the rotting wife was giving off so I had to rely on just that sense. I also knocked a few times. I figured if there were undead inside they'd make noise or respond to the knocking somehow. I got nothing either time, so I just opened the doors quietly.

Both rooms were bedrooms, one the master, the other looked like a guest room. I checked the closets as well but they were filled with closet-y kinds of things. All clear for danger.

I snagged a suitcase from the master bedroom closet and started filling it with everything I could find that was useful. Most of it was just more of the same. There was a fair amount of canned goods, which was awesome, and they had two large tins of dry iced tea mix, which would help with the variety on drinking just water. I snagged all their pill bottles, all their cleaning supplies and soapy hygiene-y kinds of things, and I took the man's clothing. He was close to my height so I figured something might fit. Unfortunately his shoes were too small for me. I take a 13, and all he had was an 11. It hadn't occurred to me until right then that I eventually would need new shoes. Where the fuck am I going to go to get those? There's no shoe store here in town. Or major retailer really. Do I go house to house looking for a dude with size 13's in his closet? I never get a fucking break.

OH! The total major score for the apartment was a pistol on the living room floor. It was a Colt M1911 which is one of the finer classic handguns. This one looked old, like from the war old. It shoots the .45 caliber round, which is a serious man stopper, but it only holds 7 bullets in the clip. Sort of a risk/reward situation with it. It'll knockdown whatever I hit with it, but it needs frequent reloads. Either way I was happy to have a spare pistol finally plus the old man left his box of bullets on the end table next to the lounger. There were 6 rounds in the clip when I checked it, and 13 rounds left in the box. I know, not much, but theoretically that's 19 dead zombies.

I got the fuck out after that. Took my suitcase filled with loot, headed to the Tundra, and left to come back here. One thing that did strike me just as I was about to leave though were the houses all around the gas station. The last time I came down I could see movement in all the houses. There was still movement, and I was totally sure especially now that the movement was just dead people walking around inside. All of those houses potentially had more supplies I could use. I made a plan to come back down and scour them for goodies soon.

Drive back was fine too. Well, sort of. When I turned onto the road the school is on there was a zombie hanging out at the stop sign. Pretty much just… chilling out there. I slowed down when I saw him and watched. He hung on to the road sign for about 30 seconds and did this drunken spin in my direction. He either saw me in the truck, or heard the motor running because as soon as he turned, he let go of the sign post and started in my direction.

He was in near perfect shape. I couldn't see a wound anywhere, and his clothing was basically spotless. It was a younger guy, about my age, maybe a little younger. Receding hairline, pasty white with a shade of bluish grey. He made pretty good time coming down the street towards me, but I had enough time to put the truck in park and get out.

I shot him in the head at 20 feet with the .45. The impact sprawled him flat out on his back as well as punched an exit wound in him the size of a coffee can. I may only have 18 bullets left for that gun, but that is gonna be 18 moments of satisfaction. Guaranteed.

Drive back after that was fine. I stopped at the maintenance truck that died on me last time and poured one of the bottles of dry gas I just got in the tank. I figured it couldn't hurt and it's not like I paid for it anyway. That reminded of the cape again where I got the truck though. Right then I resolved to make a return trip there too someday soon. I remember seeing useful stuff in the garage. I don't remember now what I saw then, but I remember thinking I should come and get it later.

Rest of the day was more of the same really. I got all the shit inside when I got back first off. I emptied the gas cans into my boy Blue, and returned one of the spare cans to the hiding spot I had it at before. I also siphoned about half the truck's tank into Blue too. That capped it off for the most part. I'm debating making runs until all the car gas tanks are full again. That would mean the fuel is here on site instead of down the road. It was less likely to get stolen from here than taken from down there. Even with the crank gone, I think I'd feel better. But again, that's just a shitload to work to do. I really need more gas cans.

I did my patrol in the afternoon and took an extra hour out of daylight to practice with the bow. I haven't fired it in weeks I think so I knew I wanted to get some target work in. I was pretty rusty with it, but after a few dozen arrows downrange I felt pretty confident again. I also grabbed the fishing pole and tackle kit and went fishing. I should actually re-phrase that. I went and stood by the shore of the lake holding a fishing pole, and a beer for an hour. Well I held the beer for much less than that, but you get the idea. I caught nothing but fresh air, and a can of cheap American lager.

And that leaves us here Mr. Journal. It's almost bedtime for me, and Otis knows it. He's down underneath the kitchen table here rubbing up on my legs like I'm made out of catnip. That's Otis-speak for "go to bed so I can crawl up your ass." He's not subtle when he communicates. Tomorrow I am going to weatherize this place. I found some of the window plastic in a staff office the other day and I know somewhere in the girl's dorm I can find a hair dryer. I'm also going to seal off a few of the rooms I don't use and somehow block the heating vents so I'm not wasting heating oil.

I'm thinking there is some sense in trying to build some kind of refrigerator outside. It'll be cold soon, and if I can find a way to keep the food away from the bears that are out there, and keep it dry, I can make ice finally. Plus I think I'm going to try and bag a deer here soon. I know they're out there, I've seen them. If I do get one I can use the cold weather to freeze the meat, and I can smoke some too. Might satisfy my meat craving! That'd be….. AMAZING.

Until we speak again Mr. Journal, I wish you safe travels!

-Adrian

November 13th

I have had too much too drink today…. I wasn't going to whrite an hournal entry either, but I can't sleep and I just need to get everything off my chesticle.

I don't know why I am doing what I'm doing anymore.

I don't think that's the beer I drabnk talking anymoe either. And yes, my grammar might be bad right now, I'm somewhat drunk still. Go fuck yourself if you can't hack a few messed up words.

I am so lonely. I wake up alone, I am alone at breakfast, I am alone at lunch, I am alone at dinner. I write these journals all alone at this fucking kitchen table, and when I go to bed at night, I am still alone. Why the fuck do I keep doing this every Goddamn day? Why am I fighting so fucking hard to survive day in, and day out? I keep marching along the edge of the cliff like a confused Lemming, unsure of whether or not to jump over with his friends.

Why was I such a piece of shit that day? Why the fuck didn't I get in my car and drive to her work and save her? I just don't get it. I'm brave. I'm courageous. Nothing scares me. Why the fuck didn't I go? I went everywhere else that goddamn day. I even went to a motherfucking garden center. It's inexcusable, and unforgiveable.

Mr. Journal, or whoeverr the fuck is reading this after I die, if they still have music wherever you are, stop reading this and go listen to the song 'nothin on you' by B.o.B. And like, really frigging listen to it. Don't mail it in. Don't take long though. I might not be here when you get back.

Do you understand now? Are you crying as hard as I am yet? Do you understand why I sit here every night and think about that one thing I didn't do? My greatest sin, my greatest failure. You can't understand. You never will. I'll never be able to find the words to describe how empty and little I feel. I miss her so much it's like all the air is gone from my world when I think of her.

I've had that song on repeat on my laptop for like 3 hours now. I've been doubled over here in the kitchen, face in my hands, unable to stop the tears. I am a broken man tonight, and all the King's men can go fuck themselves. I don't think there's any way to put Adrian M. Ring back together.

What the fuck is my purpose here? I am alive, but what for? If I died right fucking now not one soul would miss me, or even know it. If I took that .45 I just got, and kissed the barrel, and squeezed the trigger, every single problem would just vanish, right? They say suicide isn't the solution, and that all it does is hurt the ones you love.

The thing is... the only ones I love are already dead. Or they already think I'm dead, so what fucking difference does it make if I kill myself? I already shot my mother. My dad died years ago. I have no idea where my brothers or sister are, and I abandoned my girlfriend to a fate that's so horrible I can't even think about it without losing my mind. There's no one left for me to hurt.

The only things that are keeping me from painting the ceiling of this kitchen with my fucking brains are my cat, and the fear that if I do kill myself, and there is an afterlife, I'd be fucking myself over. I can't even deal with the thought of leaving poor Otis to fend for himself and there's no fucking way I can kill him before I do myself. And my mother's Catholic upbringing has me convinced that if I do eat a bullet I rot in Hell, and that wouldn't be much better than this at all. Although at least in Hell I might get the feeling I'm finally paying for my sins. I think they call that closure.

So what are my choices really? Sit here for the rest of my so called life, however long that is, all alone, with my cat? I can grow my food, maybe shoot a deer or a turkey here and there, and what? Write to you Mr. Journal in the hopes that when and if they find this laptop someone will give enough of a shit that they'll look at the "my diary" folder? That's not worth living for. Not a life worth living at all.

I'm a fucking scavenger. I am a human vulture, picking at the remains of the tattered corpse of society. I break into people's houses, steal from the dead, and return to my fucking cave here up on the mountain.

My kingdom of ashes.

Lord Adrian Ring, King Shit of Turd Mountain. All hail the King.

Fuck my life. God my head is killing me. Cheap beer always does this to me. I should've left it at the goddamn gas station. I usually try and drink the good shit, the microbrew stuff. I guess it's nothing but shit for the King of Turd Mountain now my friends. Sigh.

What are my choices? REALLY?

Stay here alone? Leave alone? Bring others here? Try to find more people and join them elsewhere? Purge the town, county, state, and nation of the undead? I'm struggling enough with keeping one gas generator powered and one private school campus clear, let alone the whole fucking town. Sigh.

I need to make amends to make my life livable. I need purpose to survive. My own survival is not purpose enough to survive this way. I'll eventually have a night where I'm so sad, so lonely, and so scared of waking up alone again that I

WILL kill myself. I know it. I can feel my sanity slipping away more and more, and my fear of spending eternity in Hell is starting to feel less scary than living my life like this.

I can't rescue Cassie. I just can't. She's either safe, or dead, and either way I can't change those situations. My sin is complete with her. I cannot dwell on what I cannot change. I can only seek to make amends for my greatest mistake, or I can visit justice on myself for it. Justice to me means my death, and like I said, I really don't want to leave Otis alone. He's too stupid and loveable to make it long. He'll rub up against a zombie the first day I'm gone and get eaten. I can already see it.

So that leaves making amends. That means I need to live my life to the best of my ability, and it means I do things in her honor, to celebrate my love for her, and to remind myself of how lucky I was to have her in my life for as long as I did. It also means I need to help others. Helping just myself is far too self serving to give me closure on this.

I need to help other people. That young couple at the gas station the other day would've been a good start too. I did help them though, really. I can't help it if the woman got greedy, and things went down the way they did. That's not on me. I didn't pull that trigger.

Alright Mr. Journal. Today is the day. Tonight is the night. I will sleep off my beer, and tomorrow I will suffer through the hangover that I deserve and know is waiting for me there, and the next day I start planning out how I will survive.

Not just staying alive.

How I plan on SURVIVING.

-Adrian

November 15th

I hope today is a better day. I can say with some certainty that my head no longer feels like it is filled with braying, kicking donkeys. At the very least that's better than yesterday.

I've begun to plan my future. Such as it is. I actually think getting hammered the other day did me some good. I think I've been in denial this whole time, and the alcohol made me come to terms at least somewhat with it. Talking to you Mr. Journal has also helped a lot. Once I got my shit together yesterday I sat down and started to sketch out a plan that allowed me to help people.

But, my plan also needed to maintain my own safety. In the interest of taking my sweet ass time and getting it right, I'm going to wait another day or two to fully lay out the plan here. I can say so far, I'm feeling like a pretty intelligent guy. I just hope I've thought of either everything, or enough to keep safe and actually make things better, as opposed to making things worse. I've done a lot of both it seems recently.

I'm feeling motivated to talk about things though, and if I'm not ready to share my plan just yet, I should continue to recount how everything got to where it is now. I know I was talking at length about how I cleared the campus and made it "safe" so I think I'll finish that story. There's still a fair amount of that to talk about.

Rest assured though Mr. Journal. I'll share my plan in a day or two. Just a few more kinks to work out.

Okay then.... clearing the campus. Lemme look back and see where I left off.

Right. I had just gotten done killing all the zombies from my sniping position in Dr. Potter's classroom. I had seen from the classroom earlier in the day that there were zombies banging on the back entrance to one of the staff office buildings. If you can imagine the campus in your head, you come across the bridge, and almost immediately to your left is the staff building, and across the street from that is admissions. The main classroom area is maybe 70-80 yards down the road from them.

The back entrance I was talking about would be on the far side of the staff building from the admissions side. Make sense? It's the door away from the bridge. There are a few trees and a lawn area in that space, so it's mostly open. I remember pulling Dr. Potter's desk out of the way, and unblocking the door after I packed my stuff up. I slung the . 22 and opted for the shotgun for the moment.

I got down through the main school building with no issues. There were bodies all over the upper hallway from when I'd shot my way in earlier, and they were starting to give off that pungent rotting smell already. I thought it was a little early for that, but I'm not a coroner.

Looking through the glass doors I could see a single zombie that had shuffled into the campus street likely from behind the school building. I sat the shotgun down, poked the barrel through the jam of the glass door after cracking it an inch or two, and popped it in the head once. One reason the .22 is so effective for doing this kinda stuff is the lack of recoil. It's easy to aim, and there's no muzzle lift. If you miss, it's easy to pop off a second shot. Plus the .22 round frequently won't exit the skull. It just rattles around inside like a supersonic pinball. Scrambles the grey matter so to speak.

I felt the .22 was better, so I reloaded, and slung the shotgun. I changed my mind about checking the staff office first, and headed over to admissions to make sure the building was actually devoid of undead. On my way out I checked the zombie I just shot, and realized it was one of my favorite students. Kid named Pete. Tall, kinda goofy, but super witty. He was the awkward kid that you just knew would be fine once they got out of the social clusterfuck that high school was. Sad.

I moved across the campus with the .22 shouldered,

doing the combat walk. All movement is from the knees down. Hips stay flat, shoulders square, weapon steady. Moving like that allows for faster target acquisition. I saw nothing and made it to admissions fine. I had to wade through bodies to get there though. I didn't count, but there had to be 40 or 50. They were everywhere. Students, staff, parents, maintenance people, folks that were totally random and unrecognizable... Just awful.

I checked through the windows and saw movement, so I switched off to the shotgun, and headed inside slowly. Lobby was clear, offices were clear, but at the door that led to the office where the Gaga CD had been blaring, there were still two zombies, slowly, absently banging at the door. One was a student, a little freshman that as I recalled was deep in the throes of puberty just last week, covered in pimples, and the other one was one of the athletics coaches, still wearing his school sweat suit. Probably came from gym class before all this happened.

I sat the shotgun down, drew the sword, and slinked down the hallway as silently as I could. Once I got to within an arm's reach, I stabbed the gym teacher in the back of the head as hard as I could. The sword lodged in something hard and went down with him as he slumped dead to his knees. I had to let the sword go unfortunately, as I didn't want to risk struggling to get it out with the kid zombie right there. The kid spun pretty quickly and started at me, but I took a few quick steps back, drew the Sig, and put two in his head. First shot was enough though. The second just put a furrow in his scalp as he collapsed. Once everything was clear and quiet, I wrenched the sword free from the head of the gym teacher. I cleaned it good on his school shirt, and put it away.

After that I moved the curtain on the floor, shut the admissions door, and decided I'd check the staff building. I had my keys, so getting in wouldn't be a problem. My only worry was what I was going to find inside.

I crept across the road with the .22 up again. I didn't see

anything, so I went to the front entrance that basically faces the admissions building. It was a heavy duty wooden door, oak I think, and it was locked. I unlocked it with my key and cracked it open. Pushed up against the door was a giant pile of furniture. A desk, a bookshelf, a few rolling office chairs…. I think there was a potted plant and maybe a sink as well. Point is there was an enormous pile of shit put there. I laughed out loud and hollered in that it was me.

I propped the door open with the rock that was beside the door for that purpose, and hollered a few more times. Eventually I heard some faint yelling coming from the upstairs offices. I couldn't make shit out, so I hollered I was coming in, and kicked in their makeshift barricade. Eventually I had to climb over the desk, and I shut the door behind me.

I cleared the bottom floor quickly, which was easy, as it was basically two large office style rooms with low cubicles. There was a bathroom as well, but the door was open. When I came back around to the stairs in the main hall, I nearly shot a young girl coming down the steps. She had snuck down and came around the corner just as I did, and I damn near squeezed off a shot right in her face. Holy crap I remember nearly pissing my pants. She went pale frigging white and screamed bloody murder when she saw me point the weapon at her.

Luckily, I checked my trigger finger just in time and just scared the daylights out of her. The girl sat on the steps once she calmed some and we talked for a few minutes. I didn't recognize her at first, as she was all messed up and covered in weirdness. Blood streaks on her face, messed up hair, clothes all screwed up, dirty. She was a mess. I recognized her as Abigail Williams. She was a fairly mousy blonde senior who was pretty damn smart as I recalled. She was wearing a fairly simple outfit that day too. Simple t-shirt from MC-Chris, and some jeans. Sadly, her shirt was all messed up and her bra was showing through. I cried a lot for her. She didn't have much to show. I know, sad Mr. Journal.

At least she was alive.

As I recall Abby was in the campus center when one of the parents coming to get their kid drove in. As she said, they were, "driving out of their fricking minds Mr. Ring," and lost control. That was the car that I saw the day prior that was lodged into the side of the one of the buildings. Apparently things spiraled out of control pretty rapidly after that. The driver died, shortly came back, and started a minor rampage around campus before someone killed him. Abby thought it was death via bat, or perhaps an oar from one of the school canoes nearby.

She guessed that the driver bit maybe two or three people before being killed, and as you can imagine, that started the cycle. Now mind you when I arrived on campus, it was long after that had happened, and I hadn't seen any zombies at that point. Which meant.... Those people bitten were still here somewhere. Abby herself had watched the crash, saw them die, then come back, then bite the people trying to rescue them. A demented biting the hand that feeds you sort of thing. Fucking weird world we live in now. I wonder to myself now how many paramedics and first responders were the first people to get bit. They're bit all the time by crazy people, and I'm sure a lot of them got bit that day, and wound up succumbing because of it. Food for thought.

Fortunately for her she panicked, and ran in there. From what she said, the fresh zombies followed other people on campus away from her, and were likely now inside other buildings. More zombies to kill I guess. When the staff hiding in here with her had enough, they left her alone. She barricaded the door, and locked herself in an office upstairs. She stayed there all night the night prior, and was waiting for whoever was shooting to come help her.

Not bad for a 17 year old kid.

She was hungry, but otherwise, unharmed, and remarkably still sane after all that. She said she actually felt much better when she heard me shooting earlier, which made me feel good. She said she knew people were here helping when the rifle started firing. For the meantime though, I had to figure out what she wanted to do, and get done what I needed to get done.

I still had an energy bar on me, so I tossed it her way, and she ate it like it was a gourmet meal. I still remember the look on her face as she savored every bite. Too funny how hunger can change your standards on food. I think she would've mowed down a cardboard box at that moment if someone gave her some salt to sprinkle on it. Once she was done I laid it out for her. My plan, not my cock you pervert. Mr. Journal the gall you have…

Heh. I told her that I was going to clean out the school campus, one building at a time if I had to. I was going to make it safe to live in, and that she was more than welcome to help, or to sit still and stay here until I was done. She considered it for a few minutes while I pissed and shit finally, but when I came back she declined. She wanted to head back home and find her parents. She said they lived an hour away or so, due west from here. She couldn't live without finding out if they were okay, and I totally understood. I totally disagreed with her though. Young girl leaving all alone with the world the way it was seemed pretty fucking dumb to me, but she was old enough, I didn't want the baggage. Speaking of pissing and shitting, do you find it irritating Mr. Journal when you pee standing, then just as you flush and start to leave, you have to poop? Drives me nuts. I mean seriously.

We chatted for a bit, I told her the basics of what I knew, and we exited via the front door. Just outside 25 feet away there was an undead student milling about. It probably heard us moving the barricade aside as we were leaving, or was drawn to the sound of the gunshots earlier. He immediately snapped to attention when we walked out, and started striding at us. I handed the .22 to her, and drew the sword.

The fresh ones are always more dangerous. They're a

little quicker, and I think they're almost a little smarter. They are still pretty slow, really dumb, and I took him down. I made an example of him to her while she watched.

I walked at him and dropped low and to the side, swinging the sword at knee level. The force of the blade sent it right through the gristle at the knee and lopped his leg clean off. With little balance anyway, the dead kid face planted. I circled him, watching her horror as he rolled around trying to get at me. It hurt to be so cruel, but she had to see here what would be everywhere out there. Eventually the zombie got on his stomach. I stopped moving, and allowed it to come straight at me. Once it was close enough, I swung down hard, and cleaved his head in two. Once again the sword lodged firmly, and I had to pull it out holding his head still with my foot.

She threw up and dropped the .22.

I calmly explained how only destroying the brain would kill them. I told her about fuel, food, water, and safety. I told her to go straight home, and find her parents. Then come straight back if they didn't have a better plan.

We picked out a car on the side of the street that had keys in it still, and she got in. I wished her good luck, told her to be safe and smart, and she drove out.

She never came back. I guess they had a better plan.

After that, I started my building to building sweep of the entire campus. Most of that is pretty mundane by my standards now, but there was a couple of interesting... occurrences. I'll detail those last few things in a journal entry shortly. I'm not sure, but I think my next entry will be my plan.

No promises though Mr. Journal. I have a hard time keeping those lately.

-Adrian

Soccer Mom

Stacey closed her eyes and leaned back, resting her head against the park bleacher bench behind her. The sun was still coming down on her face and it felt good to be outside. She could hear all the kids running around on the soccer field right in front of her, and with all the other parents right here she could let her guard down and relax for a minute. She hadn't gotten a break all day, which was usual for summer when you have two little ones at home. No school for the summer meant no rest for mom.

Stacey felt something small and soft hit her in the stomach, and she sat back up again. On the grass directly in front of her was bright yellow spongy football. Her six year old boy Tommy was running straight at her full tilt, eyes fixed on the ball he had just likely thrown at his mom.

"Mom! Throw me the football!" Tommy stopped ten feet away and threw his hands up like pro receiver, waiting for an incoming missile.

"Brace yourself buddy!" Stacey hollered, and gunned the football as hard as she could at her son. It left her uneducated hand like a banana being shot out of a cannon. It tumbled end over end and sailed ten feet above her son's head. She laughed at her attempt, but Tommy yelled in dismay and ran after the ball. Moments like this were the reason Stacey had kids. She could re-experience the world through their innocent eyes every day, and be rewarded with their triumphs almost more than they were.

Her little daughter, only 4 years old this month was one town over at her husband's mother's place. Little Sarah just loved grammy, and today they were exploring one of the area's most enticing tourist traps, the Butterfly Museum. Sarah would be talking about butterflies for a month nonstop, but at least it gave Stacey a break, and it gave grammy some precious time with her granddaughter.

Stacey looked around the field and saw a dozen kids all frolicking in the summer sun. It was late June, midweek during the waning summer vacation, and these kids were enjoying every second. In another week the parents would start the back to school shopping, and not long after that the little ones would be marched right back to their educational prisons to learn how to be bigger kids someday. As much as Stacey loved her kids, she craved some peace and quiet at the house. Normally when the kids were at school or daycare she had the run of the house. She could do laundry, clean, prepare some food, and maybe even sit down and read a decent book. Summers meant all of that was either off limits until the kids were asleep at night, or done with two kids hanging off of her like barnacles during the day.

She laughed to herself quietly and shrugged. It's not like she didn't know what she was getting into. Just then her cell phone went off in her purse, and she pulled it out and answered it. It was her husband.

"Babe, where are you and kids?" He asked her seriously.

"I've got Tommy at the park playing ball with some kids, and Sarah is with your mom at the Butterfly Museum. What's up? Something going on?" Stacey could sense some anxiety in his voice. This scenario happened a lot, especially when something was happening around town. He was the Chief of Police after all, so he always knew when something was up. Frequently he would call and fill her in on the dangerous happenings around town.

"Something very bad is going on. You need to get Tommy, head to the grocery store, and buy as much food as you can. Food that'll last too. Canned stuff. Buy lots of water too." His voice broke suddenly and he went silent.

"Honey what's wrong?" Stacey leaned forward on the

bench after hearing her husband's voice crack. Something was VERY wrong.

"Dad's dead." He choked out.

Stacey remained silent for several moments, tears welling, looking at her son playing, trying to figure out what the hell to say to her boy or her husband. "I'm so sorry David. I don't know what to say, what happened?"

"You watch the news at all today?" He asked after sniffling.

"No, been busy with the kids, was there a shooting at the shop?" Stacey dug a tissue out of her purse and dabbed at her eyes to clear the tears away.

"Well yeah, but that's the least of it. There's some kind of sickness spreading all over the place. It makes people all kinds of crazy, and they attack everyone around them. Someone infected came to the store, and long story short, Dad got bitten. The bites of the infected spread it." David sounded like even he didn't believe what he was saying.

"That's crazy. Your father died of a bite? Is this like rabies?" She was just about back together emotionally now.

"Not exactly. Danny shot one guy that was sick, but that guy's son had been bitten earlier. The kid bit two of the EMT's who responded, then he bit Dad. It was damn horrible Stacey. Phil, Dad's best friend wound up shooting Dad so he wouldn't get sick and bite anyone else."

Stacey shook her head in complete confusion. This wasn't happening. This was something that happened in bad horror movies, and books written by people from Maine. She just exhaled in response to the news. Her mind couldn't work fast enough to think of something appropriate or useful to say.

"Look honey," the Chief said to his wife, "this is spreading like wildfire. The state police are blockading the interstates, and the major hospitals are now quarantine zones. Things are going to get really bad, much worse than just Dad dying. This is end of the world bullshit. We need to get a bunch of food and water, and get the kids home immediately." He was back in cop-mode now. Authoritative, and strong.

"Okay, I can go get Sarah and your mom, then go to the store, then go home." Stacey gathered her stuff up and started to wave at her son, but her husband cut her off.

"No. You get Tommy and go to the store. I'm headed to the museum to get Sarah and mom. I'll meet you at the house. Once you get to the house, you lock all the doors, and you get the kids and yourself upstairs, and you lock yourselves in a room. Don't answer the door for anyone. And you know what? Get the spare pistol out of the gun case in the closet and load it." David sounded sure of himself. That made her feel a little better.

"Oh.... okay." She said back to him. She didn't like guns at all.

"I just cut the entire force loose. Everyone needs to get home and take care of their families. That's the priority right now. Stacey I love you, and I will see you in an hour or so. Once I get Sarah." The Chief said.

"I love you too, you be careful." Stacey started to crack a little again. They both hung up at the same time.

*****

Stacey did everything she could to hide the phone call and all the bad news it contained from Tommy. He was a little peeved they had to leave the field so suddenly, but this wasn't too unusual with his Dad being Chief. Frequently David would call Stacey and interrupt their plans so this wasn't all that out of the realm of normal. Today was a different situation though.

Stacey drove her small SUV confidently down Main Street to the grocery store. She noticed traffic seemed a little heavier than normal, and people were certainly driving a little more recklessly. At the main lights in town she watched two cars run the light, and it set off the policeman's wife in her. Stacey had half a mind chasing them down and giving them hell for driving so ignorantly. She also saw several homes along the way with boarded up windows. It reminded her of the vacation David, her, and the kids took to the Florida Keys a few years ago. They had a hurricane warning and the whole resort area was boarded up in hours. The storm missed them, but she never forgot the feeling of panic as the world seemed to come to a complete stop from something she couldn't control. Stacey was getting that same feeling again right now. She wondered to herself how all this had happened right in front of her without her knowing. Ignorance certainly wasn't bliss today.

Despite the jerks on the road she made it all the way to the grocery store unscathed and parked in a decent spot near the front. She got Tommy unbuckled and out of the car seat and kept an eye on everyone around her. It was late afternoon, maybe 5ish, and the parking lot was super busy. It was like the Saturday before the Super Bowl, or right before Thanksgiving or Christmas. Very unusual for a late June day. She took stock of all the people pushing overloaded carts out of the store to their cars as she and Tommy walked across the parking lot and into the store. Apparently she and David weren't the only ones with this plan.

Stacey swung her son's hand as playfully as she could and chatted about his time at the field with his friends. It helped her forget what was going on, and also served to keep her son from noticing the subdued panic going on all around them. They jumped on the sidewalk, hands held in unison near the entrance to the store, and started towards the automatic doors. Just as they finished laughing at their silliness, there was a loud yell from the parking lot.

Stacey only had to take one large step backwards to get a good look at what was happening. A middle aged man was walking across the parking lot only 50 feet from where they were, and he was frozen solid, hands up in front him as he yelled for a minivan to stop. The driver of the minivan, a woman Stacey recognized as a local, didn't even hesitate or try to stop. The minivan hit the pedestrian square in the legs, and plowed over him like a speed bump in the road. The van lurched up and down as the wheels rolled over the poor man, crushing his body, breaking the limbs and twisting them into awkward angles. The driver didn't stop after either, and sped away onto Main Street.

Stacey immediately covered Tommy's eyes before he realized what was happening. She stood there slack jawed, completely in awe of what just happened. Unconsciously she reached for her phone to call 911, but then she remembered that her husband had already sent the other officers home, and said two paramedics were either bitten or dead. What point was there at all in calling for help, who would answer now anyway? Multiple people in the parking lot immediately ran over to help the mangled man, and with Tommy with her, she was thankful for that. She had to get some food, and get out of downtown before this thing got any worse. More than anything though, she just wanted to get home and see her husband and daughter as soon as possible. She ushered her son into the store, and grabbed a cart.

Inside was worse than the parking lot. There had to be three hundred idiots moving around the store at top speed, filling their carts with everything under the sun. She saw one older lady pushing a cart filled with cheap beer with all her might towards the checkout. No food in the cart at all, just cases and cases of the rotgut beer. Some people just have different priorities Stacey thought to herself. She had much different plans. David said get durable food, and that meant food in cans, so she put Tommy in the cart, and started to weave her way in between the mobs of people in the store, trying to get to the canned food aisle.

As she passed the handful of aisles on her way there she grabbed some boxes of cereal, and some crackers. They'd stay fresh some time, and would be a good snack food for the kids. She also picked up a few bottles of juice on a display. The kids loved juice. When she finally reached the canned goods aisle, she had to wait. It was so packed with people trying to load their carts there was almost no space to move. After waiting nearly ten minutes she finally started to lose her nerve. In front of her, and at the end of the aisle, she could see that people trying to get into the aisle were preventing people from getting out of the aisle. She snapped.

"Idiots! Get out of the way so they can get out of our way!" She hollered at the half dozen folks all jockeying for position in front of her. They turned, astonished a woman was yelling at them. She gave them her stern motherly look and two young men backed their carts away. A few people previously stuck in the aisle rushed out, relieved to be free.

"See? We can't all fit in there, let some more out." She shook her head at the morons she was surrounded by. Poor Tommy was all flustered watching his mom get angry. She never got angry. A faint tear welled up in one eye as his six year old mind tried to wrap itself around what was happening. For the first time he was starting to realize that something was wrong around him. Stacey smiled at him and shook her head in that "can you believe these silly people?" way. He smiled back at her, and they both started to feel relieved.

Stacey was still frazzled on the inside though. After another minute or two enough people had gotten out of the aisle that more folks could enter. Everyone seemed to be trying to get the same stuff. Heavy soups, canned pastas, and vegetables seemed to be the order of the day. She took a couple cans of everything, and made sure she grabbed extra chicken and beef broth. She could always make soups out of the veggies growing in the back yard garden at the house. Finally after fighting against the current she was done, but now she had her role reversed. Now she was stuck in the aisle while a whole new group of idiots tried to fight their way in. Two blunt forces for stupidity, butting heads yet again.

She was just about to yell something when a giant man

came around the end of the aisle she was near. He looked stern, resolute. Just seeing him assess the situation made her pause her second yell. He was tall, fairly handsome (if unshaven), and had an enormous shotgun in his half full cart. He seemed serious, and he seemed like he wanted in the aisle, and it was clear he wanted that now. She was instantly afraid he'd grab the shotgun and start threatening people to get out his way, but what he actually did surprised her.

He leaned over and tapped another middle aged man on the shoulder, "Dude, move. They can't get out." His voice was low, authoritative. Not a threat issued, but a calm statement of fact backed by the same confidence she'd heard countless times in her husband's voice. The young man took one look up at the bigger man and without even thinking about it, he backed his cart away.

Stacey could see the big man had tattoos on his forearms going down to the wrist. They were colorful scenes of Koi fish, flowing water, and various tribal designs. Beautiful and scary at the same time. She was both entranced by, and apprehensive about this odd fellow. After getting the first man to move he simply went to the next person and repeated himself again. The message changed slightly every time, but it always had the same simple meaning; "move." It was the most effective and subtle use of intimidation she'd ever seen. She found herself smiling at the show of charisma. Finally one last person pushing her way into the aisle remained for him.

It was a 60ish year old woman, clearly suffering from a tragically shitty mood. She was cursing under her breath the whole time this was happening, and was pressing her cart against the back of another shopper in front of her. Just as the tall tattooed man walked up behind her, she impulsively reached over and scooped a dozen cans of food into her cart. It seemed to Stacey an action taken out of spite more than need. The tall man's brow furrowed in disapproval as he watched her do it. By now Stacey could've left, but she wanted to see how this ended.

"Ma'am, can you please back away a little so the folks in front of you can get out of our way?" He leaned over gently and said it just loud enough to be heard over the din of arguing shoppers and the beeping at the checkouts.

"Go fuck yourself buddy, you're not getting in there before me." She snarled at him without even looking at who was talking to her.

The big man just smiled, stuck his hands in the front pocket of his hooded sweatshirt, and leaned in to her again. Stacey could feel his aura of intimidation almost physically flare up as he spoke again to the old lady, "Ma'am, I am **NOT** your fucking buddy. And if you don't put some of those cans back you just scooped up, and get the hell out of the way for everyone else, I will see to it both your hips get busted right here in this aisle." His voice was as calm as preacher's at a Sunday wedding. That wasn't a threat he'd just uttered. It was another statement of fact.

The old lady finally looked over her shoulder incredulous of the threat and the color drained from her face. You could see she hadn't figured on the quiet voice coming from such a big, imposing man. She locked eyes with the huge guy, and he held firm for a moment, then smiled like a snake at her. This was a man who would do what precisely what he just said he would. The handful of people gathered nearby in the aisle all took an unconscious step backwards. The arguing died immediately as everyone waited for the old lady to respond. Time seemed to stand still.

She licked her lips, never breaking eye contact with the giant stranger. She coughed a wet cough, a smoker's cough, and looked down into her cart at the cans she'd just put in the cart. She grabbed some of those cans and put them back on the shelf. Her eyes darted around shamefully and she slowly backed her cart away, freeing up space in the aisle for people to leave.

The big man nodded to the old lady in thanks, and turned towards Stacey and Tommy. Her heart jumped a few beats as he took her and her son in. Partly it was fear out of what he might say to her and Tommy, and partly out of excitement. He gave her a genuine, apologetic smile for what just happened, and then tussled Tommy's hair. She could instantly see Tommy liked him. He was so much like his father, her husband. The big man made a show of presenting the open aisle for her exit, and he gave her a nod as they left the aisle. She looked once over her shoulder as she walked away and saw the big man was letting the old lady into the aisle ahead of himself. Despite being able to push his way ahead, he had kept his spot in line. She knew right then she liked him, and she knew he'd be just fine.

The rest of her store experience was much more benign. The biggest battle by far was fighting through the canned goods aisle. The majority of the other aisles were clear of big crowds. She was headed to the checkouts to pay when she realized they were low on dog food for their beagle Scotty. Scotty could and would eat just about anything, but she figured while she was here she should get dog food. A couple minutes later she was in line, and a few minutes after that, she was unloading the cart onto the checkout belt with Tommy's help. As she chatted with her son about how awful that old lady was to that nice man she saw him again.

50 feet away down at the produce section he was standing still with his cart, clearly in a moral dilemma. He looked at the checkout lines, ten people deep, then looked at the entrance to the store, wide open. She knew what he was thinking. 45 minutes in line to pay, or just walk out? He shook his head one last time, snagged what looked like three bunches of bananas, and headed out the sliding automatic doors. She laughed out loud once at his audacity, and went back to emptying her shopping cart. That seemed like a little bit of justice to her.

A minute or two creaked by in the checkout line. Incessant beeping coming from the barcode scanners in multiple overloaded lanes drowned everyone out. Even Stacey found herself standing quietly, zoning out, bagging her own groceries. Suddenly noise from outside slowed the beeping to a crawl. It was screaming. Several of the people near the exits walked over and looked out the doors and windows at whatever was unfolding in the parking lot. The witnesses stood in silent horror, several of them covering their slowly opening mouths with their hands. Stacey reassured Tommy she'd be right back and ran over to watch herself.

The man that had been hit by the minivan was sitting up in the parking lot. He was covered by an industrial blanket. One of the heavy kinds you'd use for moving. She couldn't see his face, but the blanket was stained through in several spots with his blood. Dark red circles and splotches were all over the thick blanket. Circling his sitting form was the man from earlier. He had the giant shotgun from his cart aimed at the man. Stacey looked on in horror as he calmly kept it leveled at the victim of the car accident. No one knew what to do. She couldn't imagine what was happening that would force the big man to shoot someone. He seemed so calm, and controlled earlier.

Just as her mind started to struggle with the idea that this stranger was pointing a shotgun at an injured man, the blanket fell away, revealing the smashed body of the victim. Everyone standing around beside her gasped in shock and horror at his appearance. His body was mangled beyond human comprehension. His torso was crushed so violently ribs were poking out of his side, ripping holes large enough for his innards to swell through. His mouth was crusted with bile and blood and his skin was ashen and pale. Something was clearly wrong with him. The young girl standing next to Stacey formed the sign of the cross and started praying fervently.

Stacey shook her head slowly, her mind refusing to make sense of what she was watching. The victim, now clearly dead in her mind, leaned over towards the large stranger and attempted to go at him. His annihilated legs failed him though, and he fell forwards, hitting his face on the

185

pavement and spilling some of his guts out of his ragged stomach. Her attention turned to the big stranger with the shotgun. Her heart started racing in fear for him as the destroyed man on the ground started to lift himself and crawl at him.

The tattooed stranger pointed the shotgun at the head of the man on the ground, closed his eyes, and pulled the trigger. The sound of the shotgun going off was still loud enough to scare the people inside the store. All of the beeping at the checkouts came to a halt.

The head of the car accident victim exploded in a giant mist of reds and browns. There was a flurry of faint thunking noises as bits of his head hit the giant window of the grocery store. His headless body fell to the pavement backwards and began oozing blood and ichors onto the ground from the many openings in it. Stacey could see the tattooed man was hit in the legs by the gore given off from his shotgun blast, but he seemed no worse for the wear. She watched him take a deep breath, assess the situation around him, and calmly walk away. He got his cart, and walked towards the back of the parking lot until she couldn't see him anymore.

Stacey's mind was wiped clean. She stood there motionless for some time, watching the pieces of the dead man's head slide down the window before her motherly sense realized she could hear Tommy sobbing from the seat in the cart. She snapped to and ran over to him. She lifted him up and held him close, whispering in his ear that everything would be alright, even though she wasn't sure it would be.

*****

Stacey left the store out the same entrance she and Tommy had used to enter it. Fortunately it was the entrance the furthest away from the decapitated man. She was thankful for that, at least for Tommy's sake. He was going to lose enough innocence today without getting a close look at the aftermath of the earlier shooting. As she pushed her overloaded cart up the parking lot row she made a largely vain attempt at distracting her son from the body on the ground. He was staring intently at the pool of blood the body had fallen in and no matter what she said, he wouldn't look away. Eventually she just covered his eyes with her hand, and pushed the cart faster to her SUV.

She used her remote entry fob and had the back hatch opened before she even got there. As fast as she could she got the jugs of water out and in the back of the truck along with the bags of cans and other food. The bags were very heavy though, and when she finally finished she felt like she had lifted an entire house. Tommy was facing her the whole time mostly because of the way she positioned the cart, and she kept looking at him and seeing little elements of her husband's face there. Little Sarah was her spitting image, and little Tommy looked just like his Dad David. Too cute. His face reminded her of her husband though, and that led to thoughts of how her father in law was dead now. Apparently shot by his own good friend by request, and with her husband's permission. She still couldn't understand what the hell was happening.

After all the groceries were stored away in the back of her truck she got Tommy secured in his car seat. The SUV thrummed to life when Stacey turned the key, and she backed out quickly. The mother and son got back onto Main Street and started towards the house. The Moore family, Stacey, David, Tommy and Sarah had a very nice colonial style home set in the hills just outside of town. By car it was normally a mere five minute drive. Today the five minutes would be much longer.

Stacey played a driving game with Tommy on the drive back. It was one they played often in the car.

"Okay Tommy, I spy with my little eye, something big

187

and blue!" She laughed as she started the game.

Tommy leaned forward in his little car seat and scanned the traffic around them. Right next to them at the light was a big blue truck, "Is it the truck Mommy?" He pointed his stubby little finger against the car window right at the vehicle.

"You got it! YAY!" Stacey celebrated with her son. He clapped his hands and gave a look of supreme satisfaction. The mother and son continued their silly little game the rest of the way down Main Street, and the two miles on Dove Street. Then, as she slowed to take the right hand turn onto Hill Street where they lived, they were hit head-on by a gigantic pickup truck rounding the corner.

The massive pickup was speeding considerably coming into the turn. The driver, a middle aged man who had just left his girlfriend's home in search of her was paying little to no attention to the road. Stacey and Tommy were ravaged by the impact. In her haste to get home the mother of two had left her seatbelt curled up in the side of the car, unused. Her small frame was crushed by the pressure of the steering wheel and airbag as the front of her vehicle collapsed in on itself. It took her many painful minutes to die. Ruptured organs and blood vessels slowly emptied into her stomach cavity, suffocating her. She couldn't even manage to turn and check on her six year old son as she bled out. Finally her body went limp, and her face came to a rest against the steering wheel in front of her.

Little Tommy, strapped firmly in his seat was almost none the worse for wear. Knocked unconscious by the impact, he sat still, face down on his chest, oblivious to the death of his mother two feet in front of him.

The senseless driver of the off-road specialized truck did not escape unscathed. His vehicle was larger, and tougher, and took less damage in the crash, but his situation was not good at all. The truck's lifted suspension was driven upwards at strange angles by the impact with the lower car driven by the mother. Something had given way and drove its way into the cab, crushing both of his legs against the dash, pinning him firmly. He screamed in pain incessantly until he was hoarse.

The man sat there sweating profusely, beating his airbag down, lamenting his broken legs, searching around the scene of the wreck for help. After what seemed like an eternity he saw the woman driver, the idiot as he called her, finally come to in her car.

"Hey! Hey! Call for help, I'm all fucked up in here!" He yelled as loudly as he could. He smacked his hands repeatedly against the cracked windshield of his truck. The woman looked dazed, out of sorts, and was bleeding from cuts all over her face.

"Lady in here, over here you stupid bitch!" He winced in agony and smacked the windshield again. He had to close his eyes and shut out the pain for a bit. When he finally opened his eyes he saw the woman had pushed her car door open, and was dragging her feet, slowly walking over to his side of the truck. His hard breathing started to slow as he finally felt some form of rescue coming to help. He rested his head against the back window of the truck for a second, then gathered enough strength to put a shoulder to his door. It protested briefly, but eventually popped open with a shriek of bent metal. The hurt lady picked up the pace and came around the front of the car near the fender, and reached at his door.

The pinned driver finally looked up at her and saw her face, and her eyes. All her color was gone. Her teeth and gums were torn out and open, leaving a bloody pulp where her mouth should have been. Her eyes had gone milky, hazy, and she clearly was not in her right mind.

"Ahhh!" He screamed and tried to wrench the door away from her outstretched hand. It was too late though, she was around it and coming in the cab at him. He pushed as hard as he could, he even punched her as hard as he could multiple times through the pain of his destroyed legs, but no matter what he did, she kept coming back. The fought this struggle for what felt like an eternity to the driver, until eventually his punches stopped pushing her back, and she was on him, ripping, biting in a savage silence.

Even with her ripped apart face and mouth she bit at him and tore his flesh with success. The driver's hoarse screams came to a gurgling end as his throat was torn apart by her jagged, broken teeth. He clawed at her, pushed her away, but his strength was gone. His fight was over.

Stacey's undead body continued to tear bits of flesh away until he stopped moving. He twitched a few times and with a savage instinct she tore into his body again until it stopped moving again. Finally, after a somewhat sad, confused moment, Stacey's undead body slowly turned away, and began to shamble down the street towards the house she had been heading towards while still alive.

Tommy, her beloved six year old son that looked just like his father, sat in his car seat, in the back of the wrecked SUV, still unconscious.

November 17th

I am the man with the plan. More accurately, I am the man, with a draft for the plan. I was going to put off starting the plan until another entry or two, but I've come to the conclusion that I think better when I'm talking to you Mr. Journal. Thus in this entry, I will lay down the basic ideas for how I plan on increasing the population here, and making amends for my greatest sin, leaving Cassie to an unknown fate. As I shared in my semi-drunken entry a few days ago, I think helping people will give me some closure, and give me purpose in life.

All philosophical mumbo-jumbo karma bullshit aside, I need to also figure out a way to do this without getting myself killed. Getting killed would totally defeat the purpose. Plus dying would suck ass.

Alrighty. So here are some bulleted thoughts that have formed the basic plan. These are still discussion points at this juncture; they aren't necessarily set in stone. Bullet points first, followed by in depth explanations. Oh yeah, here's one thing else: I've made the assumption that the best course of action is to stay here on campus, and use it as my "home." All people wishing to receive my help will be moving here.

- I must secure the campus further.
- I have to get some wood stoves up here to alleviate the dependence on gasoline and fuel oil.
- Additional food and supplies must be procured *or* I need to wait until I can get a garden/farm up and running.
- I need to secure the outlying structures headed into town of zombies. (this also potentially satisfies the additional food clause)
- I need to ensure that my own home, Dorm E, is safe not only from zombies, but from human intruders.
- I need to establish a form of communication that will allow me to speak to and vet (read: spy on them) people

before I actually meet them.
- And finally, I need to establish a set system of government/rules for when and if people come here.

That's a lot to go over. Let's share my thoughts on each point.

I must secure the campus further. What I really mean by this is finding a way to make the back end of the campus fortified. Granted, the school is very much like an island, but really it's more of a peninsula. The bridge crosses onto the peninsula more near the tip, so the back end of the campus is still crossable on land. Now the river cuts the campus territory across that area, kinda forming the island, but there's nothing stopping a wandering zombie from wading through the shallows and onto campus. It's already happened several times. I'm thinking I build a sturdy rock wall, or maybe find lumber, and slap up some simple walls. I can get 2x4's and screw them tree to tree, then attach plywood to that. That's likely enough to hold off a few strays until spring when more sturdy fortifications can be built. I'm not looking for Fort Knox here. I am also wondering how I can make the bridge more fortified. The two vans I have parked in a staggered V formation are great, but it's not perfect, and someone with a good sized truck could easily push them out of the way. Not sure on that solution just yet. I think a drawbridge is a little beyond my engineering capabilities.

This point also covers making more of the dorms secure. There are a lot of ground floor windows that are currently exposed, and a zombie walking on to campus could easily smash a window, and be inside in seconds. This increases the importance of finding a substantial amount of lumber for reinforcement purposes.

Wood stoves. Gotta get em. At least one for Hall E, or alternately for a Hall with no electricity. Understandably I can make it through at least one winter without a stove, but if I get people in here before or during winter, I don't want them in Hall E with me, and they will need heat. I need to find at least one wood stove, preferably several. I think a good way to find them might be to cruise around the farmhouses up here and scour the places with chimney or stove pipes visible. Now getting a giant woodstove back here… that's another problem I'll have to deal with. I've got the trucks for it. I just don't know if I can lift one all by myself. Plus I need to figure out exactly how to install one, which may require additional materials.

Food, supplies, and/or a garden. Ideally I'd like to get people up here before winter. However, it's already the 17th of November, and we had spitting snow the other night. It won't be long before the road out of here is impassable. Blessing and a curse really. Zombies won't be able to get up here, scavengers like me won't be able to either, but the downside is I can't leave for shit either. One idea for that is to plow the road myself. There's a plow attachment for the trucks down in the grounds keeping barn area for the trucks. But a plowed road is a pretty obvious sign of human life, and I think it'd be better to just plow the roads here on campus if I do that at all. I think there is a small plow somewhere for the ATV too.

Road situation aside, I need to get more food, and more supplies. I know there's a lot of food inside all these houses up in the area. I found a bunch just in the little apartment above the gas station, and that was a home for just two little old people. Some of the houses up here are 2,500 square feet or better, and housed 3 to 5 people. Assuming even a few of these houses have full cupboards, I'm literally just miles away from months of food. Other than the food issue, I need to find additional consumables. Toilet paper, soap, dishwashing detergent, ammunition, shoes, clothes, etc. More than anything else though, I need to find medicines, and books about how to use them. God forbid I get a cut, or an infection, or the flu. I have ZERO antibiotics, and I know fuck all about which ones to take for what.

I really don't want to think about this, but I am pretty sure I will have to go back into town to hit one of the pharmacies. Ewww.

Soo... assuming I don't get supplies, or I find out I need to wait for spring, then I should just wait to get seeds in the ground. If I do that, I think I am more or less prepared. It would be great if I had some fertilizer type stuff, which may require a trip to the garden center where I got the seeds "that day." That also could be a shitstorm of a trip though. Oh, and despite the fact I am trying to be less reliant on gas, I need a lot more gas. I will need it, until I don't need it. Does that make sense Mr. Journal?

Secure outlying houses/buildings of zombies. This ties directly into the finding supplies part. I really want to clean out all the houses within a mile or two of the dead inside or around them. If I can clean them out of zombies, get all their usable supplies, and then lock them down, it'll mean there's a drastically reduced chance of wandering zombies heading up the road to here. It will be dangerous. But you know what? So is crossing the road. Not so much because lately there's a chance I'll get hit by a car, but more likely that I'll get mauled and eaten alive by a handful of the undead. It's not like the good old days anymore kids. All we had to do then was walk to school in the snow, uphill, both ways.

I need to secure Hall E from intruders. I really feel like I'm zombie proof here. All the doors are heavy duty, doubled up on both entrances, all the lower windows are secured with sturdy wooden barricades, and I've got the one deck secured well. My worry now is if someone alive comes up here with a ladder, they're in as easily as 1-2-3. Gotta figure out a way to make sure that new people can't get in here without a bitch of a time. Call me paranoid, but I'm more worried about being shot by the living, than I am about being eaten alive by the dead.

I am thinking about totally blocking off all the first floor windows and leaving just window slits/gun ports. Possibly using cement to do it, or even brick if possible. I can always use the second floor windows as vantage points should I need to kill things outside.

Communication system to vet potential "roommates." I'm feeling clever here. Now my first thought was to simply paint up some huge ass signs, and leave them all over town. "Hey assholes, safe place to live at the end of this road." That kind of shit. What I realized almost immediately, is if I did that I was giving away my greatest asset. Solitude.

By telling people where I am, they can come here, and take the place from me. Well, the fuckers can try. Anyway, I realized before I told ANYONE where this place was, I would want to feel them out first, preferably from a distance.

Enter Steve's letter. I had completely forgotten about it, but Steve said he was going to get a CB radio, and check it every day at noon or something like that. So I thought about it, and realized that was a frigging great idea. I could leave CB radios in a couple places around town, with huge ass signs that said, "use this CB at such and such a time to find a safe place to live." That way they could radio me, we could talk over a day or two, then if I felt good about it, we could arrange a meeting elsewhere. If that went well, then I could lead them back up here and see what happens. If at any point in time I got a bad feeling, then I simply cut ties and tell them to go fly a kite. Worst case I'm out a CB, and maybe a sign. Sounds good right? I think it's a helluva basic idea to keep myself safe, and allow me and a bunch of total strangers to establish some relationship before I give them the farm. I'm thinking I can even set up the CB radios in pre-cleared safe houses with water and minor supplies as a gesture of good faith, and to impress people. After all, if they need to wait to radio me, I want them to be safe during that time.

So the last part is really complicated. Once I get people up here... how do we run the place? Do I run it and tell everyone else what's up? I was the first here, I got the place safe, and no one else knows better than I do? If they don't like it they can scram? How do I establish laws? Is it a democracy? Do I simply take a U.S.law book from the library and grandfather it in as the same old, same old?

The nice guy in me that has almost always done the "right thing" in his life says we should establish an immediate democracy by majority, and bring in every law that was on the books from before. It's familiar, everyone feels valued, and I won't have to shoulder the moral and legal burden of being quite literally King Shit of Turd Mountain.

The pragmatist inside me says fuck everyone, you're the boss. You know better than anyone else who shows up what to do, and your judgment is better than theirs. We follow simple common sense laws for the meantime, and I can always take advice if needed, and ignore advice if needed. My chief worry is this scenario: I "rescue" a family or group of 5 people. I tell them we're a democracy, and everyone has an equal vote. The first vote we cast is that they immediately are in charge, and they tell me to get the fuck out. Well that ain't fucking happening Mr. Journal. That motion is not getting carried.

I really don't know. I'm sure the final solution will be somewhere in the middle. Actually, I'm not sure about that at all. It's this question that makes me doubt doing this in the first place. I can totally envision telling a new arrival what's up, and it escalating to violence.

Alright soo… where do I start? To fortify I need lumber, maybe some brick, concrete blocks, and possibly cement. There isn't a ton of any of those items here. To get supplies I need to clear out the nearby houses of zombies. To find people I need CB's. People are the last step though. That's easy to cross off for now and do later. The only logical thing that I can think of to do first, is to clear out the houses within a mile. There are probably 40 or 50 in total, and I think I can clear out two or three a day if I move right along. I'm betting most are empty, or can be cleared fairly easily. It is unlikely that any of these houses will have more than 5 or 6 undead in them. Not too bad if I'm smart about it. The real question becomes… what the hell do I do if I find living people inside one of them? Slip away unnoticed? Invite them here ahead of schedule? Form a tribal alliance ala Survivor?

Fucked if I know Mr. Journal. It's all improv dude. More plan refinement tomorrow, then I'll start clearing out houses. Any spare time I have until that's done I'll spend trying to fortify Hall E I think.

-Adrian

November 18th

Update on today's accomplishments is first on the agenda. The weather was pretty good today, which was awesome. Last night we had one of our fall typhoons again, so I was a little anxious about how it would be today. It was cloudy, but it stayed about 50 and never rained. Perfect for work outside.

I realized early I didn't need to refine my plan. I think at the point I'm at I cannot plan any more. I need to start doing stuff, and adjust the plan to circumstances as they come up. I didn't want to start clearing houses today, so I scoured campus for building materials and collected them near hall E so they were convenient. I used the ATV and the little trailer.

I found a LOT of awesome shit stored in nooks and crannies all over the place. One of the dorms had a ton of lumber in the basement from a building project that never got started. It was mostly all 2x4's, which is excellent. I found 24 8 foot 2x4's, an ass ton of screws and nails as well. I got wood. Had to throw that in there.

In the back of one of the maintenance outbuildings I found bags of concrete, which rocks. (more accurately I guess it turns into rock) I can make great use of that. All over the place I collected 60 separate concrete blocks, and about a hundred bricks. Spares for the sidewalks I would assume.

Those will go a long way towards locking down Hall E, and making fortifications across campus.

I also found a bunch of random buildings supplies like drywall, spackle, skill saws, etc. The facilities tool shed was a goldmine. Guess I should've expected that. One of the nicer things that I found was some significantly higher quality furniture out in the staff houses in the far back of campus. I'd totally dismissed those houses after I emptied them of food back when I was clearing campus. I found a pretty sweet bed, and a bunch of couches and stuff that are much better than the shitty dorm furniture that's here in Hall E. I only moved one recliner over today, and that's where I'm sitting as I type this. I am in a little bit of heaven. I'll move more over later.

The one mildly shitty thing that did happen today was my realization I have a fucking gigantic pile of dead bodies in the back of campus. Up until now, every time I have a body, I've been dragging it back and throwing on a huge pile, way out of the way. The stench hadn't reached down to the main campus area, but when I was up that way.... holy shit it was unbearable. I decided to burn the bodies just after dark.

Adrian's helpful tip of the day: It doesn't matter how much gasoline you pour on a dead body, it doesn't burn for shit by itself. You need wood to keep the fire going. Found that out about two hours ago. I had to grab a bunch of the dead fallen wood that was dry to insert into the pile of corpses to sustain a pyre to burn the bodies away. Ooops.

Right now they're still burning, and luckily the breeze is blowing the smoke out across the river. The fire isn't visible as best as I can tell either, despite it being the size of a tractor trailer. If it burns all night, there should be nothing left by morning. Doubt I'm that lucky though, I might have to light it up tomorrow at dusk to finish the deal.

So yeah a really productive day. Very happy with myself.

Story time. I write so much faster when I'm in a good mood. It's noticeable. I love it. Right now I feel like I could write Tolstoy's epic in about twenty minutes lol. I'm such a nerd.

So I really want to try and wrap up the day after "that day" when I really dug in and got nasty with cleaning this campus out of the undead. It was pretty bad too, but most of the stories consist of the following: "entered dorm/building, found several wandering zombies. Shot some, chopped the heads off of others, didn't get bitten."

There's only so much of that I can type before I feel I'm recording needless history here. However, there were a few incidents that were interesting or unique enough to warrant a more substantial story. I'll give some details on the boring shit, then cut to the chase on the scary stuff.

The majority of the school, staff, and maintenance buildings were either empty, or had minimal zombie presence. I think I ran into perhaps a dozen zombies in those buildings the afternoon after Abigail took off for home. Most of those undead were dispatched with the .22, or with the sword. I cleared all the buildings as normal, even checking closets, cupboards, everything. (that's why I was so freaked out when that zombie jumped me in the cafeteria. I am *positive* that place was empty)

All of my serious problems came from the dorms themselves. I have no way of knowing how the situations got to where they were that day because I wasn't here for most of it. I was either downtown assembling my supplies and trying to find friends and family, or I was stuck on the admissions roof. Everything here is speculation.

I guess that the majority of the kids who attended school here got out safely. That's pretty awesome. We had about 100 students on campus for the summer session, which is fairly normal as we're an "overachiever's" kind of place. I'd guess that out of that population there were maybe 40 student zombies on site. Now mind you we had perhaps 60 staff that day as well, and I think 40 got the fuck out safely. The remaining 20 died here, and came back as zombies. The final straw was the x-factor, the parents. We had... shit it could've been 200 parents here over the course of that day, and there's no way of knowing really.

That gives us a rough estimate of about 100 undead on site. I think I killed somewhere around 40 or so from Dr. Potter's classroom with the .22 in the morning hours, which thinned the herd significantly. The remaining 60 zombies were shamblers I encountered while moving about outside, or they were locked inside the dorms.

Think about that for a second. The better part of 60 zombies inside 5 dorm buildings. Average that out to 12 per building and that's a pretty high threat density. The first neat story came when I was clearing out Hall B. Hall B is one of the three dorms that have two floors. Hall B was an upper class dorm for the girls. I cleared that dorm second to last. I should make mention that I cleared Hall E first, as I was almost positive that was the dorm I was going to hole up in after. That plan was a remnant from spending all night on the roof of admissions. Plenty of time to think.

Anyhow, Hall B physically looks like a very square colonial home with faintly industrial windows and doors. Imagine some of the fraternity and sorority houses on large college campuses and you're pretty close to it. I had gotten into the habit of doing a circle around every building to clear the entrances, and to scope out the situation inside through the windows. Hall B was totally clear from what I could see. The surrounding yard was also empty, and I was actually thinking that the dorm was going to be smooth sailing. By now you can guess how correct I was.

I entered through the front, which was one of the heavy duty fire doors molded so it looked like it was fancy wood. The door opened into the foyer, and to one side was the common area, and the other side the dining room. In the back of the first floor were bathrooms, and the dorm's kitchen. I held still for a few second, listened and took a whiff, and heard and smelled nothing. I cleared the first floor with the .22, and slowly crept up the stairs.

One wide stairway led up to an upstairs landing/hall

area that was open to the bottom floor. This dorm was supposed to hold a maximum of 32 girls, and if memory serves, there was about 20 or so living there when everything went down. Once I got to the upstairs I caught of whiff of badness. Not just a dead body rotting meat smell, it was more of a fecal smell to be honest. Ripe, pungent, and fresh.

I tip-toed and checked the bedroom doors, and noticed that one of the rooms towards the back was the source. The upstairs bathrooms were both empty, so I shut those doors, and pushed two of the chairs in the hall in front of them. I cleared the doors where no smell was noticeable. All three of those bedrooms were clear. Each room had 4 sets of bunks, and theoretically at full capacity each room would hold 8 girls. I had 3 empty rooms, and all 3 of those rooms didn't smell. 1 room stunk.

I listened at the door, and it was silent. I know, shocking right? These doors opened inward, so I tried the handle, and it opened, but when I pushed the door in slowly, it didn't budge an inch. Something was blocking the door. I put some shoulder into it, and got it to open an inch, and I damn near got floored by the stench wafting out. Straight up shit and carnage. I can't even describe how bad it smelled. My huge ass pile of a hundred bodies out back of the campus had nothing on the way that bedroom stank that day.

Now as soon as I got the door cracked I saw a bunch of movement, and the door was pushed shut and I heard a scraping on the floor. I'd heard that noise before, and it was the sound of the bunks being dragged on the hardwood floor. Kids are always rearranging their rooms, and it was a common and distinct noise in the dorms. After the creak the door slammed shut right in my face.

Mind racing I tried to piece it together. After the fact I found out my guess was right. Initially I felt that there was a bunk pushed up against the door. (correct) I also figured that there were undead inside, and when I opened the door, they likely rushed it, and pushed the bunk back up against the door, shutting it again. (again, correct)

I'm not gonna lie, I had no idea what to do. I was pretty sure they weren't going anywhere though, so I ran back down stairs, and grabbed a snack in the kitchen. There was some leftover pork chops from the dinner the night before, and I gnawed one to death and washed it down with some orange juice.

The dilemma was how do I kill the zombies inside? It was unlikely I could push the crowd inside and the bunk enough to get the door open. Even if I could, that was stupid. Then they could come out the open door and rush me. So I sat there for probably 15 minutes deep in thought until I heard a loud crack coming from behind me. I remember standing up from the dining room table and pointing the .22 out the window like lightning. Standing at the window, outside staring at me, was one of the parents. Well, one of the dead parents. It had hit the window and cracked the glass. That did it for me.

I stepped out the back door, jogged around the side of the building, and popped the parent in the head with the rifle. He slumped to the ground quickly, and I walked around to the other side of the house below the window of the room where the smell was. I dug through the bushes along the side of the house and found a few golf ball sized rocks. Ten paces away from the house later, I gunned the first rock through the bottom pane of the upstairs window. I waited, then side armed another rock through the top pane of the window. The second rock actually bricked one of the zombie girls right in the boob and sent her backwards a foot or two. Right after that, they all started coming to the window, and began clawing down at me.

I popped a .22 shell in the magazine to replace the one I had just shot, and waited for the plan to reach its culmination. It took another minute before the window frame gave way, and they started to tumble out the window, head over heels, falling the 20 or so feet to the ground. If it wasn't so horrible, it would've been *hilarious.* One right after another, a cascade of 16, 17, and 18 year old girls crashed onto the lawn, forming this demented pile of broken bones, putrid flesh, and glitter speckled skin. I backed away a few more feet, and just let it happen.

Once they stopped falling I waited for them to start separating. Once untangled, they started crawling, walking, or dragging themselves across the lawn at me. I prioritized my "target rich environment" and dropped the walkers first. I changed mags, and shot the few crawlers. After that I drew the sword and finished off the few that were really messed up with shattered arms and legs. They weren't much of a threat, so it was low risk at that point. God it smelled horrible. One of the things that really messed with me dealing with Hall B those first few days was sort of a subtle thing. One of my fondest (and vaguely perverted) memories of Hall B was the lovely smells that dorm always used to have. All the pretty young girls wearing nice perfumes, and using body washes and oils and stuff made that dorm such a nice place to be in. Smelling them in that condition that day was like pouring vinegar in my ear for the sole purpose of purging that pleasant memory.

Very unfortunate. Thinking back on it after all this time, I am starting to remember the good smells, not just the bad. That makes me happy. (in a totally non-perverted way)

Once I finished off my Niagara Falls of undead teenage girls I went back inside and pushed the bedroom door open carefully. There were two more zombies in the room, but they were in really sad shape. From the looks of it, they were just utterly destroyed by a bunch of the others. My guess was they holed up in there (good idea) but brought someone, or several someones inside that were already bitten. (bad idea) The bitten folk probably died, woke up as zombies, lather, rinse, repeat. If some of the girls put up a fight while they were being devoured, their bodies would've been demolished by the bunch. That was my take on the two left behind. They were just physically decimated. They got their heads split open, and I moved along to the next dorm.

The second story of interest happened later in the day when I was clearing Hall C. Hall C is almost identical to Hall B, and is about 40 yards away on the other side of a street. We tried to split those two dorms as much as possible because Hall B was for the girls, and Hall C was for upper class boys. Putting them any closer together would've been an STD factory.

Teen sex stories notwithstanding, when I cleared the place I had a substantial problem. It was the last dorm I had to clear, and it was just getting dark at the time. The darkness alone was giving me the heebie-jeebies. If I didn't keep my head on a swivel at all times outdoors, it was really easy for them to get alarmingly close. I'd shot two zombies that'd gotten to within 15 feet of me earlier. Far too close for comfort. With it getting dark, my vision would be shittier, and I was starting to feel real vulnerable.

I'm guessing it was maybe 8pm? Don't remember for sure, and it doesn't really matter I guess. Anyway, after the Hall B bullshit I was a little worried about more blocked off doors, so I made extra sure to check the upstairs windows as well as the downstairs. Just like Hall B I couldn't see anything in any of the windows. I let myself in the front door the same way, but this time the shit hit the fan immediately.

When I opened the door, there were bodies all over the place. I think later on I counted eight in the pile, and they were not all dead. The door stuck half open and one of the bodies right there latched onto the side of the door right at my feet, and sort of pulled itself right onto my lower legs. The damn thing's weight kind of chop blocked me and I tumbled backwards off the couple steps and planted hard on my ass. Mind you, this is the day after I smashed my back against a wall when my mother tried to kill me, and this was only maybe 10 hours removed from trying to sleep on the frigging admissions roof. I was sore to begin with, and landing right on my tailbone was insult and injury.

I mean if I want to enhance positives, the fall backwards

sent me feet away from the prone zombie that was a split second away from biting my calf. In retrospect, a busted asshole is better than being dead I guess. I remember yelling out in pain, swearing a blue streak for a second, then shooting the fucking thing in the head as it crawled down the steps at me.

By then a handful of the zombies that were on the floor had either gotten to their feet, or were crawling through the door that was ajar. From my back, as calmly as I could muster, I started shooting them down. I am pleased to announce to you Mr. Journal that zombies are not courteous folk anymore. They NEVER hold the door for their friends, which helped me substantially. I think three of them got out the door before it slammed shut behind them, and those three got dropped pretty easily.

I think it's worth mentioning that panic kills. I know it's hard to imagine trying to stay calm when you're on your back and three zombies are ten feet away, but really, if you just separate the horror from the reality of what you need to do, you find yourself not panicking nearly as much. I cleared my head, and kept telling myself shoot first. Move away after. If they're dead they can't kill you, if you crawl away, and they're faster, they'll catch you. Simple stuff really, it just escapes people in times of great anxiety. Maybe that's why I didn't get PTSD from my tour in Iraq? Dunno.

So four zombies came out the door, and four zombies got shot. I inspected the bodies quick, and it looked like three of the boy students, and either one parent, or a staff member I didn't know. At that point I didn't know how many were still inside, so before I opened the door, I got around the side of the house all sneaky like, and looked in the side windows. Through the curtains I could see a couple more standing, and a couple more scratching at the door from the floor.

Continuing stealth mode, I moved to the back of the house, and let myself in the door at the kitchen. I switched off to the shotgun as well, and slowly crept inside. The only way to get an angle on the front door was to walk through the kitchen, into the dining room, and look to the right into the entrance foyer where they were. I crept in, and peeked into the dining room just far enough to see the back of the first zombie. Once I had him dead to rights I started shooting. He got one in the back of the grape, and I took a few slow steps to the side. As soon as I moved the other standing zombie was climbing over the form of the one I'd just shot to get at me. Luckily the body that had gone down fell right at the feet of the second one, buying me time. I popped the second one's head apart with some double ought. The two crawling zombies were such a mess I took them out with the sword pretty easily.

I cleared the rest of the hall and found zilch for danger. Once that was done I had basically cleared everything but the staff houses, and the athletic fields which were a fair distance away, and with all the killing of zombies I'd done that day, I felt pretty safe.

I went back to my car, moved it as close to Hall E as I could, and got Otis out of the staff office building where I'd put him earlier. It was the same building I found Abby in earlier that day. Poor Otis was so frigging out of sorts from all the bullshit he just clung to me like Velcro as soon as we got into here that night. I don't even remember falling asleep. I just remember waking up in the room I slept in, still sore as hell, and trying to piece together if all of what had happened was a dream or not.

So surreal the first few weeks. It's like when you start school, or start a new job, there's this period where you are still kind of in disbelief that this is the new reality you have. Holy shit! I'm in High School! Or wow, I finally got the job I wanted all this time. Except this was more of a "oh dear, the world has come crashing down around me and I've lost almost everything I've ever held dear."

Hopefully you get the point Mr. Journal.

That's the bulk of the clearing of campus. Some other crap happened the next few days as I found more stragglers wandering about, and when I searched through the staff housing, but the majority of that is point, click, delete bullshit. Slow moving zombies that I keep my distance from. They get shot from said distance, and I move on to the next target.

Hands are finally getting tired from typing tonight, and I'm pretty wiped from the work around campus too. Otis is intently staring at me from the living room floor in front of me as well. It's bedtime. Otis says so.

Tomorrow I start clearing out surrounding houses.

-Adrian

November 20th

Picture in your mind a crucifix. A very tall crucifix with fairly long arms. At the base of the crucifix there is a bend to the left side. Almost like a small hook.

That's like the road that the school is on. The bridge is at the very top of the crucifix, and the road ends at the bottom of the hook, at very bottom. This is Auburn Lake Road. The stop sign at the bottom of the hook is the one near the gas station I've been to twice. The two arms of the crucifix are roads that go off from the road that leads to campus. My plan for clearing the houses started with me clearing the arms of the crucifix first. If you were to leave campus via car, Jones Road is to the left, heading up a slight hill, and Prospect Circle is the road to the right.

I did some recon this morning in the Tundra and discovered a few things about my 'hood, and the work that would be required to clear it. Jones Road terminates at a large farm and has 9 houses on it. All are larger houses, set back from the road, with long driveways, garages, and would be considered "upscale." Prospect Circle is not actually a circle. You can clearly see that a developer fully intended to make a cul-de-sac, but it was never completed.

It's more a wide curve that has an abrupt dirt end with some boulders piled up. Prospect Circle has 7 houses on it, and they look like they were stamped out of a mold. There are two designs, both bland, and it looks like the beginning of a cloned suburban hell.

Auburn Lake Road is 3.9 miles long from the bridge to the stop sign at the end of it. There are 14 houses staggered randomly along the road. They come in various styles and sizes but most are on the larger side, and tend to be farm houses, or colonials. There is one gambrel style home, which I was always partial to when I drove home from work each day. It just looked homey to me.

State Route 18 was the road that the stop sign was at. It's also the road the gas station is on, and is the same road I saw the young couple with the little kid on. It's a fairly minor state route, really just a road, but whatever. Names hardly matter now. Clustered around the stop sign and the gas station there are 15 homes within about a hundred and fifty yards.

My plan intended on clearing the houses all the way down to the gas station as well as the bunch of houses right there. If you attended 3rd grade math you have probably realized that is a grand total of 45 homes. Geez Louise, that's a shitload of real estate. So the real plan then becomes where do I start, and in which direction do I move? During my drive to count homes and whatnot I came to the conclusion I would start at the gas station area on Route 18, and move up Auburn Lake Road back to campus.

This makes the most sense to me right now because I will be creating noise, and if the noise attracts zombies I would rather attract them to areas further away from campus if possible. How far does the sound of a gunshot travel? This will tell me if you think about it. I kill the zombies at the gas station, and draw in all the zombies that heard the gunshot to that area. I kill them. Theoretically I will then have killed all the zombies in earshot, thus creating a large buffer zone around the school. After all those zombies are dead, the only ones I really should have to worry about are the ones that are drawn into the area by errant noises, wildlife movement, or say if a car drives down Route 18 and drags some zombies behind them.

What do you think Mr. Journal? Solid logic and reasoning? I guess your opinion doesn't matter because I already started. I know, I know. You're offended I didn't come to you first and check for your opinion. Relax, take a chill pill. What's done is done, and we cannot lament what we cannot change.

Jesus I should take my own advice. I could totally get on Oprah with that bullshit. You know that's a totally random question. Is Oprah still alive? Broadcasting from some nuclear bunker about her book club? I bet she is. If I was Oprah-rich I would be too. I mean I wouldn't be broadcasting from my nuclear bunker about Oprah's book club. I'd be talking about something entirely different. Like video games, or maybe the pros and cons of breast augmentation. Natural, versus enhanced? Food for thought Mr. Journal.

You know that makes a lot of sense the more I think about it. I bet she started all this in her final phase of global domination. In six months she and an army of production assistants from her show will come out of this massive vault in Illinois somewhere with a magical vaccine that fixes everything. The world will bow down to Harpo Productions and we will be forced to build shrines in her visage on our living room mantles.

Now that's a truly horrific scenario Mr. Journal. And that's coming from a guy who shot his mom because she was trying to eat him. Demented shit.

Back to the story at hand here. I forgot to mention earlier in this entry that I checked my enormous funeral pyre yesterday morning and as expected, there was still a gigantor pile of dead bodies smoldering near staff housing. I spent most of yesterday digging out decent, dry wood and getting the fire going again. I took a big risk and started the burn during dusk, but I'm fairly sure the smoke wasn't visible in the sky. Today when I checked the pile again there was almost nothing left. I shoveled it up into the dump truck, brought it down the road far away from the lake and buried it in an old crumbling house foundation. Problem solved. (knock on wood)

That was most of yesterday. When I was done doing that I was exhausted, so I fired up the generator, kicked back in my recliner with Otis, and watched a DVD. I actually fell asleep in the recliner with Otis on my chest, which was actually kind of cool. What DVD you ask? I'm happy to hear you're interested in my movies tastes. All I have here at the moment is whatever the kids had, or whatever staff had here. Selection is limited. However, I was pleased to find one of the dorkier kids in Hall C had a plethora of movies in my bailiwick, and last night I watched Office Space. Love that movie. Sameer.. Niya.... neeya..... not gonna work here anymore. Lol. Love Mike Judge.

Clearing houses. Right. Alright so in my brain I've been exhausting small details of the clearing of these houses for days now. Shoveling dead bodies.. I'm planning ahead. Lifting concrete blocks.. I'm planning ahead. I'm rubbing one out.. I'm planning ahead. You get the idea.

I'm using the Tundra. It's more agile than the dump truck and I just like it. I figure I will bring the shotgun, the .22, and the Sig. I have my hunting vest on over Dr. Potter's winter jacket. I am a little warm that way, but the coat is pretty heavy duty and it should help if I am bitten. Fuck the fleece jacket for now.

Pants-wise I am opting for cargo pocketed khakis. I've got a semi-professional first aid kit set up in a pocket, should I get hurt, and I am wearing my boots. As luck would have it, one of the kids had an enormous head like me, and also happened to keep his High School football helmet. I am bringing it with me in the event I feel like I need a helmet. I don't like the way my hearing is muffled wearing it though, so I'm hoping I don't need to be an honorary member of the Greenfield Spartans, class of '08.

I am fully ammo'd up on these runs as well as wearing my short sword. I think that's pretty good. In the truck I have a full first aid kit, as well as a few gallons of water, and some food so I don't have to drive back here if I don't need to.

I started with the house that was furthest from the gas station. I am being very careful to announce my presence to anyone inside the houses before I attempt to enter them. My great worry is someone hiding inside will see me trying to break in and they will attack me or shoot me. I did three houses today, and all went exactly the same.

Pull into driveway, honk horn repeatedly. Exit vehicle without shotgun or rifle drawn to illustrate my non violent intentions. Make a grand showing of myself and holler in that I am here to help them if they need it. If they do not want help, open a window and tell me so. I do this for 5 minutes. After that, I assume the house is unoccupied by the living, I get the .22, and clear the surrounding area. I check all entrances, outlying sheds, barns, garages, etc. I also check in all the windows to see if anything is moving inside. The first house I checked was completely empty of living, dead, and undead, which was a nice start.

Pictures on the walls showed an older couple with two teenage kids, and the bedrooms confirmed that. They had a boatload of good food. The house smelled awful though, especially after I opened the fridge. Big mistake there. No more checking in fridges. The rotting, moldy food inside was almost acidic in smell and I shut it as fast I could. It was so vinegary and nasty my eyes actually watered for a few minutes.

The second house I cleared was a little smaller than the first. One floor ranch with a two car attached garage. No cars in either yards by the way. Honked, hollered, checked the yard, found nothing dangerous. I did find a dog chained in the backyard though that had clearly died from starvation.

That really hit a nerve with me. I started to think about how many pets were left behind just like that. There must be millions of dead animals that starved to death, or died of dehydration out there after their owners died. God that makes so frigging sad. Just imagining it makes me half angry, and half heart-broken.

The shed had a bag of concrete, which was awesome, and I could see some movement through the bay window in front of the house. I'm loathe to break windows now so I didn't shoot the zombie I saw standing inside. It was an older man that looked like a suicide, or perhaps a stroke or something. He didn't look bitten or anything, so I just made an assumption. Maybe he starved like his dog.

I backed the Tundra up on the lawn right in front of the bay window and laughed as he continued to try and climb through his window. He kept falling down on the couch that was against it, getting up, trying again, and falling again. It's like that Greek dude who keeps pushing the rock up the hill over and over. Zombies and their never ending journey for meat.

I turned on the stereo in the truck and blasted a CD. My selection for this house was a Pat Benatar CD that the previous owner had in there. Not really my bag, but the music wasn't really for me anyway. I made a big show to the dead guy inside of walking right up to the window, then lowering myself out of sight so he couldn't see me slip around the back of the house. I snuck a peek through a side window to make sure he was still going at the truck, and once I saw he was, I went around back and tried the door. Mercifully it was unlocked. I slipped inside, found my way through the house, and popped him once in the head from behind.. I was sort of pissed though, because the frigging bullet went through his head and broke the damn window, which was exactly what I was trying to avoid. Oh well. Guess he'll have to file a claim on his homeowners insurance.

The house had one hallway leading off the living room

and as I started down it another zombie came out of one of the rooms. It was an older lady who was butt ass naked. Her arms were ripped open from what looked like self inflicted wounds. Just gaping rents running from wrist to elbow. I shuddered a bit, backed up a few steps, and shot her twice. First bullet hit her in the head but didn't kill for some reason. Small brain? Thick skull? Who knows? I've seen people shot with AK-47's that hopped up after like it was a bee sting. The world is filled with weirdness.

Turns out she had come out of the bathroom, and when I went in there the tub was half filled with coagulated blood. My guess is she took a bath, slashed her wrists, and that was it. Another sad story that doesn't fucking matter. I dragged their bodies out into their yard near the dog's body, killed the Pat Benatar soundtrack, and went back inside to scavenge their shit. Not nearly as much worth taking, but still good stuff. Lots of Spam. Don't laugh Mr. Journal. It's a refined and classy meal when the world has fallen apart.

Third house was larger, and was totally empty like the first. This house belonged to a fairly good sized family, and it was pretty well stocked. I was really pleased with the haul of just food crap I got out of it. I think I added maybe 20% to my existing food supplies just from these three houses. Very exciting. Not too dangerous either. There was a note on the kitchen table that was written hastily that explained that the family had gone to their in laws up north, and that anyone looking for them should go there.

I packed up, made sure everything was good to go, and headed back up here. Doing all that took up pretty much every bit of daylight I wanted to spend down there, which worked out perfect. Once back I got everything inside and organized.

Major items of note that are cool: 120 cans of various foods. Lots and lots of the canned pasta crap, which is pretty yummy, and surprisingly nutritious for shitty food. I got the concrete, 20 more blocks and a handful of bricks, as well as 8 sheets of plywood from the 2nd house. Major score on the plywood. He also had a handful of 4x4's and 2x4's.

Toiletries were a heavy score as well, and someone in the third house was a nurse or something, because their hallway closet upstairs looked more like an emergency room than a place to store linens. I was a little bummed I didn't find much in the way of medicines, but between the three houses I did get a lot of pills like aspirin, Ibuprofen, ex-lax etc. Lots of rubbing alcohol, bacitracin, and hydrogen peroxide too, which is great. Household remedy stuff. I got a bunch of razor blades for shaving, extra socks out the ass, some properly sized boxers for my ass, and best of all, about a hundred new CDs and DVDs.

Mr. Journal, a wonderful day. I secured all those supplies and cleaned out three houses using only 3 bullets. I plan on doing more of the same the next few days. If I can keep this pace up, I will have the entire neighborhood clean in 14 more days. Mmm… doubtful.

Well, I gotta get something to eat here, and Otis looks hungry too, so I am off. I'll write more entries in the next few days as I get time and energy. Hopefully things will go well and I can talk more about some of the other crap that happened before I started writing in this diary. There's a few good stories left in me still. Plus I haven't even scratched the surface with anything about me really. Although I'm not a terribly interesting guy.

Have a good night Mr. Journal.

-Adrian

November 22nd

Guess who is Oprah-rich?! Mr. Journal I bagged a motherfucking deer. Right out the second floor window of

Hall E as I was getting my frigging shoes on this morning! I sat up, scratched Otis's head for a minute, got my feet dressed, stood up, looked out the window and saw a good sized buck at the stream. Snagged the hunting rifle, slowly cranked the window open and about 15 seconds later I was balls deep in venison.

Mr. Journal I hope you aren't a Bambi fan because venison is fucking delicious! After I dropped it I got all geared up and headed out to gut it and get it back here to dress it up. I'm not an expert at dressing deer, but I did a great job all things considered. It's frigid out right now still so I think the meat will freeze if I get it outside and leave it in the shade. That means most of today will be spent getting the meat preserved, and finding a way to store it.

Fresh frigging meat. Omfg. Seriously.

-Adrian

November 22nd (2nd entry)

I am doubly Oprah-rich. Got me some potting soil today! Oh man, what a day though. I turned one of the small brick sheds into a smokehouse. Pretty easy really. Got everything out and stored in a different building, then strung up some of the wire I found months ago to hang the meat off of. I made sure to cut the deer up into small enough chunks that it'd smoke/dry a little quicker than normal too. Hung all the meat from the rafters, then went out and found a maple tree. Conveniently maples are more or less everywhere up here, so I didn't have to go far to find one.

Unfortunately I had to use the little chainsaw again, but campus has been empty of zombies for a long time now. I haven't seen shit on my patrols lately, so I'm thinking it'll be okay. Anyhow I got the maple down, chopped it into logs, got some in the center of the brick maintenance building, and started a really slow smoldering fire. Now wet, fresh wood burns smoky, and that's exactly what I want. I want a little bit of heat, but mostly just the smoke to seal the venison and preserve it. Plus the maple flavor will get into the meat too. Mmmmm.. maple flavored venison. Boing, boner.

I had enough salt in the cafeteria tubs as well to brine up a few of the venison chops. Those will last a few weeks too and it preserves a lot of my variety in what the venison choices are. I don't want all the venison to just be maple flavored. I can't remember exactly, but I think it's 2 or 3 days of smoking will preserve the meat. Brining is done already, so that meat should keep in a plastic bag in the cold outdoors indefinitely.

Enough of that. Before I went off campus today I dug out the propane grill from staff housing and cooked up a venison steak. I really don't have words. It was transcendent. I gave Otis a few little bits too and he was rolling around and rubbing up on everything. I think he got his own kitty sized boner. We were the happiest people in the whole world earlier. God that was good. I mean so good. I could theoretically have fresh venison for like 4 or 5 weeks easily. Straight to January, assuming I live that long. I'm going to have an erection over this for days. I am fucking tent poling it. I need sweatpants.

Feeling positive though all things considered. I have meat now, and I got some potting soil earlier which means I can start a little indoor garden in some pots. Fresh tomatoes and herbs sound pretty sexy. Gotta figure out what to do about growing shit tomorrow night after I get in from clearing houses. I am typing 900 miles an hour right now. So excited.

After I got the smokehouse set up I ate the shit out of that venison. I don't mean that I went out to the deer corpse and ate the poo in the deer's butt, what I mean is that I voraciously and eagerly ate the venison I cooked on the grill. I felt that needed a little extra explanation. After that I had enough time to clear one house. Sticking with the plan, I went back down to the area of the gas station, and went to the house next in line to the one I did last yesterday. Speaking of yesterday.....

Cleared 3 more houses on the 21st. I previously mentioned there are 15 houses around the gas station that needed clearing, and I had already done 3 of those. I cleared three more yesterday, which leaves 9 remaining on Route 18 coming into today. Yesterday's haul was decent, but not as overwhelming as the first day. Little bit of food, bunch of cleaning supplies and minor medical crap. The best thing that came out of yesterday's clearing was two five gallon spare gas cans. That'll improve my gas runs. Speaking of which, I should probably do one soon again. I've had to run the generator much longer during the day than I would like to keep Hall E warm. It has gotten very cold very quickly this year.

So yesterday I didn't encounter anything dead, undead or alive. Just empty dusty houses. I think the three families or residents or whatever cleared out and took the majority of their shit. Lots of stuff missing from the houses that you would expect to see. Picture frames, lots of office drawers open with paperwork missing, and empty fridges. Yes I know I swore I wouldn't check fridges again, but two of the three houses had the fridges open already, and I couldn't resist opening the third one. Refrigerators are my Pandora's Box apparently.

Anyhoo, moral of the story is I didn't kill anything, but I also didn't find much of anything. They can't all be winners I suppose. Did I tell you I got venison? Win!

Today was different on both counts. I knew from looking around yesterday that one house had several zombies in it, and I kinda made a plan to hit that house today. I thought it was a good idea to remove them before they broke a window, or managed to get a door open. Contained zombies (at least on paper) are a little easier to deal with than the roaming ones. Less likely to sneak up on me.

So the house with the zombies, the one I went to today is

a cape. It's got a detached two car garage, and has cedar shingle siding. Dormers on the second floor, very nice really. I would even say it's upscale. There were four zombies inside that I could see. Two adults and two kids. I tried the truck plan again, but it didn't work for shit. Backed it up into the yard like normal, and jacked up the Pat Benatar music, but I couldn't get them to come my way and stay that way. I'd get one or two over at window, but after a bit they'd walk off, or when I tried to slip away, they'd follow me around the house. Kinda sucked. I even brought a small selection of CD's with me from the other day, and tried a few different bands. They were not fans of Chevelle, Crosby Still & Nash, or Rihanna. Sad really. No taste these dead guys.

Plan B was to set the house on fire and say fuck it. But once again I realized that the only thing that scares me more than zombies is zombies that have been set on fire. I could just picture the house burning down enough that the zombies would escape, chase me down, set me on fire, and then eat me. Sort of like what happened to that deer this morning.

Sooo… plan C. I did not have a plan C. Plan A worked to so well up til now that I hadn't really developed a way to deal with this. The dead family was wandering around on the first floor, so smashing out a window and having them fall seemed decent, but not as effective as when I did it on Hall C back when I was clearing campus. I thought of ramming the house with the Tundra, then letting them come out and running them over, but I didn't want to risk damaging the truck. I also thought of opening the door, backing away, and hoping they came out single file.

None of those ideas appealed to me, and finally I decided to tank. Mr. Journal if you're unfamiliar with the term, it means to use your body as a meatshield. You block doorways and prevent your foes from escaping. I know, it wasn't ideal, but I had my Greenfield Spartans football helmet handy, and I was feeling a little invulnerable with a full belly of venison. Did I tell you I got venison? It's delicious!

I went to the side door of the house near the garage. I situated the Tundra so it was aimed out of their driveway, and I got the passenger side door open so that if I had to bolt, I could run and dive into that door and be off in a jiffy. I got the shotgun, slapped the helmet on, and propped their screen door open. This side door opened into their kitchen, and I could kinda see down a hallway, and sort of into the opening that led to the living room. The mother came to the door as I was getting ready, and started scratching and hitting the glass pretty hard, so I leveled the gauge off at her head through the window, and annihilated her face. Point blank like that with the glass in the way it was just frigging spectacular. Not in the creepy gory way, but..., you know actually there's no way to say spectacular in regards to decapitation by shotgun and not have it be in the creepy gory way. Disregard all of that Mr. Journal.

Her head blew the fuck up.

It was at that point I realized I didn't have to open the door. If I just stood there and waited, theoretically I could shoot all of them just like that, as they came to the door. So I took a step back, and let it happen. 15 seconds later, their little boy came around the corner from another room, and came at the door. I couldn't bear to shoot him with my eyes open, so I closed them once he got to the door, and shot at the space I thought his head was in. He was bumping into the door, reaching up through the shattered glass at me, cutting the flesh on his arms to ribbons. Thankfully I got lucky on the first shot and hit him right in the head. I think the venison high is keeping me sane today. Right after I shot the little boy, their daughter came straight down the hallway, and I had to do the same thing. Just couldn't pull the trigger while looking. Reminded me too much of seeing dead kids in Iraq. I am concerned about being rushed by a bunch of kid zombies now though. I'm not sure how I'll react to that.

Gotta keep telling this story or I'll dwell and get all depressed about it. Sickens me. Dad zombie never came to the door. Maybe it was creepy uncle zombie? I never found any family pictures in the house either, which was weird. I'm starting to think that these people didn't live here before all this shit went down. Maybe they were squatters who stopped for some reason. You know that does make some sense, because there were no cars in the garage, or driveway.

Anyway, squatter zombie dad (or creepy uncle) never came to the door to get shotgunned conveniently. I reached inside the shattered window on the side door, unlocked it, and let myself into the kitchen. The center island provided a good barricade, so I went around it the long way to have cover from anything coming out of the living room. I couldn't see him in there, so I slowly went down the hallway. I got about halfway down the hall when I started to hear this.... chewing, crunching noise. It was coming from room at the end of the hall. I kinda hastily cleared the room in the center of the hall, and moved down to the end, shotgun up.

All I could see at first was the dad zombie crouched down in the doorway, holding something to his mouth. I figured out instantly he was eating something, and he was totally absorbed in it. I slung the shotgun real quick and pulled out the blade. One quick downward stab at the base of the skull and he went flat on the floor. I had to curbstomp his face a couple times to get him to stop twitching, but eventually he was down. Turns out he was eating some kind of mouse or something. Couldn't tell really seeing as how he had it mostly fucking chewed up by the time I killed him. Stomping on his head most likely didn't help either. Bet that was why he never came to the door. Found a more convenient meal. You know that really frigging befuddles me. How the hell was he fast enough to catch a mouse, but they're too slow and stupid to get me? Have I discovered the better mousetrap? Hm.

Cleared the rest of the house with no issues. Basement was creepy as a motherfucker, but it was empty. It had the open stone foundation, and had a low ceiling. Cobwebs all over the place. No electricity meant using my little flashlight, which does not make for a comforting experience. Finding a zombie in a dark ass basement with a flashlight might give me a heart attack. I can see it now. I come around a furnace, or a pile of boxes, I'm sort of distracted by falling dust, I look away, and when I look back BOOM! There's a bloody zombie right there in front of me. I won't need to be eaten alive at that point, I'll just drop fucking dead of a heart attack. Luckily, no coronary seizure today for me.

The house had very little in the way of food or supplies, which lends more credence to the idea that the original folks left with everything. I did find a few little useful items here and there, but nothing really outstanding. However... when I checked the garage, I hit the "mother load." Apparently the original residents had a garden, and they were very serious about that garden. There were an assortment of fertilizer bags, top soil, ulti-chem-nutra-food or whatever you call it, and tons of tools, pots, dowels for propping up plants, and even two or three really good books on gardening. Mega score in my book. The ubah.

Heavy as shit though. Loaded up the truck, did a once over of the house again, moved the bodies outside into the garden area, and came back up here to get everything all settled. I did a quick patrol of the grounds just in case. I was a little paranoid about using the chainsaw earlier, but nothing was up here that I saw, so I think I'm all good. Oh shit I forgot to mention that house had cat food! So Otis is still in supply for his needs. I was a little worried the bag of dry food might've been rotten, but I checked it earlier and it'll be fine. There was also a half dozen cans of the wet food, which I'll save for special occasions for him. Thanksgiving is coming up after all.

As for tonight, I think I am going to burn a handful of CDs for my house clearing enjoyment. I found a stash of burnable discs back when I was searching the dorm rooms a few weeks ago. That seems like something to do. Maybe I'll throw some Gaga on there for experimental purposes.

Strictly scientific reasons of course.

Still need to figure out what to do with this boner though.

-Adrian

November 25th

Happy turkey day Mr. Journal. Here in America we call today Thanksgiving. On Thanksgiving we usually eat turkey, hence the turkey day greeting. Today though, I am eating venison. Why break with tradition you ask? Well, I don't have any turkey, and because venison is fucking delicious. Really yummy. Wouldn't lie. I guess the point of Thanksgiving is to take some time out of our lives and realize what we are thankful for.

I thought I would talk about what I am thankful for with some of this entry today. I don't think I ever sat down and really, truly thought about what I was thankful for before the world came to an end. Well, the end as we know it. The world is still moving along I guess, we're just disappearing off of it. I'm off track here.

I am thankful for being alive. I don't even know how many people across the world have died because of whatever is happening, but I am thankful that thus far, I have avoided being eaten, or getting sick, or whatever causes this.

I am thankful that I still have Otis my cat. Otis is my homeboy. No one really ever got along with me as well as he did, and the fact that I still have him with me keeps me far saner than I would be otherwise. I'm thankful for his purring when I scratch him, I'm thankful for his killing of mice, and I'm thankful for his warmth on cold nights.

I am thankful for all the weapons my man Phil at Moore's sold me the day the shit hit the fan. I am thankful

223

for all the ammunition. I am thankful for the spare magazines. I am thankful for the additional ammunition and the rifle I got there when I went back. I am also thankful for the .45 I found at the gas station.

I am thankful for all the food I got at the grocery store the day the zombies first appeared. I know I took more than I needed that day, and I know I was kind of a prick to the people there, and I do kind of regret that, but at least I am still alive, and thankful for the opportunity to try and help others. I am thankful I survived the trip back there right after all this shit started too. What a fucking nightmare that was.

I am thankful for my family. Well, I am thankful that while I still had them, they were for the most part good to me. Mom, Dad, three brothers and sister. I don't think I have ever fully listed their names off anywhere actually. Here's the list Mr. Journal; Margaret and Thomas are (were) my parents. In order, we are; Caleb, Myself, Thomas Jr., William, and littlest sister Rebecca. There you have it, the Ring clan. I am thankful for their merciless beatings (eat my ass Caleb), their blaming of their mistakes on me (fuck you Tommy), and all the detentions for beating up my sister's suitors. (love you Becca.)

I am thankful for having been in love with someone. I think there are far too many people in false relationships that stay in them because they think they are in love. There's such a thing as being in love with someone, and then being in love with the IDEA of being in love with someone. Teen love is usually the latter. I loved Cassie, and I know she loved me back. For that I am eternally grateful. I am sorry I didn't do more for you baby. I will always be sorry.

I am thankful for the deer that came to the stream the other morning. I am thankful the meat from him was delicious. I am thankful it has preserved itself well. Very thankful.

Enough being thankful. I'm starting to feel all preachy Mr. Journal, and I am not a preacher. I can give a sermon for sure, God knows I've lectured the shit out of the kids here a

few times, but I've got other shit to talk about now. Alright…
so it's been a few days and I have a fair amount of catching
you up to do.

It's now Thursday evening. Continuing with my plan to
clear houses and do all the things needed to make campus
inhabitable by others, I have been a busy dork. The day of
the 23rd I spent clearing houses down on Route 18. I
managed to clear 3 more empty-ish places. Yesterday I
cleared the remaining 3 houses on Route 18. Officially, all 15
of those homes are empty of zombies, and have been
stripped of the best supplies in them. As you might imagine,
it went not according to plan.

The three houses I did on the 23rd were completely
mundane. I found more of the same old, same old. One
house had almost entirely been stripped clean already. It
looked like the owners packed up and moved. The other two
houses were just kind of poorly stocked. A somewhat
disturbing find was a cupboard filled with jars of dusty baby
food. Made me wonder where the baby was. Hopefully safe
somewhere with the parents. I took the baby food just in
case. I might meet someone with a baby, or God forbid, I'll
be around people who start making them.

Yesterday was a little more problematic. When I returned
down to Route 18 to do the last three houses there was a
handful of walking zombies moving around the area. I saw
them when I came to a stop at the stop sign near the gas
station. Most were milling about, moving in the same
general direction, due west. There were eleven of them,
which was the most I'd seen since my trip to the grocery
store the first week of July. I'd kind of hoped to never see a
batch that large again, but I guess that just wasn't in the
cards.

Here's the dilemma. Get out of the truck and shoot them
from as far away as possible? Go all Grand Theft Auto on
them and commit some heavy duty vehicular
zombieslaughter? Or search for a flamethrower and burn

them to a crisp? I think by now Mr. Journal you understand that I am painfully afraid of zombies that have been set aflame, so I got rid of that idea quickly. Well my phobia of burning zombies coupled with a total lack of a flamethrower.

I was worried about damage to the Tundra, but I was more worried about wasting ammo. This truck had 4x4, and excellent ground clearance, so I opted for a slow-roll GTA experience. Three of the walking dead were to the right of the stop sign, almost right in front of the gas station. They were already moving towards me, so I turned towards them, accelerated to about 15 miles an hour, and aimed for the closest zombie. I think it was a younger guy, and I hit him square with the grill. Wanted to save the headlights. Slow hits don't launch the bodies up quite so much, and it seems like you're more likely to run them over at that speed, which was the goal here. I bonked him good, drove over him, and steered into the other pair. Two females. Mixed ages. One of them was a complete wreck, almost entirely naked, missing an arm and half her face. I plonked the two of them just like the dude, and hit reverse to make sure they were mangled so much they were a non-issue. I noticed in the rearview the batch of eight down the road were turned around and heading my way, so I sped it up and got turned around.

By the time I maneuvered the truck around in the road and aimed it at the small horde of approaching undead they were right on top of the truck, banging on the hood and coming around the side. I threw it in reverse and backed up 15 or 20 more feet, then slammed it in drive. I hit the gas a little too hard though, and slammed into the pack of zombies faster than I wanted to. Two of them directly in front were men, both of their chests and throats eaten open and exposed. They were tall enough that when I hit them they flew up and over, as opposed to getting knocked down and ran over. They tumbled across the hood, and one of them hit the windshield hard enough to send cracks all through it. Fortunately it was the passenger side. That irritated the piss out of me. The other guy just left a huge bloody streak on the hood and fell off.

That dead guy who hit the windshield managed to get his clothes hooked on the frigging wiper blade too, so as I drove forward and over the other zombies I'd managed to knock down, he stayed stuck to the hood firmly. I remember clearly him flopping about, trying to hold on, all the while staring intently into the cab at me, white, pus-filled eyes fixated on me. I swear I felt total hatred coming from him. I slammed on the breaks though, and his clothes gave way, and he shot off the hood and spun on the pavement in front of the truck. I gave it some juice and drove over his haterade ass. Don't hate the player Mr. Zombie, hate the game.

I pulped up the rest of the walkers by simply going back and forth with the truck in the middle of the road. I had to get out though and finish off a few of them that I couldn't run over. One of them spun out pretty bad when I hit him, and he landed propped up against a tree, well off the road. I had to shoot him with the .22 too. A bummer, wasting bullets like that. But, he came at me pretty quick when I went at him with the sword, and he was a big motherfucker and I didn't want to die. I guess killing a zombie with a bullet can't be a waste. It's a dead zombie right? Using the sword would be more resource efficient, but using a bullet isn't a waste. There, I feel better about it. Rationalization for the win.

As best I could I got the bodies out of the road. I didn't want it filled with obstacles made out of bodies, and I also didn't want to draw too much attention to the area. A dozen dead bodies in the road might raise someone's suspicions. So after clearing out the completely random zombie herd I focused on getting into the three houses I wanted to clear. I followed the same pattern as before. Honk repeatedly, make my presence known, etc etc. Nothing came out, and I didn't see anything moving inside, so I entered the houses and cleared them as normal. The first house was a pretty standard farmhouse design. Three floors, white with black shutters. Huge ass attached barn. Not much in the way of great supplies to be found, although they did have a couple

12 packs of decent toilet paper. Doesn't seem like much Mr. Journal, but I assure you if you use sub-par toilet paper too long your asshole WILL get chapped. No one wants a chapped ass.

Barn had some cool outdoorsy tools but again, not much to celebrate over. The house was a bust, right down to the creepy ass basement I had to clear with my fucking small flashlight. Surprisingly Mr. Journal, I have not yet found a decent flashlight in any of these houses. I wonder why that is? One of life after the zombie apocalypse's small mysteries. Where did all the flashlights go?

Second house was much smaller but had a few things worth taking. Whoever lived there frigging loved video games, which is cool because I am a fan as well. They had the whole setup including a 50 inch flatsceen HDTV, PS3, Wii, and Xbox360. Fortunately I am a pretty strong dude, and I was able to get the tv into the truck by myself. Up until now I was just using an old school crappy tv from one of the dorm common rooms. Now my limited television and video gaming time is greatly improved. He also had a ton of good movies and CDs too, which amps up my collection for entertainment.

That house also had some pretty sweet snack food. Video gamer dude was a really big fan of chips. There were about 8 bags of assorted corn chips, tortilla chips, and cheese coated puffs. He also had a few full boxes of snack cakes and about 10 full 12 packs of sodas. Jackpot Mr. Journal? You be the judge. I'm stoked for the junk food, but it's junk food. Empty calories for the most part.

House three was the best of the bunch in terms of straight up loot. That's saying something considering house #2 scored me a 50 inch flatscreen. I am mostly concerned with having enough food to survive the winter right now, so any food I find is good, and any food that's canned is worth its weight in gold. House 3 was a mini Fort Knox for me. I found zilch in the house proper. They had a reasonably well stocked pantry filled with lots of usable foods. There were multiple boxes of cereal, and most amazingly, 5 boxes of dried milk, one of the things I had forgotten to grab any of at the grocery store. Who ever lived here really liked dry milk. I haven't had real milk in some time, so this will be a big treat going forward.

Downstairs was the real treasure trove. Large tin cans of juice. There were multiple cardboard flats of 6 cans stacked neatly in the corner. They had tomato juice, pineapple juice, grapefruit juice, apple juice, fruit punch, and a few other random flavors. I think that's the real jackpot Mr. Journal. Without a regular heavy dose of vitamin C I'm actually at risk for getting scurvy. It's not just a pirate's problem Mr. Journal. Arr.. it happens to survivors of the apocalypse too! Arrr! Sorry that was…. lame.

Problem solved though. Plenty of good vitamins in the all those juices. Really stoked for the tomato juice. Makes me want to get the indoor garden started, which I haven't yet. I think I'm going to maybe do one or two houses tomorrow instead of three and use the rest of the time to relax and get the pots going. I'm starting to really burn out lifting all this bullshit all day long. I'm strong, but I'm not a machine.

I cleared out the house and the vault of juice in the basement. I was pretty much pulling out of the driveway when I noticed a shed in the far back of the property. I had to check it, so I stopped the car, backed right into the back yard, hopped out, and walked back to shed. It was shaped like a barn, with the angular yet rounded roof. It was even red. One of the aluminum deals you could get at a lot of hardware and lumber stores back in the 80's and 90's. Junk really, but they worked for folks without a lot of cash. I got to within 10 feet of the door and saw it was ajar. Normally not that much of a red flag, but right about then I caught a whiff of something wretched inside.

I used the shotgun barrel to push the door wide open. Once I got done throwing up I sat down in the cold grass in the yard for a few minutes. It's kind of hard to talk about this Mr. Journal. Weird. Inside the shed I found about 15 dead animals. All had been strangled, as best as I could figure. Sitting in the far back of the shed, buried in the carcasses of the dead animals was a frail little old lady. The top of her head was sheared clean off by some large blade. On hands and knees facing this macabre shrine, naked and covered in blood was a teenage boy. Somehow he had driven a knife up under his chin, through the roof of his mouth, and into his own brain. I think he fell on it that way. Purposefully.

I have no idea how this came to be, or why this happened. I just don't get it. I kinda forgot about it up until right now too. I was so excited to tell you about my haul today I'd sent the memory away.

Man.... Fucked up.

I am thankful I still have my cat. I am thankful I wasn't around when whatever happened in that shed went down. Fucking atrocious.

I think I sat like that in the middle of their lawn for 10 minutes before I heard a car coming. I was still kind of in shock, so I just sat still, frozen. I could only see the car a little as it drove by, but it was an upscale sedan of some form. A black BMW or Mercedes. It bombed by down the road at like 50 miles an hour, and never stopped, or even looked my way. I could see a brief glimpse of at least two people in the car. I clearly saw a long shock of red hair on a female passenger.

People. Survivors. Moving through the area.

Exciting? Horrifying? I just don't know.

I left the house and came back here. Got everything in, got the HDTV set up, chilled out for awhile, had some food, and spent the majority of last night playing Playstation. Put off getting the pots together for my indoor garden until today.

As for earlier today, I got up at the crack of dawn, geared myself up, and headed down to the gas station again. I was curious if there would be more of the roaming undead again. There was. I pulled down the hill to the stop sign a bit slower today, and stopped far before it. There were 5 zombies, doing the same thing as the bunch yesterday. Milling about, slowly moving, but today they were headed to the east. I think they were following the luxury car I saw drive by yesterday. If the mob yesterday saw the car heading west, they might've followed it for some time, eventually maybe losing interest, or who knows what. Same thing today, only when the car comes back through.

It certainly raises the question of whether or not the undead follow cars. Once they get moving in a direction, they seem to keep moving in that direction until something gets their attention. If nothing else does, they just keep moving forward indefinitely. That's sheer theory Mr. Journal. I have no proof of this.

Definitely scary though. If it's true, then it confirms my fears that anything that comes through the campus with a zombie behind it will drag that zombie behind it. I really wonder if one zombie will get the attention of other zombies? I haven't seen them attack each other ever, and I've seen them alone, and in groups. I wonder if they unwittingly form groups because of some base, evil instinct? Fucked if I know.

Point at hand was there were 5 zombies meandering slowly towards town to the east. I was comfortable with using the truck as a battering ram again, so I aimed at the cluster right in the middle of the road and gave it the gas. Ran over them pretty solidly, and turned around down the road for an encore. Hit the last two walkers after they got bunched up with each other, and finished the ones that didn't get their head busted with the sword. As safely done as can be imagined. I dragged the bodies off the road again.

I am… really starting to think about putting the school's plow on one of the dump body Fords. It's got the attachments for it, and I helped Doug the maintenance dude do it a few times. I could do it pretty easily. I'm thinking I could do some serious damage with a snowplow. Mmm. Snowplow. Mmm. Zombieplow. That doesn't sound right at all. *thinks of bunnies*

Much better now. Palate cleansed.

After that I decided I'd clear oneb house on Auburn Lake Road. There was one house fairly separate from the others that was actually the first house on the street. Typical white house, black shutters. Huge wraparound porch though. Must've been a great hangout for sunsets and early mornings with a hot cup of coffee. Maybe next summer I'll come back and do just that.

This house had a large barn in the backyard, and after I made my presence known, I cleared that first. Yet another disturbing find. This barn was big, with a giant loft filled with hay. Hanging from one of the barn beams was a dead guy. He had clearly hung himself, and started to kick and scratch at the air as soon as I entered the barn. Must've been desperate to end his own life, but I'm not gonna judge. There must've been millions of suicides. I can't even fathom the despair the world felt, is still feeling.

I cleared the barn real quick, and retrieved the .22 from the truck. I popped him once in the head and his jerky movements came to an abrupt stop. His limp body just swayed back and forth in the crisp breeze. He'll swing like that until his neck disintegrates.

The house was empty. Well, empty of people and zombies. I spent an inordinate amount of time opening doors though. Every single fucking door in that place was shut and locked. I know I said I wanted to use the shotgun to blast doors open, but it became apparent that'd be a huge waste of ammo. I would up sniff testing every door, knocking loudly, waiting, and then eventually booting every door in. My legs are killing me from all the kicking.

Luckily, the house was empty of the dead. In terms of crazy loot, there wasn't a lot. I think my hanging buddy holed up in here for some time. His trash barrels in the back were filled with cans, and his shelves were more or less bare. The big haul was a giant still sealed container of instant coffee. He also had some little stuff, but nothing really mind blowing. It was almost a waste of time. I am glad I got to shoot his body though. It would've been weird to find a zombie walking around with a noose hanging off its neck. Fucking creepy right?

Um. Yeah not much there really. Some coffee. Few cans of shitty food. Another creepy open stone foundation. He did have a five gallon gas can in the back of the barn though, which I guess is pretty neat. Starting to get a little concerned with the amount of fuel I could have laying around campus here. My boy Blue is bad enough.

I called it quits after that. Headed up here, got my meager spoils into Hall E, cleaned myself off, and made some dinner. I opened yet another can of potatoes, a can of carrots, one of those yummy cans of brown bread, and I fired up the grill for a bit to cook up one of the racks of venison short ribs. And if you didn't see this coming Mr. Journal, I opened up one of the cans of cranberry relish I got from my mom's place. I gorged myself almost to the point of nausea. Heavenly.

Today was a good day Mr. Journal. I am thankful for that. I still can't get that redhead in the car off my mind.

-Adrian

November 27th

Wassup Mr. Journal? It's Saturday, and I'm pretty exhausted. It was nice to have a relaxing afternoon on Turkey day, but as the old saying goes, there's no rest for the wicked. Going to have to take a day or two off here. My back is starting to act up, and I'm fairly sure I sprained a thumb when I caught it on a doorframe earlier. Sore as hell. Still too much to do though, and that means I'm right back at it.

I wound up waking up pretty late from my venison and vegetable rufee cocktail, so I decided to just do two houses and call it a day. I stuck with the houses on Auburn Lake

Road and just did the next two in line after the farmhouse where I shot the zombie that hung himself. I'm moving along in a geographical sense. Instead of just doing all the houses on one side of the road, I'm doing them as I come to them. The two I did yesterday were right across the street from each other, which saved me a lot of time.

The haul was mediocre. Fairly good amounts of durable foods, but the biggest items of note were a brand spanking new crock pot, and a perfectly new set of pots and pans. Doesn't sound like much really, but crock pots are the SHIT for lazy bachelors. You can cook almost anything with little risk of burning or overcooking, and it almost always comes out awesome. Fucking A, crock pot. The pots and pans are just a big upgrade over the industrial crap I've been using here in the dorm. Just nice to have better crap. Probably shouldn't call it crap though, seems counterproductive. Just nice to have better things.

So that's about it. Oh wait that's not true. One of the homes I went to yesterday had a reasonably well stocked liquor cabinet. Lots of half drank bottles of the cheap stuff, but honestly, beggars can't be choosers. I don't think I'm going to drink any of it. I'm starting to think after seeing that car that having extra of stuff, and stuff I don't need/want is a good thing. Barter materials. I might need to strike a trade someday and I know there were a lot of drunk assholes in this town. They will probably trade good and trade hard for the cheap shit.

After clearing both places Friday I came back, swapped the pots and pans out, and got my indoor garden up and running. I am starting fairly small time though. I got 10 pots filled with soil, earth, seeds, and some fertilizer. I started mint, thyme, rosemary, basil, 2 things of cherry tomatoes, 2 pots of cucumbers, and 2 things of green onions. Not sure exactly how this will work out, but they're planted, and I am not a total moron, so I should yield something edible. Just gotta keep them warm during the day, keep them watered, and make sure they get enough light.

Three more houses cleared earlier today. Zero undead. Moderate foodstuffs, the same as yesterday. Monotony for the win. Biggest haul out of today was finding a full propane tank for the grill. I'm hoping sooner or later one of these houses has one of those mega backyarder grills in it too. The one I'm using is a Walmart budget special. It works, but it sucks. Probably won't last long either. I want one of those chrome and stainless steel ones you see on display in the front of the DIY stores. That'd be nice.

So yeah, not shit today worth finding. Little bit of food, little bit of clothing that might be interesting. The definition of marginal. However, now that I've eaten a decent meal, I feel like talking about the past. I still have a lot to talk about when it comes to the time before I started the journal, and I think now is as good a time as ever to start that process up again. Feels like it's been forever since I talked about it anyway.

A lot of it is a blur, I'm going to be honest. I'm sitting here struggling trying to figure out what happened on what day, and to be honest, I'm still not sure I have it right. What I can say, is that right after the shit hit the fan, I came up here. I spent that evening, and the following day killing the undead all over the damn campus. I know I found Abigail that day after, the young girl who wound up leaving for her parent's place. I recall pretty clearly that I spent at least two days, maybe three here. I swung down to the athletics fields, found a few additional undead, and dealt with them the same as the others. I was using mostly the .22 for everything early on. I didn't have the full confidence yet to just march across a field and hack the head off. Takes some serious stones to do shit like that. Now, I'm pretty much okay with it, but back then, no thanks.

At the early stages of all this bullshit I didn't really know what was going on. Was it an infection? Was it a virus? Was it a biological weapon? Contagious? No idea. Half the shit that I learned from the CDC turned out to be bogus, so I wasn't feeling 100% confident in anything yet. I'm a lot more comfortable now, but early on, I was much more cautious and afraid of doing anything. Using the .22 meant I could kill from range, and that meant I felt much better about things.

I hesitate to say I was wasting the ammo though. I did have 2,000 rounds to use, and there's only about 8,000 people in the entire town, so I felt like it'd last a long time. Don't forget too I had 50-60 rounds of 12 gauge then, and a few hundred 9mm's as well. I'm lower on almost everything now, but at that point, I felt like I had enough to last.

So far, so good. Still have plenty of ammo. Plenty is assuming I don't get assaulted by either a ton of people, or a ton of zombies. If that happens, you can burn through ammo hardcore. Standard load for ammo on patrols was 7 magazines plus one in the M4, and we routinely took far more than that for areas that we knew we were gonna get attacked in. That's 250 rounds for a single firefight, give or take. My point is you can seriously burn through ammo when the shit gets thick. Peace through overwhelming fire superiority.

And... speaking of shit getting thick. So after my two or three day period of laying low, I made the decision that I needed to get more food. In retrospect, I probably didn't need to go back to the grocery store, especially considering the other food resources around here. I had the gas stations, the houses all around the campus, etc. But, this is only a day or two after everything started, so my mindset at the time was grocery store = food. Typical consumer thought pattern.

I think a lot of that decision came from desperate thinking. The first couple nights I didn't sleep at all. I was worried people were going to come to campus and try and kill me, or that I didn't have enough food and ammo, you get the picture. Basically I was just scared shitless that I would starve. I spent a lot of those days re-thinking everything I'd done, and wishing I'd done just about everything differently. However, I couldn't then, and still can't change the past.

I made the decision a day or two into the shit to head back into town, and try and get more food. I knew that people would eventually panic and want more food. I knew they'd probably panic soon, so I needed to get the food before them. I also knew that many folks would try and "ride it out" and had decent food stores. I wanted to get to the store before those people ran out of their own food. I was expecting the apocalypse. Madness, panic, zombies everywhere, fire, zombie on fire, wild dogs, high prices and inflation, and honestly, I thought I stood a pretty good chance of getting a rash. I was scared of finding... everything downtown. Wholesale evil. Worst case imaginable.

As it turns out, my fears weren't that far off from the truth. I went back downtown in my car, a grey Toyota Camry. Man I loved that car. Mr. Journal you will note the past-tense reference. I geared up like I was ready to rock the fucking apocalypse. Had all my clips loaded, had the guns cleaned, put my vest on, got the shells loaded into it, filled all my pockets with loose ammo, grabbed water, energy bars, had pretty much everything I needed. I decided that it'd be best if I went down early-early in the morning too. I felt that going early gave me the best chance to avoid running into other people vying for the same food as me. I was wrong, but at least my logic was decent.

I left campus at the crack of dawn. The grocery store is perhaps a twenty minute drive if you drive the speed limit, which puts it at perhaps 9 to 10 miles from campus. It is east down Route 18, couple turns left and right, and shazam, you're on Main Street, right in the middle of the retail area of town. Grocery store, hardware store, a few restaurants, plus three or four of the major manufacturers in town are in a little industrial park there. Really it's our version of Grand Central Station.

The drive down to the grocery store was pretty normal. Most of the time my drive on this route was early in the morning when I was getting out of work. Normally at those hours the roads are pretty empty anyway, so things seemed normal. Once I got through the largely wooded area just outside downtown, things got a little weirder. I saw two houses on fire. One was already burnt out and down, and the second was still raging hardcore. Obviously that was unusual. I also saw a handful of bodies in driveways, splayed out in ditches, and generally just strewn around. Seeing bodies around is also unusual. For normal country at least. I'm pretty gracious when I call America normal, incidentally.

No zombies though. Didn't see any of those until I got into the more urban area of Main Street. There's a few fast food eateries, regular restaurants, a couple pharmacies, a handful of strip malls, you know the deal. Once I was in that area, there were quite a few of the walkers. They were all slowly moving in the general direction of the grocery store too, which was a bad sign that I didn't pick up on until too late.

I kept my speed low. Mainly I didn't want to drive into a mess too fast and not be able to adjust. Plus I was worried I'd hit a zombie and smash a window, thus making the relative sanctuary of the car null and void. I pulled into the parking lot doing maybe 10 miles per hour. Almost immediately I noticed things were off. There were cars parked in a chevron pattern at the two entrances to the parking lot. The way it was set up was clearly defensive. If someone rammed the two cars parked like that, they would get pushed back into two more cars parked at right angles behind them as well, pretty much guaranteeing that you'd trash your car. You'd have to hop the huge ass curbs to get into the lot, which wasn't an option for me in the Camry.

Without saying a word, it told me people were in the grocery store. Adding fuel to that fire, there were about 20 zombies meandering around the parking lot. It was decision time. Park there, and run to the store to get what I could? Or turn and leave? Going in meant I had to deal with the dead, and likely some of the living inside as well. Leaving meant no food. In the end, my fear of starvation was greater than my fear of the zombies. I parked the car, gathered my weapons, and started to clear the parking lot.

The first few zombies I killed were the ones nearest the car. Behind me in the street were a solid half dozen that I'd driven by just a minute prior. I used the .22 and moved down the line landing my headshots pretty smooth. I think I might've missed one or two shots due to nerves, but all in all it was excellent marksmanship. After they were down, I swapped mags, and started shooting the shuffling dead that was heading across the lot towards me. I had more time to deal with them mostly because of the arrangement of cars as a blockade was between them and I. I emptied my 2nd magazine pretty quickly doing that and sat back down in the car and started to reload my empty mags out of the pocket of ammo in my vest.

That's when I heard the distinctive boom of a high caliber rifle. My car's windshield spiderwebbed instantly and I actually heard the zing and the snap of the bullet going by my head. Mr. Journal, have you ever been shot at? There are three completely different ways to be shot at. This was what I refer to as a "stage three" shot.

Stage one: You hear a gunshot. Ka-pow. End of story.

Stage two: You hear a gunshot. Immediately afterward, you hear a "zinging" noise. Stage two shots mean the bullet came close enough to you that they are aiming in your general direction.

Stage three: You hear the bang. You hear the zing. Almost simultaneously you hear a "crack" or "pop" as well. That's the sound of the bullet breaking the sound barrier near enough for you to hear it. That means that they are either really lucky, and you got accidentally close to the bullet's flight path, or they are TRYING TO KILL YOU.

As a general rule of thumb, you don't start getting really worried until you get to Stage two.

Of course the dead giveaway was the quarter sized hole

punched in my windshield about 4 inches from where my face was. Evasive action! I dove flat out of the car onto the pavement and busted the shit out of my chin. Split the bitch wide fucking open. It also rang my bell like a motherfucker. That digger made me think that when I got knocked on my ass in Mrs. Goodell's classroom I might've gotten a concussion.

I scrambled as best I could right up flush to the cars blocking the parking lot. Unlike in the classroom I didn't drop my weapon this time. I quickly finished reloading the clips while I got shot at a couple more times. Both of the new incoming rounds hit my car again, really and thoroughly fucking up the windshield, and the hood. Big, loud PONG noise as the bullet punched into it. Good news is that meant the shooter didn't know I was behind the car they'd arranged as a blockade.

I snuck back some, peeked up through the car interior, and saw a shape leaning over the roof of the grocery store. Pretty clearly a shooter aiming in my general direction. I set my trap. Likely the asshole was using a bolt action, or lever action rifle. The caliber sounded big, so I was pretty sure of that. That meant their first shot would be fast, and pretty accurate, but their second would suck as they chambered a new round. I took off a shoe, and tossed it about five feet to the side towards the other car in the blockade.

The shooter saw it, and let loose one loud round at it. He missed the shoe, and as I watched, he started to throw the bolt on his rifle to reload. Fucking clown shoes. Ridiculous. I leveled off at his profile, and quickly squeezed off a handful of shots. Remember how I said the .22 was great because of the low recoil? I didn't have to jack the bolt, or swing a lever to reload. Squeeze and fire. I saw the form tumble backwards onto the roof, simultaneously dropping the rifle forward over the edge into the parking lot. I remember laughing in celebration as I got my shoe back on. I didn't see any other shooters on the roof, so I proceeded to kill the remaining zombies that had gotten alarmingly close to me. I wound up having to drop the rifle for the last three, as I was dry on ammo in the mags. I closed in and used the pistol for the first time since clearing the campus.

Safe parking lot. Relatively speaking. I reloaded my magazines yet again, scanned the lot and the streets for zombies, and decided to cross the parking lot to get into the store. Now by this point I knew I had living people trying to shoot me. I decided moving to cover was the best option. Enough cars were left in the parking lot that I could easily move behind them, so that's what I did. I used the slow and smooth walk, and kept the rifle aimed at the entrance to the store nearest me. I noticed then that the entrance looked somewhat boarded up.

No one shot at me again during the run across the lot. Smooth sailing so to speak. I made it to the front of the store, right near where I'd shot the very first zombie I'd seen "that day" and I took cover. The doors were boarded up solid. Someone inside had taken the time to build up some damn sturdy plywood and 4x4 barricades over the automatic glass doors. I yelled and screamed for someone to answer, but no one did. I took a quick look around the front of the building, and saw that the majority of the glass windows had been shot out. Shot out pretty severely actually. It looked like downtown Fallujah up close. Pretty clearly there had been a massive firefight in the parking lot between someone outside, and someone inside. Glass was broke in both directions, and there were dozens of the tell-tale pockmarks from bullets in the brick façade.

Bad news bears kids.

I peeked inside the store through the busted out windows and saw a goddamn mess. Most of the shelves were either bare, or tipped over and ravaged. There were a solid dozen bodies draped over the registers and carts at the main checkout and I could see at least ten or more walking zombies moving in and around the aisles. Not cool at all.

Not gonna lie. Did not have a plan. I remember being all pissed off and getting angry and shit, but after a minute or so of sulking like a bitch I got myself together. I had already burned through too much fucking ammo in my opinion, but that just meant I was pot committed. I couldn't fold without seeing the river and the river was inside the store.

I needed to kill everything inside without going inside. I was at a busted window, and had clear lines of sight to about ten of the zombies, so I decided to treat it like a firing range. I checked the parking lot for any zombies that might've wandered in behind me, saw it was clear, and started popping off the dead folk in the store. The expression fish in a barrel is pretty appropriate here.

I saw about ten, but shot nearly forty. After I went through all my magazines for the .22 there was still a few clambering to get though the window at me, and I stood there reloading as they slashed their own arms to ribbons reaching over the smashed glass in the frame at me. They left wretched streaks of dark blood and bits of muscle, skin, and ligaments all over the building. Watching them mutilate themselves with no regard for their bodies still creeps me out. They are so single minded and driven toward murder. The smell coming from the inside was stomach turning. After I reloaded the rifle I finished them off at ten paces like a gentleman.

I waited a solid five minutes before I attempted to get the barricades open. No go there. I peeked around inside the windows and saw they had the makeshift doors padlocked and chained shut, and I would either have to blast the fuck out of the door with the shotgun, or go through the window. I chose the window. Right nearby was the damn blanket that someone had thrown on the body from the accident on "that day." Remember Mr. Journal? The moving blanket? I grabbed that, smashed the glass in the frame out, and threw the blanket over the frame. I climbed up and through, and switched to the shotgun.

Initially, I wanted to blow chunks. It was a motherfucking bloodbath. Blood was thick as pudding on the floor for Christ's sake. There were dozens of dead by now, and some were still oozing stuff, and others clearly had oozed all their stuff at a prior date, likely just earlier that day, or perhaps a day or two ago at most. Last stand kinda bullshit. The grocery store Alamo.

I slowly made my way over to the produce section and walked down the front of the store, checking each aisle for anything moving. It wasn't until I got to almost the very other end of the store that I saw something fucked up. Way in the rear of the shop I could see the door to the stockroom. Surrounding the door, scratching, clawing, pressing, was a small mob of zombies. Three deep at least.

Of course you know what that means by now. Something worth eating was on the other side of the door. Something living. I had enough shots between the shotgun and Sig to kill all the zombies gathered at the door. At this point though, I wasn't sure if I wanted to do that. From my cursory examination of the aisles I knew there was plenty of stuff worth taking already without adding any additional danger to this trip. Of course my thoughts led me think I'd tip these zombies off to my presence if I tried to be sneaky, plus I just couldn't leave these people, whoever they were, behind the door like that.

I crept down the aisle that was a straight line to them, and started shooting once I got to about 20 feet. Head level shotgun blasts are flat out terrifying. The spread of the pellets combined with the proximity makes for just a massive amount of damage. With just the shotgun I was able to drop all the zombies before I had to start backpedaling. Once they were all down, I drew the sword and finished the two or three that didn't die. To be honest, I was sort of in a panic wondering what was on the other side of the door anyway, and I wanted these fucking things dead before I had to deal with that.

I think I'm psychic. No sooner than I'd yanked the blade out of the ear of the last zombie the swinging doors flung open, and a huge prick jumped out with a double barrel shotgun leveled at me. He was about five and a half feet tall, nearly as round as he was tall, and was wearing dirty bloody slacks and a button down shirt that was still buttoned and tucked in. It was spattered with blood, but it was still tucked in. His round belly hung over his belt sort of comically.

I also recognized him as one of the managers of the store. He looked scared out of his fucking mind. He instantly started laying into me with threats at 140 decibels.

"Move and I'll fucking blow you away you motherfucking prick!" I think was the first thing he said. In response I just stayed frozen holding the sword. I think I even shrugged a little at him. Didn't defuse the situation, pretty much made it worse. He took two or three steps at me, stumbled a bit over one of the zombie bodies I'd just stabbed in the head, and started going down. When he impacted the floor, half on a zombie, both barrels of the scattergun let loose, and he shredded a zombie torso into bits.

Double barrel shotgun. Ruh roh asshole. You're outta bullets.

So I forget exactly, but I think I kicked him in the face three, or maybe four times. Not super hard, just really hard. Hard enough that he knew I was pissed at him, and he knew I could kill him, but not so hard that it did kill him, or knock him out. I put the sword away and grabbed his ass hard. I pinned him up to the wall in a sitting position and got right down in his face.

"What the fuck is your problem you asshat?" Was the first thing I said to him. At that point he pissed himself, and started talking incessantly through his busted lip and fucked up teeth. Turned out I probably kicked him too hard in the face. He could lose weight, but his face would be fucked up forever.

To paraphrase his conversation, he essentially said he had "hired" local people to protect the store. During the worst of the end of "that day" people started coming in and just stealing shit. He offered free food, water, and money to anyone that'd help him keep the store safe. About twenty folks joined in over the course of the day. They kicked everyone out, fortified the place with the barricades, and had a pretty good thing going. Late last night though, another group of locals came to get food, and a gunfight ensued.

Best I could piece together from Chubby McSmashface was that there were heavy losses on both sides. Most of the people died in fact. The zombies inside here were the people that holed up with him, and the dead outside were likely the majority of those that died in the assault. Once the first batches inside started going down... well, you can probably figure out what happened then. Dead bodies make zombies, and zombies bite people...

He and the single other survivor made it into the back room. He stayed at the door, making sure they didn't get in, and his remaining Alamo buddy went to the roof to make sure they weren't assaulted again. I'm guessing that was the shooter who tried to kill me on the roof. Shitty news was that the shooter had taken all their spare guns and ammo up to the roof, and that the ladder to access it was pulled up. Couldn't get there from here.

I'd heard enough by that point. I understood his situation, even sort of agreed with his plan and whatnot, I just couldn't give a fuck. He just leveled a shotgun at me, and to be honest, I fucking KNEW he was going to try and kill me if he hadn't tripped. Thank God he was a nincompoop. Yeah that's old school Mr. Journal. Trying to bring it back. Nincompoop. Try it out it's fun.

I pulled his ass to his feet, picked up his shotgun, and flung it over my shoulder towards the front of the store, and told him to get his fat ass marching. If I so much as saw him again, he'd get all 12 gauges to the goddamn face. I can still remember his lip quivering when he took off running. I waited a few minutes until I heard him grunting to get out the window, making his final escape.

After that I checked the backroom. By then it was mostly empty. Usually grocery inventory was stored there, but it was long since gone. I'm guessing they just restocked over the course of "that day" and by that point they had what they had on the shelves. Once I knew it was safe, I went shopping.

There was enough food in the store to fill three carts. Most of it was total shit, but I couldn't afford to leave anything behind. Cans of generic beans, box after box of frigging Jello, luckily there was a few jars of peanut butter left, and there was a surprising amount of the organic aisle stuff there too. I guess even with the apocalypse occurring people still weren't interested in eating healthy. Fuck em. I'll eat the shit.

I realized with a sort of dim anger that the prick I'd just let go probably had a key to the padlocks holding the doors shut. Whatever. From the inside it was easier to hit the hinges on the doors, which I did with the shotgun. Literally blew the doors off the hinges Mr. Journal. Funny stuff I assure you.

One cart at a time I sprinted across the parking lot and loaded it into my car. First cart was no sweat, second cart was no sweat, and just as I loaded the third cart into my car, things started getting sticky. Mr. Asshat manager was coming back. He was running right down the middle of Main Street, full tilt, with at least 20 more zombies following him. He didn't make it though. He gassed out and collapsed right on the solid yellow line and had every single last one of those undead fall on top of him. His screams were long, and shrill. Hearing him die was not as satisfying as I imagined it would be. It's not cool to go that way.

I got my car loaded as fast as I could, but they killed him and ate what they were going to eat very fast. It was about then that I realized that they don't sit and eat for long. Once whatever they're after is dead, they seem to lose interest. Eating is almost like a secondary thing for them, it's just an effective weapon I think. I don't know exactly. Not sure about much anymore really.

I got in the Camry and started it. I backed out as fast as I could, but I backed up a wee bit too much. The ass end of the car plowed into the first handful of zombies that were coming my way, and the car backed up, and onto the bodies. Here's my ground clearance story.

Bodies underneath cars with low ground clearance, mean the vehicle's wheels make little to no contact with the ground. Wheels that aren't on the ground cannot make a car go forward, or backward. I was stuck, parked on top of five or six zombies, with at least a dozen more right on their heels. So to do a quick callback to the pros and cons of ground clearance on vehicles in the post zombie apocalypse car market.... I highly suggest investing in cars with enough room underneath to drive over a dead body. End of callback.

I ran like a bitch. I ran like a sissy boy in a prison shower. I ran like the wind. I ran like Secretariat. I ran my ass right back into the grocery store. Now these motherfuckers can't run, which is one of the biggest saving graces. They have two speeds: slow, and stop. Sprinting back to the store gave me the time to gather my wits, make sure my guns were loaded, and start to shoot.

Now like the moron I am, I left the shotgun, and the .22 in the front seat of my car. All I had was the Sig, and the two spare clips. I count my blessings here because inside earlier I managed to drop all those zombies at the back door without having to use the pistol. How fucking clutch was that huh? You know my being alive at this point is by the slimmest of margins, and largest piles of shit-ass luck.

Sometimes Mr. Journal… a little luck is all you need.

I opened fire once I got my wind back. It took me every fucking bullet I had to drop the remaining 15 or so zombies. In fact, when I started to run low, I switched to shooting at their knees to ensure I'd hit them and drop them. Their legs move less than their heads when they're walking, and I figured I'd just kill them with the sword anyway. Which is just what I did. Empty gun sitting in my holster, I waded carefully into the pile of half-dead undead, and did what I had to do. Fuck my life right?

I started back across the parking lot when I heard this super ugly thump/crunch from behind me. I spun around and saw a twitching body right at the front of the store. I was totally like what the fuck? Then I realized it was the shooter from the roof. I had shot him, he had died up there, and in his IQ impaired zombie state, he walked off the edge of the roof trying to get at me. It must've been a good 40 foot drop, and he was pretty well dead for good when he hit. I got a good chuckle out of that. It also forced me to look in that direction, and that's when I saw the rifle he dropped earlier.

I jogged over, saw it was busted to shit, and got pissed. However, in some freakishly bizarre twist of coolness, the scope on the rifle was pristine. Whatever, right? My .22 needed a scope, so I took the rifle, emptied the shooter's pockets of ammo (.30-06 if you're curious, which was cool because later on I got a good rifle in that caliber) and got back to the car.

All of the zombies underneath it were either pinned, or dead for good. I did need a different car though. I had to search pockets and parked cars for more than an hour until I found keys and the corresponding car. Totally hit a homerun though. Ford FOCUS! BOO YA!

World ends, free cars everywhere, and the best thing I can get is a Ford Focus? Really God? Really? All I'm saying is that something a little nicer would be pretty sweet, right? I shouldn't bitch. With all the luck I've had so far I have zero fucking ground to stand on.

I had to push the cars out of the way in the lot to get the Focus into the road, but I did, and got the groceries moved about. I waved longingly and lovingly to the car that had served me so well, and I came back here.

What a shitty ass trip Mr. Journal. Shrug. I did get a lot of food. Even if it was just Spam, Beans and Jello. Of course it took two or three weeks for my split open chin to knit shut. Butterfly bandages and gauze and all that jazz. Still have a pink ugly scar along my jaw line from it.

Ta-ta for now big guy.

-Adrian

November 29th

Not a happy camper today Mr. Journal. Nope. Unfucking happy Boy Scout right here. Not sure why, but I was woken bright and goddamn early by banging on the front door of Hall E. Hard banging. Intentional banging. Clearly not sexual banging.

I frigging leapt out of bed like a crackhead near a soup kitchen and snagged up the .22 near the bedroom door. I peeked out the window and saw not one, nor two, but three zombies down at the frigging door, smashing their little heads off to no end.

Gonna use the whole words here… What. The. Fuck. I threw a fucking hissy fit for REAL. Once I was done with my three year old temper tantrum I threw the window open, and proceeded to shoot the dumbass walkers trying to beat down my front door. Wasn't too pleased either because one of them was juuuuust enough around the edge of the building for me to literally yell and scream to get him to walk around the corner to get a clear shot. You want to talk about irritating. Idiot zombie wouldn't walk into my line of fire like a good side of beef.

Not asking for much God. As if it wasn't enough to have all these fucking dead people walking around you have to make killing them a challenge too? Do you not fucking like me? What'd I do in a past life? Cornhole a nun? Cornhole a bus filled with nuns? Fucking A.

AND IT WAS WHILE I WAS TRYING TO SLEEP. I get no fucking breaks.

Phew. End of rant.

So. Here we are with this.. awkward thing going on between the two of us Mr. Journal. You think I'm all dangerous and edgy, and I could explode into a rage at any moment. So you're thinking to yourself, I'll just be quiet, maybe lay low, play the listener role for a bit, let him get his anger out somewhere else. Smart call really. I could explode again. I could blow up like a Pinto's gas tank.

I'm harmless I assure you. I haven't shot a real person in at least a month. Probably longer than that. Shot plenty of dead ones though. Working on setting that high score.

My thumb is still really sore. Definitely sprained it the other day. When I woke up the day after it was all bright red and swollen. Hot to the touch as well. I iced it, took some ibuprofen, and kept it elevated. Within a few hours I was in pretty good shape, and decided I'd do just two houses yesterday. Need to take a little bit of a breather. That and the weather has sucked balls. Lots of sleet and cold rain. Early in the morning the sidewalks and roads have been covered in black ice. That is one of the things I do not miss about driving back and forth to work. Cold as hell.

Anyway, keeping with the plan of clearing Auburn Lake Road, I worked my way up that road and did the next two huge houses in line. Newer development style bland houses that were pushing 3,000 square feet. I won't bore you with the details, but both houses were empty of danger. Riveting stuff right there.

I'm sure you're interested in what I found though right? That's almost always good news right? Well Mr. Journal, surprise! Didn't get shit. Both houses were bare right down to the damn floor tiles. That's an exaggeration. There was plenty of shit in both houses, but nothing worth loading into the truck and taking. To enhance positives though, I found empty doghouses at both places, which tells me they took their pets with them. Happy for that at least. It's the little things, right?

After that I wasn't feeling like doing much of anything, so came back here, ate a reasonable dinner of bland canned food, and decided to fire up the Playstation. Seemed like a great idea right up to the point I had to use my sprained thumb. Plan B was a bad horror movie, which just left a sour taste in my mouth considering the current events of the world, so I settled on watching The Hangover again. Good times.

This morning I awoke to my lousy ass neighbors beating on the door. Really unpleased about that. Can't really describe how unhappy that makes me. How did they know I was in this building? All the other buildings up here are just as likely to have living people in it, so what drew them to me specifically? Did I leave some form of trail I haven't realized yet? Did I make noise at some point that led them here? Were they led here by someone else? I've got so many questions, and so few answers.

Once I got done killing the idiots downstairs, dragging their bodies way out back to my previous body pile, cleaning the doorsteps of Hall E, and getting a bite to eat, I decided I should just go back to bed. Fuck it.

I woke up a couple hours later. Refreshed, yet with a fine layer of still pissed off about life. It's a wonderful life I have here. Tedious toil, constant danger, shitty food, marginal living quarters, and a never ending stream of injuries to show for it. It is so much like Iraq it isn't funny. Except the already dead people are the dangerous ones. Weird.

Royally effing miffed about the zombies literally knocking on my front door earlier I decided I would do a single house today, zip down to the gas station to fill up all my available gas tanks, and then come back here and throw my feet up. I'll die of exhaustion if I don't give myself a breather here and there.

When I hit the gas station the lower neighborhood area was devoid of signs of life. No walking dead, no black luxury cars with redheads, and no other signs of activity. The single home I cleared this afternoon was the cape that I got the Tundra from. I had a bad feeling about it, and just kinda thought it would be wise to stick with just that house today. Now if you recall I referred to the zombie family as June and Wally. The Cleaver family right? Well it's been pissing me off since that night because Wally was the goddamn other kid. Ward was the dad. I didn't kill Wally, I killed Ward. Attention to detail Adrian, attention to detail. Shit like that bugs me.

As you'll recall from the October 13th entry, I wound up taking out two adult zombies and one young undead girl at the house. Their bodies were still outside the house where I'd left them all that time ago. I've been keeping an eye on them as well every time I drove by. Fortunately at least the twice dead stay dead nowadays.

Their garage door was still open, and I was reasonably sure the house was devoid of the living. I didn't bother honking or letting anyone inside know I was there. To be honest, I felt like bringing the goddamn pain anyway. After my rough start to the day I was looking for a fight.

I let myself in through the garage, and used the shotgun as my weapon. I can't remember if I mentioned this or not, but generally I use the shotgun when house clearing. It's just too devastating a short range weapon. The garage entrance to the house opened into the kitchen, which was to be expected. I could see into the living room and dining room from there, as well as a second family room. Very open concept in design. I could see a door that looked like it led to a basement, as well as the railing on the stairs that led inside.

There was a fairly large amount of blood on the floor in all of the rooms. It started out as a dribble in the kitchen, but turned into a pretty substantial bloodbath in the two family rooms. There were smears all over the walls, broken lamps, knocked over furniture, you name the sign of the struggle, and it was there. Something went terribly south in here. I cleared the first floor as quietly as I could, and slid up the stairs to clear up there.

Sniff test fail.

I was no more than 5 feet down the central hall before I got a whiff of something rank. As was the case, I couldn't hear anything, but it was pretty obvious what was going on.

There were four rooms in the upstairs. Two doors were open. One bathroom was evident, and one bedroom. The two bedroom doors that were closed had scratch marks all over them. Bloody streaks running north-south as well as a few lodged fingernails deep in the wood. It looks an awful lot like my heavy duty front door of Hall E this morning. Pretty clearly a zombie or zombies tried to get in these rooms. I wonder why. Could it be because there were living people inside?

After I checked the two open rooms and made sure they were safe, I checked the first shut door. The door knob was locked, and as soon as I rattled it, I heard shuffling on the other side, and the door got pushed forward in the frame. I stepped back and watched for a few seconds as it got pushed forward over and over insistently. Mindlessly. I thought about it for a second, then leveled the shotgun off at chest height, and blasted a dinner plate sized hole in the door.

There was a sick, wet, thump noise as something heavy got flung across the room. I took a deep breath, leaned over, and looked through my new peep hole. Ripped apart in the middle of the room, propped up against a queen sized bed was the decayed body of a young boy. Not a day over 10 years old. My shot hit him too low to finish him though, it just ripped his chest apart. What was left of his body was falling over on the floor to crawl its way back to the door, to eat me. I stifled a wretch, reached inside the hole in the door, unlocked, and pushed it open.

Honestly I'd lost my urge to fight at that point. I didn't want to kill kids today, even the undead ones. It still turns my stomach. I drew the sword, and busted the young kid's head open to put him down permanently. I wound up throwing up some in the sink as I wandered over to the other closed door. I don't know if it was because I had just ripped a ten year old in half with a 12 gauge, or because I fucking had the worst feeling the other room would just the same as the first. I don't know.

The second door was locked too, and as soon as I gave

the knob a twist, there was a soft ramming from the other side. Over and over and over. I rested my head against the bloody, scratched door and felt it push against my head a dozen times. Took me a long time to build up the nerve to do it, but I blasted another hole the same as the first. This shot's elevation was more appropriate though, and I killed the little kid on the other side.

I can't tell you if it was a boy or a girl. It was wearing neutral style pajamas, and was probably about 7 years old. The body itself had already been eaten substantially, and there wasn't enough… parts left to tell one way or the other. My head shot wrecked any chance of seeing a face.

I am so fucking weary of this. Every day, day in, day out, more of the same. Mind numbing violence, destruction, and emotional wreckage. I tell Otis my troubles almost every day too, and as great a listener as he is, it's just not the same. It's days like today that make me wish I had more people to sit and talk to. At least we could bitch at God together, right? It's the little things. Maybe I should start giving praise to some flavor of the almighty, and flip the script. Change my tune. Bite my heretical tongue.

Fat fucking chance. I have no filter. I swear all the damn time. I once told a gay guy at a poker tournament that my hand was "very homosexual." I fucking knew he was gay too. Just didn't occur to me to shut my face before I said it. Had no intention of hurting his feelings. Went over like a fart in church. I had to let him hit me a few times just to let him get even. True story.

At any rate, after that I checked the basement, and it was thankfully devoid of demon possessed undead children. No spinning heads, no green pea vomit, and no flesh eating monsters.

I sat down at their kitchen table and just blanked out for fifteen minutes to get my shit together. I don't know what it is about killing kids, but it leaves me empty inside. I have no will, no motivation, no nothing after I do it. Fucked up shit. And I know I will have to kill more as time goes on. These zombie bodies don't seem to decay at all. If they are, it's really fucking slowly. There could be zombies around forever. There's a scary thought Mr. Journal.

I emptied the house. It looked like they were staging their escape as shit hit the fan. Most of their food and water was already in the kitchen or the living room, so I didn't have to lug it all around. They had a lot of really good entertainment crap, which was nice. DVDs, CDs, etc. Food wise they had a lot as well. I think all they fed their kids was canned shit and boxed macaroni and cheese. They had condensed milk, lots of sugar, and I shit you not, a full case of hot chocolate packets. It's the little things. Oh, and Ward had a fucking A awesome flashlight. Finally, a decent fucking flashlight. Heavy duty police style Maglite.

There were a few other neat things as well, but I'm not gonna spend a paragraph listing the mundane, yet useful items. TP, PT, soap, bleach, blah fucking blah blah. Add nice towels to the list too. High thread count sheets. Makes me want to go get my bed again. I think I'll put that on the list of shit to do.

Sooooo...... End of the afternoon. Came back, unloaded my shit, tended to the plants, refilled the generator gas tank, took a hot shower, fed Otis, refilled my boy Blue, cleaned the shotgun, made myself something to eat, and now I'm writing in here. And that's an easy day.

Tomorrow... I will deal with tomorrow. Tonight I watch action movies from the 80's.

-Adrian

p.s. nincompoop.

December 2010

December 1st

I am in much better spirits today. I have found and focused my inner happy place Mr. Journal. Hopefully my newfound reservoir of patience and bliss lasts me. Almost held a straight face through that. Lol. Couldn't hold it though.

It's now Wednesday, December 1st. Yippee. The Christmas season has begun for me. I'm starting to think I'm going to skip Christmas shopping this year. I think I'll gloss over my Hanukkah obligations as well. Kwaanza seems like a waste as well. I just don't feel like dealing with the kind of crowds I'd expect nowadays at the malls. God can you imagine how bad it is at the malls? In any of the urban areas where the populations are more dense? Christ. It's bad enough here, and there's less than ten thousands folks in town.

The city had over 20 times that. And that's nothing compared to the really large places like Los Angeles, Dallas, Chicago, Boston, or D.C. What a nightmare. Of course those cities probably had a more structured police response, so for all I know, I'm sitting out here like a fucking tool fighting all these dead guys and the cities are these peaceful utopias. Somehow I doubt that. I bet the cities were fucking slaughterhouses.

Glad I am not in the cities Mr. Journal. I can make do with my suburban lifestyle. Even if my carbon footprint is much larger than if I was to be in the city. I wonder what all the assholes paranoid about global warming are worried about right now, assuming they're still alive somewhere. I'd drop a paycheck that their number one issue is global rampant undead cannibalism. That or the distinct lack of patchouli incense. I'm thankful that soapbox got kicked out from under people. Not that I'm not all for saving the world from ourselves. I just hate people.

Something that always bothered me about zombie movies was dental hygiene. You ever sit down and watch a zombie movie, and at the moment that the person resurrects, they sit up, do this animalistic hiss, and bare their teeth? You tell me Mr. Journal how many of those hissing, teeth baring zombies have brown or black teeth when they sit up and do that shit.

They fucking ALL DO! It makes no sense. It's like wearing a condom when you piss. Doesn't make any sense. Why did so many special effects guys paste on brown and black sludge onto their actor's teeth? I mean, after some time, sure the zombies are going to have crappy teeth. I have yet to see a zombie brush their teeth. They have so much to do! There's no time to brush.

They have 24 full hours of shuffling around and stalking living prey to do. No breaks allowed. God help us all if the zombies decide to form a labor union. Local Zombie 403. Shortly after that the fuckers will have a good health plan too I bet.

Zombies have the same dental quality in death that they had in life. Just wanted to clear that up if anyone was still curious Mr. Journal. Tell all your friends. Tell them twice if you have to.

On a more literal and informative note, I have been lazy. My thumb has been really sore, but was a little better at the end of yesterday. After my pre-school shotgun spree on Monday I didn't have it in me to clear houses. I don't think I would've been able to pull the trigger on a zombie if I'd run into one. Just too much stress built up after killing those two kids in that house.

So yesterday I took it easy. I ran the generator all day to keep nice and warm, and I tended to my plants, which are now sprouting a little bit. I feel like a proud papa. Otis has been a little bitch about it though. I've caught him several times now sniffing the baby plants, and whenever he does that to something, eating it is usually not far behind. I've moved the plants into their own room upstairs, which I'm now calling the greenhouse. I know, clever.

Other than tending my plants yesterday I didn't really do much. Decent weather, as in no snow, rain, or sleet, but the temperature is 20F. If you aren't aware Mr. Journal, that's testicles into ice cubes cold. It'll get worse this winter too. I can feel it in my bones. And right on cue, it started to drizzle outside. Sigh.

During my lazy day Tuesday I fired up the Playstation, and stared at about five hours of Prince of Persia. I have a hard time getting into the violent games right now. If I want a first person shooter, I'll walk the fuck outside and make some noise. Lately, I want something unreal and fantastic. Knights in shining armor. Cubes falling from the sky into piles on the floor. I don't know. I just know I'm sick of hearing guns go off in the real world. Plus there's a big part of me that doesn't want to get into the habit of shooting like a video game teaches you.

In the real world, running, jumping, crouching, and firing incessantly gets you killed almost immediately. At the very least you burn through ammo much faster than you need to, or can afford to. I don't want my good weapon habits ruined by a stupid video game.

I'll probably change my mind though when I get a hankering to play through Fallout 3 again. I really wish Fallout New Vegas came out before the shit hit the fan. I was really looking forward to that game. Shrug. Lots of things I was looking forward to. I always wanted to see the Pyramids too.

There is a certain satisfaction I get whenever I do something that I don't want to do. I remember back in college I frigging hated writing papers, but when I buckled down, and fired up the laptop and got it done, I always felt good about it. I got a more thorough satisfaction from doing the things I didn't want to do too. Doing the shit I wanted to do had no reward really. It was what I wanted to do, and was a reward all in itself. Crossing something unpleasant off the to-do list meant I had been a good little person, and that

I had done something because it had to be done, not because I wanted to do it. It validated my work ethic.

I feel that way about clearing houses. I hate doing it with a passion now, but it needs to be done to secure the area for my safety, and the safety of any people who wind up joining me up here. Plus I've accumulated a wide array of loot here that will help me survive not only much longer, but in a higher comfort level. Better food, better tools, better clothes, etc.

I did three houses on Auburn Lake Road today. That drops the grand total remaining on Auburn Lake Road down to 2 houses. I plan on doing those remaining two tomorrow. That means all that I have left are the 9 houses on Jones Road, and the 7 houses on Prospect Circle. Once those houses are done, the entire road and all its tributaries are clear. Exciting, yeah? I know I'm stoked.

So my day today was pretty good all things considered. I was fortunate enough to not find any dead bodies, human or otherwise in them. I also was lucky enough to not have to kill any more zombies, adult or otherwise. Every day that goes by where I don't shoot a bullet, or swing my little sword is a good day in my book.

What was the haul you ask Mr. Journal? I got a pretty good assortment of canned food, cleaning agents, consumables etc. As far as nice gadgets are concerned, one house had a BITCHING coffee maker. One of the fancy schmancy Italian deals that makes espresso and lattes. It even steams your milk for you. If I had normal milk, that would be awesome. Not sure if it works with the powdered milk though. Same people also had a French press for coffee too. They loved coffee. Fucking loved it. Absolutely adored the shit. I'm happy though because that means as long as I can boil water, I can make coffee with the French press. I can always boil water, even if the generator dies, and even if I run out of gas.

The other two houses had two kind of neat things inside. One of which has absolutely no practical value, but I had to take it anyway because it was cool. The other was radical. As in, "dude, this is RAD."

I found a baseball card collection. Actually it was a sports card collection. Not a little one either. Eight huge white boxes filled with row after row of meticulously organized sports cards. Each carefully slid into a plastic sleeve and labeled. There were six binders filled with plastic pages to hold cards too. Unreal. I haven't gone though them yet, but I saw stuff going all the way back to the 1940's. I saw some Mantle cards too I think. Pretty neat shit. I'm like a historian now, gathering things of value to pass on to future generations. In a strange way, it makes me feel good about raiding these houses. I've got the cards stacked up in the living room here so I can sort them when I take a break. Maybe after I finish writing this entry.

The third and final house I did earlier was a bust in terms of food. There was almost nothing left inside, and the place looked like it was cleared out in a big hurry.

Right square in their kitchen, pretty as a gold ingot, was a cast iron woodstove. Hallelujah. It's fucking enormous. Two or three feet deep at least, and probably almost six feet wide. It has burners, a warming shelf, multiple zones for keeping areas of the stove warmer than others... It's perfect. I just need to figure out how I'm going to get it back here. After I do the last two houses on Auburn Lake I think I'll try and tackle the stove issue.

I also need to try and find a way to get the damn thing installed somewhere. Do I put it in here to save on the gas, or do I put it in one of the other dorm buildings so that they have adequate heat? I'm leaning towards option B because I don't NEED a stove in here right now. I shouldn't have said that. Six hours from now the generator is going to explode. I always jinx myself with shit like that. Wish me luck on that regard Mr. Journal. I need to figure out how to install the pipes, and make sure I don't set the floor or walls on fire as well.

Unless I meet and befriend the Hulk over the next few

days, I will have to find a way to take the stove apart and transport it back piece by piece. Should be no sweat right? And there's my second jinx of the entry. Man I am stupid sometimes. If I'm not careful I'll keep talking like this and find a way to give myself the Clap from jerking off. I'll be the first motherfucker in the post apocalyptic world to find a way to get an STD all by myself. Sigh.

So yeah, that's where we are today. Few added supplies, a new coffee maker of epic proportions, a giant stack of baseball cards to sort through, and a located woodstove. It's exciting. I like days like today. They give me that fictional thing... you've heard of it I'm sure.

Hope.

-Adrian

- About The Author -

CHRIS PHILBROOK is the creator and author of *Adrian's Undead Diary* as well as the popular webfiction series *Elmoryn* and *Tesser: A Dragon Among Us*.

Chris calls the wonderful state of New Hampshire his home. He is an avid reader, writer, role player, miniatures game player, video game player, and part time athlete, as well as a member of the Horror Writers Association. If you weren't impressed enough, he also works full time while writing for Elmoryn as well as the world of Adrian's Undead Diary and his newest project, Tesser; A Dragon Among Us.

- Find More Online -

Visit **adriansundeaddiary.com** to access additional content. Learn more about Adrian's world, contact the author, join discussions with other readers, view maps from the story, and receive the latest news about AUD.

Check out Chris Philbrook's official website **thechrisphilbrook.com** to keep tabs on his many exciting projects, or follow Chris on Facebook at **www.facebook.com/ChrisPhilbrookAuthor** for special announcements.

Read more by author Chris Philbrook in *The Kinless Trilogy*. Explore Elmoryn, a world of dark fantasy where death is not the end. The story begins in *Book One: The Wrath of the Orphans*, available in print, Kindle, and online. Visit **elmoryn.com** to learn more about Elmoryn, view concept art, and much more.

Follow Chris Philbrook's latest epic series as it unfolds in *Tesser: A Dragon Among Us*. Meet Tesser, the Dragon. He who walks in any form, and flies the skies free of fear. He has slept for millennia, but now he has awoken in a world ruled by human hands, where science has overshadowed even the glory of old magic. Follow Tesser as he seeks to understand why he slept for so long, and where all the magic has gone. Visit **adragonamongus.com** to learn more.

Can't get enough of AUD?

Visit the School Store at **adriansundeaddiary.com** for stickers, hats, and a wide variety of awesome shirts!

Stickers!

Hats!

T-Shirts!

CPSIA information can be obtained at www.ICGtesting.com
Printed in the USA
LVOW10s1901061014

407483LV00001B/369/P

9 781493 568710